THE BOOK OF EPIPHANIES

THE BOOK OF EPIPHANIES

Gamal al-Ghitani

Translated by
Farouk Abdel Wahab

The American University in Cairo Press
Cairo   New York

First published in 2012 by
The American University in Cairo Press
113 Sharia Kasr el Aini, Cairo, Egypt
420 Fifth Avenue, New York, NY 10018
www.aucpress.com

Dar el Kutub No. 17809/12
ISBN 978 977 416 546 7

Dar el Kutub Cataloging-in-Publication Data

al-Ghitani, Gamal
          The Book of Epiphanies: An Egyptian Novel/ Gamal al-Ghitani; translated by Farouk
     Abdel Wahab —Cairo: The American University in Cairo Press, 2012
          p.   cm.
          ISBN 978 977 416 546 7
          1. Arabic literature
     I. Title
          892.70803543

1 2 3 4 5   16 15 14 13 12

Designed by Fatiha Bouzidi
Printed in Egypt

In the name of God, the Beneficent and the Merciful.
I seek Your forgiveness and approval, most forgiving, most generous.

I returned, unable to be patient any more, for how could I be patient about that which has not been revealed to me? When my return was complete, I sat by myself, recalling and remembering as catastrophes loomed. I was in a state of total loss, unsettled and unhinged, both moving and still even though earlier I had been more like a bird than a man, flying from branch to branch. Except now it was the branch that was doing the flying away from me. I returned, bound after I had been unbound, confined after I had been free. To be confined is to be limited and to be limited, impotent.

I returned, after I was both seeker and sought, lover and beloved. My departure had been to seek myself. My flight was from myself, within myself, and to myself. I almost captured the secrets of the fire, the light, the night, the day, the sun, the moon, the lightning, the breeze of the east wind, the birth of the dew, the reverberation and the echo, the ultimate ends, the legendary beloveds Salma and Layla, the dimming of the twilight, and the succession of seasons. I was two bows' length or nearer, but a veiling mist came over my eyes. I didn't have the patience to wait. How could I bear that of which I had no knowledge?

I returned, having enjoyed the most beautiful company, after my master had blessed me by allowing me to stay in his presence, after he had imparted to me knowledge of what I did not know.

I returned after being away from family and home, after I crossed deserts and conquered obstacles, after all the barriers that humans normally cannot overcome had fallen before me one by one. I returned even though I was given to constant travel, neither staying put nor settling down. I returned and I was loath to lose all I had seen, so I sat down and started writing, hoping to shed light on some of the things I had witnessed. In the process I was sometimes crystal clear, giving all the details, and at other times I merely hinted and intimated. Sometimes I even obscured and held back. But after I got it all together and was almost done writing, a thought occurred to me: to wash my hands of this weighty matter for fear of falling short, of being unable to be precise. So I made up my mind and tore up all I had written down, scattered it in the wind, and made it as if it never was. It was totally gone and forgotten, leaving no trace whatsoever, although it had been there in black and white. I wondered: were I and my epiphanies not even there? At that point all my determination was gone, my resolve totally evaporated. The blackest of memories engulfed me, leaving the bitterest taste in my mouth. Then, all of a sudden, at that moment when the dawn broke, that mysterious voice called out to me, "Gamal."

I came to and a bright light shone in the night of my soul, a light so unlike any other that I thought I had come back to the core of the radiant Diwan. At the heart of the light I saw three figures and at a little distance behind them another three and right in the middle distance between them, a single figure. In the middle of the first three stood my beloved, the light of my eye, companion of my epiphanies, my refuge in hard times, the one giving me succor in my missteps, my imam, al-Husayn, Master of Martyrs. To his right was my father and to his left Gamal Abdel Nasser. As for the three standing behind, their features kept changing: at times I saw Ibrahim, Mazin, and Khalid, at other times I'd see my mother, my brothers, or my children or my grandmother and uncle and some friends, a few of those I loved or those who showed enmity toward me. Or I saw some persons that I had known for a long time and some with whom I had been briefly acquainted or even some I'd only glimpsed as I passed by a coffeehouse or looked up at a balcony. As for the one standing in the middle, I recognized him as my other master, al-Sheikh al-Akbar Muhyiddin ibn Arabi. Al-Husayn fixed me with a beautiful, piercing glance so I was unable to speak and yet I recited to myself:

It's a wonder that I long for them
And miss them even when they are with me.
My eye weeps for them even while they are in its pupil,
And my heart complains how far they are even though they are in my chest.

The Master of Martyrs gave his permission and al-Sheikh al-Akbar Muhyiddin ibn Arabi approached me. He took a step toward me even though he didn't move at all. I also did not move from where I stood and yet there we were, face to face. We looked at each other for a long time, in silence. Then I lowered my gaze and we separated without uttering a single word. I had, however, understood and received the glad tidings. The light faded. They left. Yet I obeyed and began to commit to paper that which I had written before and out of it came this book, which contains my epiphanies, interspersed within which are my voyages, stations, states, situations, and visions. It is a book that only those with understanding and hardy perseverance can understand. Should someone show signs of incomprehension or censure, I recite from the Holy Qur'an: *He [Moses] said, "So what have you got to say for yourself, Samaritan?" And he [the latter] said, "I perceive what they do not perceive."*

First Epiphanies
Which are the Epiphanies of Separation

Luminous Epiphany
If I knew where separation lived, I'd seek it out and disperse it.

The Epiphany of Fullness
After forty revolutions of the planets my father appeared to me in that wonderful spot outside place and time: a horizon contained rather than expansive, with dimensions perceived rather than seen. The walls in that spot were built with materials that we are not familiar with. They are neither wood nor brick. As for the ceiling, it was made up of scarlet rays. There was an isolated, singular step. My father sat there, giving me the side of his face in a posture I was not used to from him. I took a few steps toward him, my heart beating fast, anticipation impelling me forward. Yet at a certain point I came to a halt, knowing I couldn't go any further. I didn't dare. My father appeared to me dressed in clothes of this world: a black wool shirt and black pants. His hair was smooth, straight, and long. His features were young, relaxed, contented. I conjectured I was seeing his face when he was twenty years old: no wrinkles or signs of worrying. He looked at me and I looked at him. He got his fill of me but I didn't quench my thirst.

But that which felt like an eternity was now at hand. I asked permission to speak and astonishingly he spoke, his voice reaching my ears in a monotone, unadorned. He spoke to me like someone making a broadcast statement to an audience he couldn't see or to strangers he didn't know. He spoke and I listened and understood. The beloved spoke and I wrote it down. He said, "O Gamal, don't worry about me and don't grieve. My death was restful and I did not suffer. Time, both ancient and new, was over in seven minutes. What your mother said and what my brothers told you was correct. So don't fret. More important, tell me, what are you going to do?" My father was gone.

Explaining That Epiphany
He looked out from the balcony. I waved and he and the others waved back. I continued on my way and at the corner of the street I turned and saw his face looking at me. He stood still, watching me. My weary mind entertained no thoughts, and my circumscribed sight did not penetrate the unknown, so I went on walking. The following day I started my travels: I moved about, I saw, I met, I took delight, I worked, I enjoyed, and from time to time I thought of him and I remembered. Finally I came back. At the airport my wife met me, happy and all smiles. I inquired and she said everyone was well. They were all fine. When I got home, when I kissed my sleeping child and spread out the gifts, I noticed her distracted glances. So I asked. She hesitated and I grew apprehensive. I persisted and she looked ill at ease. I got more and more agitated and kept persisting. She looked at me with her big eyes and said, "Your father, may his life continue in yours."

A Lightning Epiphany
When the foreign land spread out before my eyes,
   I had the yearning for home that a she-camel has for her home pasture.

6

The Epiphany of the Impossible

I saw Gamal Abdel Nasser in a specific place and at a specific time. I saw him in Dokki Square in the early eighties, which at one time seemed quite far off but which now were retreating as if they were ghosts of yesteryear. I had seen him up close only once before, crossing Ramsis Street. I was standing on the sidewalk and he passed in front of me. He seemed very close to me. I imagined he saw me from behind the glass window of his car. Before that I used to see him on the two feast days, Eid al-Fitr and Eid al-Adha. The two feasts wouldn't be complete before we stood on tiptoe, awaiting the motorcycles and the security cars, then the photographers' car, and then he would appear before the gathered crowds. There was some gray on his temples surrounded by a halo that made him stand out as if he were the only one to see. Those days my father would carry my younger brother then would put him on his shoulders to give my brother a better perch from which to watch. In this epiphany I saw Abdel Nasser without guards, without photographers, and without the old pomp and circumstance. Yet he appeared to tower outside the usual earthly time, his invisible presence exceeding that of his physical appearance. People around him were going about their business, no one paying any attention or turning their head in his direction. I rushed toward him and he saw my enthusiasm. He turned his eyes toward me. I noticed that he was weary, exhausted. I spoke, my voice charged with an inexplicable longing and buried wounds. I said, "Hey, how are you? What's wrong?"

"Do you know me?"

"Who doesn't know the one who needs no introduction?"

He shook his head. Now I could see that all of his hair was gray.

"So, I am in Egypt?"

I was taken aback. He shouted, "But I am seeing what should not exist!"

He paused for a moment then began to utter words that he seemed to dredge from a reservoir of perplexity and troubling questions.

"Have the Israelis penetrated the front?"

"No," I said.

"Did their armies reach Cairo?"

I said, "No."

His questions kept coming, "What's this I'm seeing, then? Explain it to me. You came after us, but we were here before. Answer me: Are these not their flags? Aren't these their tourists? Aren't these their books and newspapers?"

I said, "This is true. I am against it but I don't publicize my objections out of fear and prudence."

"What happened? Are things upside down?" he asked.

His voice sounded strange, as if it were not real. I had asked myself once whether I had actually lived during his time, whether I had really seen him and what he had done. But there he was, in front of me. I noticed that people were gathering, some staring. I also realized that some people had understood what I said and drawn near. As the crowd grew I said, "I'll explain to you, but no matter how much one knows, there's the One who knows all."

Epiphany of Wishes

God Almighty has said, *And wishes have deceived you.* God indeed has spoken the truth.

Wishes are things you do not have. Those trafficking in them are losers who delight in them for a time but when they check with themselves, they find nothing in hand. Their fortunes are just as the mindless author described them: "If these wishes were to come to pass they'd be the best of wishes; if they don't, then at least we had a good time with them."

The Epiphany of Victory

I traveled at night in the green light, during the long-anticipated time of flowers. I saw myself leaving the beautiful city of Rabat on the Atlantic coast of Morocco, going forth and crossing borders without obstructions or obstacles. I entered eternal Sinai and saw the relics of the old war, the chassis of dead tanks. I recalled the moments when shrapnel pierced a human form and the cry of pain. I remembered my days as a military correspondent reporting what was happening to people I didn't know, telling them what our compatriots were doing. I could have died in those days that no one remembered now; I could have been totally forgotten in these terrible times and the time of the epiphanies. I continued my night voyage through the green rays. I crossed Sinai. I traveled on paved roads to Palestine Time. I saw the signs in Arabic, the coffeehouses, and the laughter and daily life. I passed by towns that seemed like dreams for us because they had been separated from us for so long. I saw remnants of Hebrew letters on yellow signs left in place as reminders. Everything was back to what it was. *And if you repeat the crime, we will repeat the punishment*, as the glorious Qur'an says. My guide said, "Why do you read and forget? Have you forgotten that several kingdoms had been set up here under the sign of the cross? Kingdoms that lasted for close to two centuries, with armies, postal horses, administrative systems, propaganda media, princes, followers, and knights? Then all of that was gone. People living at the time did not accept the facts on the ground." I noticed the angry tone in my guide's voice. I also noticed that the green color was growing faint, that the time of the epiphany was about to end. I saw my father; he was my guide. He looked tired, just as I had always seen him in the last years, in the years that I hadn't realized were the last years. I noticed an old building with a strange entrance that looked as if it led nowhere. Its walls were made of rubble stone with no windows. He said, "I warned you, but you didn't pay heed. I gave you signal after signal but you didn't understand. I alerted you, but you ignored it. I tried but you pretended to be blind. Why the sadness, then?"

He turned away his sorrowful face. His voice grew distant from me, then its sounds became indistinct and vanished. "In any case, sadness will run its course, then everything will go away." I was about to respond but my tongue grew heavy.

An Epiphany of Certainty

Nothing stays the same. If that were to happen, nothingness would come about. Everything is in a state of constant separation: the fetus separates from the womb, a person departs from this world to an unknown everlasting afterlife. Sight leaves the eye for a visible object then it leaves the visible object for the eye. Night departs from day and day departs from night. An hour leaves an hour behind. Time leaves time. An atom constantly departs from another atom. A body embraces a body then leaves. The penis enters the vagina then leaves it. Luscious green leaves cling to branches then fall off. An idea does not catch up with another idea. An image doesn't stay in the mind. Winter comes, spring comes, then summer and autumn. Each leaves in due time. Everything is constantly separating. One self leaves another self. Even things that we believe are permanent; even the days that we thought would never change or be replaced or vanish. Everything. Everything is in a state of separation. Everything changes. Everything. Let us understand clearly!

The Epiphany of the Attempt

Abdel Nasser appeared to me again. He seemed angry, but this time he was acting on it. He ordered the enemy's flags lowered and removed from Cairo. He ordered the arrest of all enemy personnel in the country: the ambassador, members of the embassy staff, delegates, representatives of organizations, and spies. He declared all of them to be prisoners of war. He ordered and ordered but he had no official stamp or pen with which to sign. He went around from square to square shouting, yelling at the top of his voice, for he had no means to carry out his orders. There was little he could do; his strength had left him among strange faces with unfamiliar features. Today was different than his days and the times had changed. He could see what others could not and he was terrified to no end. What he was seeing had been inconceivable, not even in dreams, let alone in broad daylight when he was awake. It was cruel beyond measure. He crossed the river and saw the pyramids looming from afar.

Gamal Abdel Nasser was now in the large square. Others beside me saw him. They couldn't believe their eyes. Some took to their heels in panic. Others clung to him. They put their faith in him and followed him. Some confided in him. Others complained to him. An old blind woman who recognized his voice remonstrated with him. The news spread far and wide among the gathering crowds. Foreign newspaper correspondents scampered to the scene. They investigated, asked questions, stood in close circles around Nasser. The news made it to various news summaries. World currency exchange markets plunged: the U.S. dollar was shaken, as was the pound sterling. The yen gained ground. Both NATO and ASEAN were put on alert. Leaders of the Israeli parties the Herut and Mapam and the like, declared it to be war. From the alleys and side streets women came out with their heads uncovered, clapping, prayerful, and complaining. A crowd gathered here and another crowd there. Police precinct commanders refrained from making any decisions, waiting to see how things would go. In the crowds chests throbbed with anxiety and apprehension, hearts raced with optimism and anticipation. There were disagreements.

Suddenly there arrived a large squad of soldiers, all about twenty years old, commanded by an officer in a jet black uniform: a strange suit with many pockets and rounds of ammunition visible. This young second lieutenant seemed to take arrogant delight in the two stars on his shoulders, indicating his recent graduation, and in his newfangled showy uniform. He brandished a dagger and poked Gamal Abdel Nasser in the chest and gave a signal whereupon the soldiers rushed forward and took Nasser away. The crowds dispersed. A heavy, unwelcome silence descended on the square. Trouble blossomed in the hearts and rivers of catastrophe overflowed with new waters.

Recitation

And they sold him for a measly price, a few dirhams, for they held him in low esteem.

. . . And God has full power and control but most people do not know that.

11

The Epiphany of Debility

I saw Muhammad Ahmad ibn Iyas al-Hanafi al-Misri. He looked venerable and from him the fragrance of basil that grew on tombs wafted. He was exactly as I had imagined him while reading his major history of Egypt during the waning days of Mamluk rule.

"I came to you before," he said.

"I remember your return, the year of the defeat. But you abandoned me," I replied.

"A wise man leaves his friends when the home turns desolate," he said.

"The heart is all right and filled with great affection," I said.

"But I see that you are weary," he noted.

I said, "My father died while I was away from home. I didn't see the closing of his eyes. I was not a pallbearer nor did I witness his interment. I didn't know and I can't conceive what he might have seen in the final moments or what images or specters may have appeared to him or were shown to him."

He said, "Do you have a sign?"

"My heart is heavy unto death," I said.

He said, "O Beloved, don't let puzzlement mask other puzzlements. How can the finite grasp the infinite?"

I said, "Please enlighten me some more."

He said, "Continue with the epiphanies. A person asleep sees more than those who are awake!"

Then he was gone.

A Moroccan Epiphany

I had an epiphany of myself on a voyage. I was standing on a platform in a railway station. I got on the train. I saw my father on the platform. He was older than at any time he appeared to me before. His eyes were sunken. He was that age when the white of the eye mingled with the black. He bent over, holding the hem of his gallabiya with his teeth. He was carrying many bags, all filled with books. I cried out, "Will I need all these books, Father?"

He made a gesture. I could read his lips, "You're on a long journey."
He looked around. His load seemed heavy, even though it was my load. I wondered at that. Then the train started moving. I got farther away. I was no longer near him. The time of separation and loss had started before I could prepare for it. Darkness fell. Then my father appeared inside an old palace with ornamented walls. In it were palm trees, cactus, basil, and unfamiliar yellow flowers. The palace belonged to one of his relatives, an uncle of mine. How did I know? I don't know.

An invisible barrier separated me from him. Around him was a green silk rug. The sky had colors for which we had no names in the languages of our world. He told me that we had not been completely honest with each other during his life, and that he had departed with many things about him unknown to us. I said, "Give me an example," and he replied, "I had two brothers, the elder of whom died in child-hood of an unknown cause. The other died early in his youth when he was pulling a cow. It dragged him suddenly to his death." I said, "You didn't tell us that." He said, "You didn't care. You didn't ask me." Then he said, "Look closely over there and you can see both of them." I tried in vain to see and hear but couldn't. I realized the distance between us was becoming greater. I took in the palace that had absorbed me: it was a Moroccan palace with Andalusian miniatures. He turned his face away from me, and spoke as if addressing others, "I was your father and you were my children. You grew up. You became men responsible for your own households but you knew nothing about me."

An Explanation
Why is it that humans persist in ignorance and blindness? Why is it that they walk in the dark in places where there is no shade or water?

The Epiphany of the Land and Changeable Time
There's a small patch of land, at the intersections, and let me tell you about intersections! It's on the path I used to take. That patch has been trampled by feet I haven't seen and will be trampled by feet still unknown. It used to be sand and rocks and before that it

was in flames. Right now it is paved with asphalt but just after the construction of my city it was irrigated and covered with green, a playground for the horses, then it became a pleasure garden until the early part of the last century. It was built up densely, then came the cable cars. But time passes, buildings do not remain standing forever nor do intersections stay the same. Some buildings would rise and other buildings may not be constructed. Perhaps people would use it as a launching pad for travel to outer space, chasing celestial bodies in their orbits. Perhaps my father walked on it many times in his daily comings and goings. One of my children might walk on it. Perhaps it will be trampled by one of my great-great-grandchildren, one of my own progeny who would not hear of me nor understand what I have suffered in these bad times because my name would fall like a dry leaf from the family tree, just as my forebears from the distant past had done. If only I could have an epiphany of one of them who had lived thousands of years ago! Who was he? How did he live? Who did he marry? I listen to some-one saying, "And if you repeat, we will repeat." I realized that going back was impossible because the world was constantly separating from itself. I looked at the patch of land in its travels through time that I would not witness. I could see the flow of movement on it after my final departure and I wished I could affix a message or a mark for those stepping on it, crossing it. If only that were possible.

A Mysterious Epiphany
I saw Gamal Abdel Nasser, vulnerable, hatless, and unkempt. I approached him and when he spoke, it was my father's voice speaking.

"Yes," he said.

"Yes," I said.

His face lit up and he smiled because I understood him. But when I realized the reason for his cheerfulness I said, "No." He shook and his face changed colors and it seemed his self-confidence was shaken.

He asked me, "How have things been for everyone?"

"It couldn't get any worse," I said.

A thin veil rose between us.

I asked him, "Why?"

He muttered and mumbled and couldn't answer.

I repeated, "Why? Why?"

He seemed too preoccupied and I said in remonstrance, "Why? Why? Why?"

The Epiphany of Sadness
This is the parting between me and you.

The Epiphany of the Martyr

I saw myself on a boat without a sail. I looked at the waves of the sea. Suddenly I saw someone in the distance. He was walking on water. I recognized my father's gait. He spoke and I listened to the voice of my friend who was martyred on Friday, October 19, 1973 during the war that was said to be the last war. I was astonished and confused: the body was that of my father. I could never mistake the way his shoulders drooped. As for the voice, it belonged to the friend I had known and with whom I had taken cover in the dark of the night behind the dunes when we crossed the Gulf of Suez and its canal to enemy lines.

He said, "I am angry with you."

I said, "Why? You've been killed by the shrapnel of the enemy that has now become a friend."

He said, "Because you don't visit my wife and children." Then he disappeared.

I saw myself going to visit the family of my friend, the martyr. I entered the house after a seven-year absence. I sensed stability in the home: good home cooking, furniture pieces arranged in the shade, the smell of insecticide and air fresheners. His wife led the way. Her face looked rosy and around her eyelids was a touch of makeup replacing the dark rings that had surrounded them after his final departure. I noticed that the wall did not have any of the diplomas and certificates for the many medals and decorations that my friend had earned. The daughter came. She was now a voluptuous young lady wearing jeans and an artificial flower tucked in her straight hair. There was a lot of chitchat, mostly about trivial daily matters such as the new time schedules, the crowding of sports clubs with new members, the disappearance of locally produced detergents and the availability of imported ones, how newspapers did not have any interesting news, the mushrooming of foreign investment firms in the suburb because downtown was already saturated, the high rents and the occasional power failures. I got up, took my leave, and left.

In the street, I walked among people, paying no attention to them at all, as if I had just realized for the first time that my friend was gone for good. Not once did the widow or the daughter mention the book I had written about him, which I had sent to them. I could see that the world had forgotten my friend. During the past seven years he had appeared to me several times and I honored his memory by myself. When the enemy became a friend, when things changed and the flags that we had lowered flew high, I imagined his reaction. My consolation was that my feelings echoed his. I kept on walking and the recent past revealed itself to me: my friend appearing in his fatigues, his penetration of the enemy lines at night, the risks he had taken and his surprises. I saw him attacking and I saw him retreating, but others hadn't seen him, hadn't even caught a glimpse of him, and hadn't kept his memory alive. I listened with a heart assailed by agonies and disasters, a heart that had become totally despondent. I was afraid that he might reveal himself again to me and that I might have to tell him the unpleasant truth, so I hoped he wouldn't return.

An Explanation
And we have set a bar before them and a bar behind them. We have covered them so that they do not see. And whether you warn them or do not warn them, they will not believe.

Epiphanies of the Diwan

When I understood what I understood and learned what I learned; when I ended up being where I was; when I realized that the eye could see but that comprehending what it saw was immense; when I was certain that a human breath was precious and that the breath exhaled would never return and that it should be expended only on that which was dearest and most precious; when I was certain that that which was gone would never come back, that everything changed, that there was a great difference between reading something and living it and being burned by it; when I thought long and contemplated time: eras, epochs, years, seasons, months, weeks, days, hours, minutes, and seconds; when surrounding conditions had changed, my father departed and my killer put his feet in my homeland and trampled the land that my head had touched first; when that enemy extended his shadow inside my home and threatened my rest with desecration; when conditions got worse and my whole life grew sullen; when my father's shadow receded . . . when, when, when, I did not retreat. I resisted my weakness and struggled with my major worries now that my pleasure had departed. Strangely enough, my desires blazed. So I made up my mind to see what no other human had seen, to live in a manner that never occurred to a human to experience, epiphany after epiphany after epiphany. I took to heart the advice given me by my sheikh, Ibn

Iyas, when he told me to continue with my epiphanies, and that a person asleep sees more than those who are awake. Thus I strove and kept striving until I came to the sea of the beginning.

I stood on a seashore, listening and hoping to hear, staring and hoping to see. I sharpened my senses, hoping to feel. I waited long. I stood for such a long time that I almost went back. Suddenly that voice called out to me, "Gamal."

At the moment when *dawn and the ten nights* are determined, my heart throbbed so hard it almost left my chest. I was terrified but I didn't blame myself, for a human was apt to be terrified, especially when hearing that voice that came only at momentous times to convey the weightiest of matters or to warn of some great calamity, but didn't divulge or disclose. After I got hold of myself and regained control of my soul, a different voice, wondrous and strange, came to me from I knew not where, as if it had come from all cardinal points, "What do you wish?"

I didn't get tongue-tied despite the great commotion in my soul. I said, "I am full of grief for what had to pass. It gives me great pain to think of what has transpired and what is transpiring. Is there a way?"

"Why now?"

I said, "What happened has shaken me to my foundation. I am requesting an opportunity. I'd like to see the past, to travel into the future."

I was asked in a kindly tone, "Why now?"

First Completion

I said, "On the morning following my return from abroad, I sought to visit my father for the first time in his new abode. This was my father who walked, strove, yearned, related, suffered, and who looked out for what we needed and tried to fill that need. I didn't know where he was buried because in the city we had not built our eternal abode, not through negligence or because we didn't care, but because of lack of means and hard times. I was accompanied by my brother and our neighbor, the two who had witnessed his final interment; they saw the shovel removing pile after pile of dirt. We took the road encircling the city, extending outside its limits and leading to its entrances. At a specific point I saw a traffic circle with old shops at its corner: a carpenter, a tire repair shop, and a modest grocery store. The fourth shop sold paint supplies at a short distance from a lime kiln. The fifth was a bread store, and the sixth was closed. The seventh store had no features indicating what it did or sold. We entered a walkway that passersby would easily miss: it was narrow, dusty, and deserted. With it began a road that cars could not enter, bound on the right side by yellow walls, silent, interspersed with rusty closed doors. At every moment I expected my brother and our neighbor to stop and point to a specific entrance but they just kept going and I followed them. After a ten-minute walk, it was time. We turned to the right, then to the left. We stopped at the entrance of an open courtyard. My brother pointed to a patch in the ground without a fence, covered with dark sand but not plants, neither cactus nor basil. He said that our relatives, the owners of the tomb, had built two spaces that they did not mark with a fence. My father was the first to be buried there. I drew near; I recited, I wept, then moved away and returned. They stood by my side. I said to myself and to no one else: isn't this unfair? Isn't it cruel? After such a life and long suffering? All those days and nights? Do they all end here and get totally forgotten? Will his traces, his face, and his story get lost here? Will he end up as if he had never been there? The more I thought about it the deeper I got into it, so I sought the task of finding the answer.

A Question Posed
But why? Why now?

Second Completion
I said without fear or hesitation that I had lived in the time of war, that I had faced death, that I had seen shrapnel hit the

target. I saw buildings and armored cars blown up. I saw the pain of wounds the moment they were born on faces. I was frightened by the flight of fighters and bombers so close to the ground that I could see the colors of the pilots' helmets. I saw a woman whose features, height, black clothes, and green tattoo on the chin I still remembered. She was living near the water. Back then the water meant something: the dividing line between us and them was at the two banks. Water was full of significance. If a head was raised more than it should be, the snipers' bullets got it. Reaching the water was in itself an adventure, an act of heroism, a remarkable feat. As for provisioning the soldiers stationed there, it was something that only the brave of heart could do. In the agricultural patch of land Umm Dayf Allah and her five children lived. She dug a trench with her own hand that was adjacent to the house built with mud and bamboo stalks. She hung at its entrance a yellow canvas curtain. Why? So that nobody could invade their privacy during troop movement or raids or cannon fire exchange. That was what she told me.

All of that was now behind us, erased. The images disappeared as if nothing had ever happened. Does time erase time?

A Section
I was told, "The request is difficult to grant but your path is not totally blocked. Submit it to the Diwan." I asked, "What Diwan?" and was told, "Don't be hasty. There are many things you do not know and were the results and fruits revealed to you without proper preparation, much harm would come to you. Be very patient, Gamal, for to those who are patient, good outcome and reward will come. Your epiphanies are hard and take you to paths hitherto untrodden. Make your way to the Diwan that is charged with running the affairs of our finite world. Seek you the lady who presides over the Diwan. Once you understand, you will attain your goal and that will be the success you seek."

Total silence ensued.

Some Cities in the Epiphanies

After a long wait fraught with wishes, doubts, and discouragement at times, I decided to take the plunge into the sea of the beginning. I wasn't afraid of drowning and I didn't dread getting wet. I sailed for a long time. The time it took one to travel by sea was different from what it took to travel by land. In the case of epiphanies it was different altogether since beginnings and endings existed side by side and at times were intermingled. I did not know how much time passed when there appeared to my eyes a city bathed in a tranquil light, enveloped by the sea just as the white of an egg envelopes the yolk. The light was not that of day nor was it like that of the moon nor, nor. I found out as I drew close to its gates that the night here did not penetrate or overtake the day, that time did not change as it ordinarily did. Rather different periods were there side by side in succession, then started all over again, also in succession. Then there appeared to me a towering building emanating from the city center. I couldn't make out the details. I went around the walls that were so high that my eyes could not see their tops. There appeared to me a small door to which a massive bridge made of turquoise led. I went through the door and I was totally dazzled, and my heart started racing when I saw the buildings made of colored specters that my limited comprehension tempted me to keep walking through. A gentle but firm resistance, however, suddenly kept my steps confined to the crystal pavement. At the intersections, the echoes of the lights and the shades of the colors met. As for the climate, it was September-like, unchanging. The month with which autumn began lasted all the time. The beginnings of autumn, before one's thoughts turned inward as usually happened in the winter, led to preparation for that introspection. It felt like the beginnings of a curve, neither fully venturing out nor recoiling back. It was neither hot nor cold, no blazing brightness or depressing darkness. I saw short, low-built walls, with bricks of rays: one brick of light, one of shade, a brick made of twilight, and another of brightness, or so I thought, for my senses were limited to that which I knew or experienced. The new knowledge that was imparted to me was measured and the process was gradual. After I took a few steps I discovered that distances were getting shorter. I did not know how long it had been, but I didn't hesitate, nor did I think of turning back. I told myself that possibilities were endless, so try to imagine what impossibilities would be like. After a while I saw a round tower of green light in the middle of which was a rectangular door with a rounded top. The door was ajar. After I stole a glance through it there appeared to me a path of shadows. I didn't draw near but stopped and waited. My wait was not long. I was called.

Avowal

I was called from an invisible place. I stood politely and bowed my head. A voice asked, "What do you want?" I said, "I seek the president of the Diwan."

"What do you want?"

I said, "My concerns are myriad, but I will sum up what I hope for: to recover that which is irrecoverable."

I was told, "Your request is difficult, but you have reached this stage only because you've tried." The voice fell silent. I walked through the tower. My sight grew weary from the brightness and the lights and the colors for which we had no names in the world of the possible. I walked and after a few steps, I realized that all beings were in a state of constant dialogue among themselves.

A Useful Lesson

According to authenticated traditions of the Prophet, peace be upon him [pbuh], all animals prick up their ears on Fridays for fear of the Day of Judgment. Once the Prophet, pbuh, was riding a mule that bolted, almost throwing him off its back, as they neared a grave, where it heard the lamentations of the grave dweller who was being punished. About Mount Uhud he said, "This is a mountain that we love and which loves us. Pebbles sang the praises of

God in his palm. This was a stone that he greeted. On the Day of Judgment a man will leave his home and his thigh will tell him what has happened back at his home after he was gone. Hides of animals have said, 'We were made to speak by God who has made everything speak.' God Almighty has said that the shadows, those in heaven and on earth, the sun, the moon, the stars, the mountains and the trees and all animals and many humans, leaving nothing out, prostrate themselves before God. In the Qur'an God says, *There is not a thing that does not sing God's praises, but you do not understand what they sing."*

Completion

I was called, "Gamal."

I paused. I was asked, "Have you struggled?"

"I have tried," I said.

I crossed the square at a leisurely pace. I passed by trees of interpenetrating memories, low hanging images, forgotten desires, and unrealized wishes. I realized that I had gone too far and that turning back was impossible. I had no choice but to go on. I became aware, and the realization flashed through my mind, just as the fragrant smell of sweet bygone days would catch us unawares, that I was two bows' length away. So I patiently bore my exile so far away from home. Then there appeared in front of me a narrow road whose pavements were made of white musk and whose sides were made of amber, or so it seemed to me. At the end of the road I was called, "Have you sought knowledge?" I said, "I've tried."

A tranquillity and peace descended upon me. I was able to see what the buildings contained, on the whole though not in detail. There was not a movement in the world that did not have its equivalent here. No inanimate object or plant, no fixed or moving thing lacked a picture or a model here. No sound lacked an echo, even the moment one wave touched another wave. I perceived but I did not see. I acquired the knowledge that the houses of the city were inhabited. Every house accommodated something exclusively: a house for echoes and a house for sounds; a house for hearts and a house for veils; a house for excess and a house for shortages; a house for loss and a house for reunions; a house for emotional life and a house for the removal of doubts; a house for hoarded generosity and a house for oppression, injustice, and tyranny; a house for mysterious signs and a house for readiness and preparedness; a house for taking by surprise and a house for granting and withholding; a house for grace and a house for inspiration; a house for moments of farewell and a house for the last moments of seeing loved ones; a house for crossing bridges, a house of tenderness, a house of compassion, and a house for thanks; a house for loving glances to embrace and a house for gentle touching of hands and a house for strong gripping of hands; a house for thanks and a house for harm; a house for despair, a house for victory, and a house for defeat; a house for profit and a house for loss; a house for the sources of light and a house for bright eyes; a house for trembling eyelids and a house for the parting of the lips; a house for intersections and a house for travelers' stations; a house for affection and a house for divine protection; a house for undoing harm; a house for happy people and a house for unhappy people; a house for strangers and a house for the lost; a house for injustice and a house for palpable torment; a house for lineage and a house for symptoms and amulets; a house for positions and a house for quantities; a house for misgivings, a house for sight, and a house for heartbeats; a house for birth and a house for death; a house for the part and a house for the whole; a house for what has been and a house for what is and a house for what will be and a house for what will not be; a house for pictures of continents and a house for oceans; a house for rivers and a house for gulfs; a house for ravines, a house for towering mountains, a house for valleys, and a house for caves; a house for cities that have been and a house for cities that will be; a house for sleepy hamlets and a house for expansive villages; a house for extinct street corners and a house for entrances that lead somewhere; a house for suburbs and a house for squares that were one day and those that will be; a house for narrow lanes, alleys, doors, and stairs and a house behind which lovers live; a house for tunnels and a house for domes; a house for towers and a house for citadels; a house for fortified hideouts and a house for temples; a house for shady corners and a house for gardens; a house for evenings and a house for hands holding flowers; a house for chance meetings and a house for that which will not be repeated; houses that lack stability and houses whose inhabitants have no stability. I perceived all the houses in their totality but not their contents. I didn't stop. I didn't hear yet I felt joy and was optimistic. I was called, "Gamal."

"Yes."

"Did you comprehend?" I was asked.

I said, "Woe is me for what I have missed!"

A Connection

A feeling of utter contentment filled me. I lived the moments after the light rainfall in faraway suburbs nestled in the midst of green leaves. I was certain that I was close to attaining some of what I had striven for. Our earthly world was summed up, abbreviated here: the beginning and the end. There was no distant past or faraway future. That which had been and that which was yet to come were adjacent: that which had not been but which will be and that which had been but which will not be. Everything was there in great detail. Suddenly things revealed themselves before my eyes: I saw the Diwan. It loomed from afar as I drew near. It was towering like nothing in our world. When I saw it, I saw it from all four cardinal points as if I were looking at it with eight eyes. I took in all the details as if I was seeing it from above and from below. I couldn't find the letters or the words with which to form speech. My mind tried to liken it to what I knew and it recalled memorial monuments commemorating those who had died in wars but whose names were unknown. I conjured up façades of Asian temples with complex structures and the entrances of mountain passes. I realized that this was the center and the axis. No voice called out my name and no sudden mysterious caller startled or terrified me. I was not frightened by anyone touching me but I imagined that I was carried, that I was floating in a sunset space without clouds. Below me were domes, crescents, crosses, and pointed spires. I was told, "Everything is here; your days and the days of others. There is, however, one thing (if one can call it a thing) that you cannot see no matter how much you try. You will never attain it regardless of what effort you put into it. You will never fathom its essence no matter how much you suffer."

I was assailed and enveloped by a heaving human sorrow. Before any attempt at inquiry on my part, I was called, "You who have been, you who are, and who will not be."

I bowed my head in silence. So, I will appear before the pure lady, guardian of purity, the president of the Diwan and the two luminous members.

An Explanation

The Diwan is the center that controls our earthly world. In it are decided the broad outlines of destinies and the major directions. That which is decreed ends up before it, from the weightiest events to the whispers of a child who hasn't experienced the world yet. The sessions are held every Saturday evening (world time) and last from sunset until the break of dawn. During the session it is decided what will come to pass within the seven coming earthly days and petitions are looked into, punishments decided, and a stone is given justice from the one who has split it. Therefore those wronged take refuge there, imploring the pure president, crying, "O president of the Diwan!" No appeal ever gets lost on its way to her, no matter what its source or place might be or what time it is made. The president of the Diwan, Sayyida Zeinab, listens to the complaints and moans of all creatures, even as the trees moan complaining about the stinging wind. She is assisted by two members; one to her left, the master of the youth of paradise, al-Husayn, pbuh. To her right sits his older brother, the one who died of poisoning, the pure of heart and conduct, al-Hasan, pbuh.

26

The Diwan

I entered a dune of white amber. I was dazzled by a light that flowed through my eyes on the surface but which coursed through my nerves and my whole body on the inside and in the most delicate parts of my soul. I became an eye and an ear. I saw with my whole being, unbound by any single direction. The president of the Diwan appeared to me draped in a cloak of the dew to be found on the tips of flower leaves. To her left was al-Husayn and to her right, al-Hasan. In front of them were what looked like large sheets of paper. I was dumbfounded, but when the president of the Diwan looked at me, I was cheered.

"What brings you here, Gamal?"

"A finite existence and a desire for an infinite existence," I said.

She said, "What made you go out?"

"My perplexity, my pain, and my desire to come in," I said.

At that point al-Husayn, the master of the martyrs, the one who fell in Karbala, turned to me. I was pleased and my pain was eased and my heart rejoiced. I held myself back from rushing into his arms, out of politeness and awe.

"What kept you awake at night?" he said to me.

"That which was and that which will be," I replied.

Then I couldn't help myself so I blurted out, oblivious to any barriers between us, "My father loved you."

He didn't embarrass me for being so forward. He gestured, "I know that."

I said, "You are the first fragrance in my life. I lived next to your resting place the most secure days of my life."

He gestured, "I know that."

"We used to perform the prayers of the two eids in your mosque. There I saw Gamal Abdel Nasser and his processions early in the day."

He nodded, "I know that."

I grew bolder and said, "My father spent the whole time by your mausoleum, always circumambulating it. He never missed a prayer time except when sick or out of town or during times of great calamities. He sought refuge by your side in hard times and he would tell those with whom he was pleased that he would read the Fatiha for them at your tomb."

He said, "I know that."

I continued, feeling no barriers holding me back, "Your aura enveloped my childhood and my youth. My father would hold me by one hand and my brother by the other hand and then we would go to visit you. We would take off our shoes and enter your mausoleum, kiss your threshold, and go out to stroll down the nearby streets there to see the vendors of incense, prayer beads, multicolored handkerchiefs, Holy Qur'ans, books relating saints' lives and epics, chewing gum, frankincense, skullcaps, amber in small thumb-sized tins, and perfumes. We would drink carob juice then head for the nearby coffeehouse attached to an old hotel where some men of our village would stay. My father would visit with them, and they would talk."

The master of martyrs said gently, "I know that."

I said in pained regret, "Those days are forever gone."

"For each thing there is a season," he said.

I turned to address his older brother, "From the far corners of my childhood I can see a printed multicolored poster in which I can make out green, yellow, and red colors. In the middle is your father, peace be upon him, wearing a green mantle, in his hand there is a sword in its sheath, above which is written in Arabic: 'God's victorious lion, Ali ibn Abi Talib,' and to his left al-Husayn is standing and to his right, you are standing."

Al-Hasan nodded. It seemed his eyes were closed. My heart was immediately at ease. I saw his smile lovelier than the vision of the beloved, and more tender than a child at peace. My trepidation left me and I was tranquil. I thought of what would become of me. The president of the Diwan looked at me. She came into full view draped in the shade of dew at dawn, radiant, beaming, affable, playful, noble, and sagacious. She said, "What's troubling you?"

"Things keep changing," I said.

"And what else?"

"Things decay and are transitory."

"And what else?" she said.

"Certainty is ephemeral."

"And what else?"

"My obsessions with wishes and no time to see them fulfilled."

"And what else and what else?"

"Changes, mutability, and vicissitudes. Things puzzle me as they disperse and gather, as they differ and agree: obedience and disobedience, profit and loss, enslavement and freedom, life and death, arriving and missing, day and night, the straight and the crooked, the even and the odd, health and illness, beginning and end, joy and sadness, the spirit and the ghost, earth and heaven, synthesis and analysis, the many and the few, lunchtime and late afternoon, whiteness and blackness, sleep and insomnia, the visible and the invisible, things in movement and at repose, the rigid and the supple."

I paused. I was finished. The president of the Diwan said after an interval of silence, "Because you have tried, because you have struggled, a portion of a portion but not all in its totality will be revealed to you, because you are limited to a finite existence that will not be extended. There will be revealed to you glimpses and signs. From time to time the master of the young denizens of paradise will accompany you. So, be patient, for if you go on and continue your quest for facts your hand will grow weary, your pen will be dulled, and your notebooks and slates will be full."

She extended her hand bathed in gentle dew and touched me. My sight became very sharp and my abilities immense. Then she said, "There is one matter, if it can be called a 'matter,' that will never be revealed to you. Don't ask about it because you will never be granted knowledge of it no matter how much learning you acquire. You will never penetrate its intricacies. And don't be hasty, for man is given to haste."

I said, "My heart is filled with astonishment, perplexity, and hope. There's no room for anything more."

The Epiphanies of the Voyages

The First Voyage: Birth

Fact
Everything is in constant travel.

A Statement
My father's life itinerary is strange and my itinerary in my father's itinerary is strange.

A Signal
The world is one of the traveler's abodes; it is a bridge spanning the banks of a huge, raging river.

Getting Ready
The one who fell in Karbala, the master of the youth of paradise, looked at me with magnanimous eyes, a radiant forehead, and the gaze of a kindly lover. I was too embarrassed to look at him: his tenderness and the kindness he bestowed on me were not things I was accustomed to. I was pleased; I was part of a great crowd. I drew near and I smelled a pleasant fragrance wafting from him and from his breath. He asked me, "Where do you wish to go?"

I said, "Are long distances a factor?"

He said, "The difficulties of the beginning do not diminish unless one knows the noble destination."

Taking his hand moistened with delightful dew, I said, "I am surrendering myself to you but I am longing for moments of birth."

Section

Everything turns: days turn into weeks, weeks into months, months into years, and years into epochs. Day turns into night and night into day. Planets revolve, humans revolve, words revolve, and happiness revolves. Summer comes and goes, winter comes and goes, autumn comes and goes, and spring also. Toil follows rest, sadness follows joy, and birth comes after death.

A Basil Leaf from Our First Voyage

My village in the deep south of Egypt was revealed to me in its original colors. The source of the light was hidden. It was the light of dawn except there was no dawn; twilight red but not twilight. There was no heat or cold. It was just the right moment, even though the day had no name, the month unknown and the year too. It was a distant day, very far, self-enclosed, unconnected to any other day. I arrived at it after a long absence. The houses were revealed to me close to each other, leaning into one another on a rise to stay away from the river water during the time of the flood. It was surrounded by thick clusters of date palm trees, fields, dusty roads, waterwheels that had not yet started to turn, doum trees, sycamores, acacia, and old eucalyptus trees. There were fig trees with a strong sweet smell that was overpowering in the bends of the village roads. I surveyed the houses, the north well, the southern cemetery. I traveled through the village at night, my eyesight sharp, with no blinders on, relaxed, my sense of hearing heightened, my heart wide open, and my senses on high alert.

I knew that no one could see or hear me, that no one could communicate or talk with me. I was very curious and knew that the moment was at hand. I entered the house. I saw three women standing, wearing black clothes. One of them was short and thin with frizzy hair and a round green tattoo on her chin. I saw my grandmother lying down in their midst, great pain showing on her face. I saw blood. I averted my gaze but soon enough I stared. The short woman said at short intervals that relief was at hand, that contractions were quickening, and that everything would be blessed with God's permission. I saw another thin, tall woman come out of the parlor and ask a man who wore a felt turban around which he had wound a brown-colored woolen shawl to invoke God's name so that relief would come. I recognized him as my father's father, my grandfather whose face my father could not remember because he died only two years after his birth. For some time I was greatly interested in conjuring up his features to see to what extent they related to me or I to them.

On an earthen bench next to the oven a six-year old boy stretched out next to his younger brother, my uncles whom I didn't know because I'd never met them. My father told me about them for the first time after his final departure and appearance in the epiphanies of separation. I tried to envision them but to no avail, even though I could see what no other human could. It was strange that I missed small images and little details.

I took a look inside the parlor and I saw the short woman whose name I didn't know, holding my father who had just been born. She hit him lightly and softly on his buttocks and back. The first cry came, thin and brief. I was frightened. I drew nearer and marveled at the fact that I passed through the third, fat woman who was silent the whole time. I didn't know her name either. I turned to the right side of my heart and saw the one who fell in Karbala, my guide, my master, and my companion. He disappeared when he was not in my thoughts and would reappear when I thought of him, even in passing. He would put my mind at ease if I faced a dilemma or was afraid. He was always two bows' length or closer. He never deserted me but was always kind to me and did not hold back anything. I was so apprehensive and frightened that I couldn't say anything or reveal anything. It was as if it was I, as if I were the branch from which its root had come, as if I were the echo which produced its original sound, as if I were the boy whose father was his son, as if I were the bow that touched its arrow, as if I were the shadow that created its own source.

I was so stupefied I recoiled into my own soul. My beloved brought me back to my surroundings. He motioned with his pure head that was once severed from the back of the neck and murmured something with his luminous lips that the noblest of creation, the Prophet Muhammad, once kissed and which Yazid ibn Mu'awiya later desecrated. Al-Husayn motioned toward my just-born father, urging me to look long and closely at the departed beloved and I did. My father was now a baby a few minutes old, eyes closed, head bruised. The short woman rushed him out of the parlor, swaddled in an old man's gallabiya. She brought him to his father. He raised his head with an expressionless face. It was the first moment of confrontation. My grandfather seemed keen on not showing joy or sadness, as though if he were to show any emotion it would be a weakness unbefitting a tough man. I preoccupied myself by looking at my father. I saw a great similarity between his features and those of his father. His eyes were closed and he was silent. The woman pinched his delicate nose gently and my newly born father cried. That was his second cry. He opened his eyes, facing the light for the first time. My grandfather smiled and exclaimed, "Hello, silly boy!" At that point my father was gone. I didn't know the day, the date, or the year even though I saw what I saw. How paradoxical!

An Apparition
The compassionate one turned and motioned with his beautiful head, as if he had guessed what I was thinking about, to the patch of land that my father's head touched the moment he came into the world. My beloved reminded me that all beings in existence,

the original elements in my voyages and epiphanies, had the ability to speak and to respond to me. Here I heard what I was not accustomed to hearing, what I could not describe for anyone, that which the letters of language were incapable of conjuring in any tongue. I affirm, as my voice is breaking, that that patch of earth spoke to me. It was whispering, saying that, all told, my father had touched it only once—the moment he was born. Strangely enough he spent several years in that house but he never crawled, stretched out, took a stroll, took even one step, touched it, played, or stepped on it. During his last visit to the village one month before his final departure, he had come, entered all houses, greeted everyone, reflected, recalled, and remembered. He had even shaken the hands of the women. He spent a night in the house in which he was born, the house of his father which unfairly ended up being the property of one of his uncles—this would take too long to explain and will be covered in detail in time. He spent his night in the outer courtyard.

"He did not set foot on me. He did not sit near me, not because the house had been expanded and the placing of the rooms had been changed and the fact that in my place now is a wheat silo. No. He didn't even look at me. He left me for good the moment he was born."

The patch of land fell silent. I kept on gazing for a long time. The question would occur to me and before formulating it and uttering it, the answer would come. That was how it responded to me. It said that the father of my father never set foot on it even though he had passed by it countless times, but that he would either place his foot before reaching it or after he had already passed it. The same was true of his grandfather, but that there was a distant grandfather who lived in the old time who used it as his sitting place, never leaving it for ninety years. "He would only leave to answer the call of nature at a certain spot in the midst of a thicket of palm trees that withered and died a long time ago. When he came here the first time, he was over a hundred years old."

I looked to my right side where my guide al-Husayn was. He did not show any objection but made a gesture and things were revealed to my heart. I recovered the time that was lost. I saw my grandfather. He looked solidly built and youthful but when he stood up he bent in such a way that his head touch the middle of his chest. When he walked he staggered and when he glanced he frowned and when he pointed he shook. He spoke in whispers and wore black rags. I learned that he had sound, sharp senses, and that he saw in the dark and had keen hearing even through the din of a storm. He had healthy teeth. The patch of land told me they were the teeth that grew again after the age of one hundred, that they became visible after his return from his sojournings. I asked, "What sojournings?" and the patch of land said that it could tell me only what took place on it or under it, that if I wished I could inquire from his foot tracks. But I did not wish to leave the place that my father touched when he came into the world so I asked it to tell me what it could.

The patch of land spoke briefly and cryptically. It said that that ancestor of mine had signs and miracles associated with him since birth, that was how those sitting nearby at the time described him. They said that he always stared at the faraway sky, that during Ramadan, the month of fasting, he suckled only at night. Once when he was sick his mother raised her hands in supplication toward the sky asking for him to recover and a mysterious voice answered her saying, "Amen."

As he was growing up my distant grandfather did not commit any sin or act of disobedience. On a cloudy winter day someone posed a question to him, "The ostrich: is it an animal or a bird?" He didn't answer but thought hard and deep and then toured the whole region asking and inquiring. What he heard did not satisfy his curiosity. So he decided to travel in search of the answer. He disappeared from the village, the whole region. No one saw him and no one heard anything about him. He was deemed lost and people forgot all about him. He traveled the world over for a hundred and twenty years before coming back and settling in the very same patch of land that my father's head touched. He spent another hundred and twenty years spinning wool. As people passed by him, they moved away or acknowledged him with a nod. As for the children, they raised a din, asked who he was, what his name was. Some of them were his own great-great-grandchildren, who didn't recognize him and whom he also didn't recognize. Some threw little stones or date pits at him but he made no effort to defend himself. Toward the end of his days, before he totally disappeared, a tall man with a gray mustache and beard and a radiant forehead, wearing shimmering clothes, came to him. He asked my grandfather whether he had found an answer to his question. My grandfather shook his head from right to left and disappeared the moment dusk appeared. Then the patch of land fell silent and the epiphany faded out. I asked eagerly, "What's my grandfather's name?" but I got no answer. My beloved did not come to my aid. I saw the changing of the dust specks, the succession of days and nights, the niggardly rainfall, the stinging winds, the passing heat and cold. The patch of land said, "No human has touched me and no one has set foot on me except your distant grandfather and except for receiving your father's head at his birth, even though I am in an inhabited place." Hoping to continue the conversation and to receive more revelations, I said, "And what is the name of my distant grandfather? What day was my father born?"

I saw my just-born father suckle for the first time as his mother propped up his head while his mouth tried to cling to the milk-filled breast. I saw him sleeping, then moving his arms and legs. I saw him staring in my direction, looking where I stood. I was backing away slowly, my voice inside me muffled without whispering and without revealing myself.

A Murmur
If he appears to me, I am all eyes.
If he speaks, I am all ears.

A Connection
In the company of my beloved I saw myself transported to Wednesday, May 9, 1945. My mother appeared tired and resigned. I saw myself

being born the same moment my father was born. I didn't know what was happening inside me and I was not aware of the extent of my knowledge or what my senses perceived. I heard my grandmother saying to my mother, "Congratulations! It's a boy." My mother opened her eyes and looked at me. They carried me for her to see me. I drew near to see myself. My head was bruised, my body bluish, and my face resembled my father's the moment he was born. But there was no resemblance between me and my distant grandfather. My grandmother said, "What name are you going to give him?" My mother, weary after her labor and delivery of a new baby, said, "We will not give him a name before you send a letter to his father in Cairo."

It was now dawn, the night was departing as a strong wind shook the door that my mother's brother was leaning back against. The dry reeds were about to scatter and be carried away by the storm. It was unseasonably rough weather. My grandmother looked at a woman they called "Duda the Worm," whom I had seen frequently in my early years. Her husband was a government watchman. I used to sit with her as she tended the oven, dispatching loaves of dough through its mouth and stoking its fire with reeds, dung cakes, and other combustibles. She told me stories. She was a good woman and I loved her. She died years ago and I didn't give her her due, what with my being away from the village and all, and my infrequent visits. I had forgotten what she looked like. She was lost in the maze of my childhood. I only saw her again in this epiphany with the master of the young denizens of paradise. She now seemed younger and fuller.

"The Worm" was the first person to hold me, the first to see me, even before my mother, my father, and my grandmother. She was the one to slap me to elicit the first cry. I saw blood covering a pile of green grass that they had spread under my mother. As soon as I was born my grandmother said, "Go, Duda, to Weld Hamid. Tell him to write a letter to Ahmad in Cairo."

I looked long at my just-born body with its delicate limbs in its confinement. I saw that my eyes were closed, that I couldn't face the light. I wondered at that and said, "Is that me?" My beloved al-Husayn nodded and motioned to me, saying, "You are surprised. But that's not your first form." For some mysterious reason I didn't understand, I was overcome with a mild case of terrestrial melancholy full of gentleness and pity. It was as if my master and companion figured out what had come over me and he began to stroke my hair. I calmed down and was at ease. Once again I continued my travel through the epiphany.

I saw Weld Hamid writing a letter to my father. I saw the letter arrive and an employee whose name I didn't know reading it aloud to my father. I saw my father's confusion, his happiness, and the slight tremor of excitement coursing through his body to his facial features. I didn't look for very long. The master of the martyrs conveyed to me the reassurance that I would see him many times later on, that I'd have my fill of him. I saw my father's confusion when he couldn't find the ideal way to express his feelings. It saddened me to see him confused this way so I called out to him and I stepped toward him. But the master of the martyrs stopped me gently yet firmly, indicating that it was no use, that contact was out of the question and that entering that world was impossible. I said, "What a pity!"

I saw my father dictating a letter to someone I didn't know, in which he asked my mother, my uncle, and my grandmother to name me Abdel Ra'uf. I saw my mother embracing me. I saw my grandmother reciting an incantation and holding a paper doll, piercing the place of the eyes with a needle several times, each piercing in the eyes of each envious woman. I saw myself throwing up. The infant me was gaunt and tiny and trembling. I got worried that something bad would happen to me. Then I caught a glimpse of my intercessor's smile and realized that I was alive. I wondered: how could I be afraid that the newborn who was me would die?

I saw my mother crying. I realized she was remembering her two sons who had departed before my arrival. I saw that she was in fear of loss. I was about to reassure her, to tell her that I would live. I almost spoke then I remembered, so I remained silent. I remembered what my beloved said in the Diwan that each thing had its own season.

My mother said, "Write to Ahmad to select a name other than Abdel Ra'uf. If he continues to bear this name, he will not live." My grandmother reassured her, but she insisted. That was what she had seen in a vision. She didn't want to say any more, but she would lose the boy if his name was not changed. "Write to his father." I saw my father receiving the second letter, listening to its contents and then I saw him dictating the reply, asking them to name me Gamal. He didn't think for a long time. The name just occurred to him. I saw the person that he wanted to name me after, a close relative of his, a young, tall, and stout man who lived in a house close to the Nile and who studied law. He died seven months after my birth. I saw my father mourning him and thinking of me as the older Gamal was being interred. He returned from the cemetery to the al-Husayn neighborhood and bought for me a gallabiya, a skullcap, and a pound of sweets that he sent to the village with a blind traveler.

I saw my mother contented and carefree, as she rocked me and sang lullabies to me: "Go to sleep, sleep my love, and I will buy you a turtle dove." I was swaddled in black rags. I couldn't see my face or features and I didn't know what was wrong with me. I guessed I was suffering from some sort of malaise. I didn't know how many months it had been since I was born. Then I distracted myself from looking at me by inquiring after the three women that attended my father's birth and I found out that they had long since departed, that my mother did not remember them or even know them. I turned my attention to the distance between this patch of land that my father's head had touched and the one that mine had. It had a green ground cover and measured seventy cubits.

My mother fell silent. I realized I had gone to sleep. She bent over me and kissed me. I was overcome with an oppressive sadness that shook me through and through. I bowed my head and took a step toward the master of the martyrs, moving away from my mother who was carrying me as I slept, with a strange kind of resignation written all over her features. My beloved patted me on the head. My melancholy deepened and I abandoned myself to grief.

A Fact

My father did not witness my birth and I did not witness his final departure. Between the two negative markers lies our alienation.

The Epiphany of Travel

We remain in a state of constant travel from the origins of our beginnings onward, forever. If you see a house you believe to be the ultimate goal, it will lead you to other paths and other goals. Many a time you believe that you have reached the most desired destination but once there you soon find yourself on the road again. How many phases of creation have you gone through to turn into the blood of your father and mother? The two got together for you, intentionally or unintentionally. The sperm turned into a clot, and that into a lump then bone, then the bone was clothed with flesh which was then transformed into another creation. That creation came into the world, turned into a child, and then an adolescent, then a young person, then into a full-fledged adult, then a middle-aged person, then an old person, then senility kicked in, and then out into the isthmus between this world and the next. So there was never stasis to begin with but constant motion, day and night.

The Connection of Travel

It was as if my master, the witness to my days, had comprehended what I was going through and my innermost thoughts, so we stopped at the upper floor of the Dar al-Shifa Hospital in Abbasiya, Cairo. I knew the day and the moment quite well. The fourth floor is devoted entirely to obstetrics. I saw myself wearing a gray suit at the age of thirty-one years, six months, nine days, and four-and-a-half hours. I was standing in the tiled corridor with no sound reaching us from the isolated room. My father-in-law stood in silence, as did my wife's brother. My father was not there, as if time had fast-forwarded him, and for a year he had been moving in the world as a stranger or we had moved as strangers in his world. Even though that was not proper and should not be allowed to happen, it did happen and there was nothing I could do about it except to roam, to coast, to suffer and to strive, to pursue epiphanies, to travel, to experience exile and its pitch-black nights, to drown in its obliterating seas, to suffer the burden of futile longing, to be captive of an irrevocable loss, to taste the bitterness of a separation that never ends in reunion, a departure unmitigated by an arrival following it or ending it, to cry over that which was gone forever and what I lost without any hope of recovery. If only I had known what I came to know. I would have listened and not stalled or procrastinated, I wouldn't have done what I have done. But how could I have foretold destiny? I was ignorant. I was hasty, and *man was made in haste,* according to the glorious Qur'an. There was nothing left for me to do in these dark days except to seek epiphanies, to strive, to take refuge in my beloved's intercession, in the hope that he would approve, or alleviate, or even save me.

I saw the door open and the doctor come out. He looked calm. He took me aside and told me that it was a natural birth, but that he had to perform a minor surgery that should not leave any scars. Then as if suddenly remembering, "Congratulations. It's a boy." He told me that the fees were eight pounds plus twenty for the anesthesia. I saw my hand offering the envelope containing the money. He said, "Thanks," and left. After a few minutes the nurse with the white uniform came out embracing a bundle. She stopped in front of me and asked my brother-in-law to close the window, as a cold wind was blowing. She pulled away the edge of the bundle and I could see my eyes gazing at my newborn son: head rectangular, eyes closed. I saw the moment I first came face to face with my son. I was startled by the fact that he looked like my father, so much so that his face looked like a miniature of his. The nurse pinched his nose gently and he let out two cries one after the other. She covered his face again and stood waiting. I saw my hand extended with a tip, five pounds. She took him to the newborns' room.

It was Thursday, the ninth of December of the year one thousand, nine hundred and seventy-six. Between the birth of my son and that of my intercessor and guide al-Husayn were one thousand, three hundred and ninety-two years of the Hijra and between his arrival and the birth of Gamal Abdel Nasser were fifty-eight years of the Common Era. Between his birth and that of my father was a number of years, months, and days unknown to me. I looked at my beloved, my imam. He smiled gently in a kindly manner and shook his head as if conveying to me that it was a fruitless pursuit.

"Did your father know how old he was?"

"No," I said.

"Has anyone tried to find out?"

"No," I said.

He said, "How would you know that now? And why?"

I didn't say anything because I felt there was a tone of reproach or rebuke in his voice; the tone of someone who knew but who didn't want me to know.

To me was revealed the moment of my father's birth, the moment of my birth, and the moment I saw my son for the first time. I saw myself present three times in three different places, seeing with one set of eyes and understanding with one mind. I didn't want to bother my dear companion so I asked myself: were events similar at the points of beginning then different when the journeying began and we developed separate and distinct pictures at every different stage? Did only the hidden similarity, that comprehended neither by the senses nor the intellect, survive? Did even these hidden similarities fade away and vanish totally in the sunset of life and old age? Why did I not achieve tranquillity and why had my master not come to my aid? Inside myself I could hear an answer: that was one of the mysteries of the voyage. I realized there was no answer.

I saw that I hadn't left the fourth floor. The hall was empty. There was a sign asking for silence so as not to disturb the patients, as well as the smell of medical disinfectants. There was quiet in the dusty light so I calmed down. Then I heard a strange voice with unusual tones and rhythm addressing me in my own language. I realized it was coming from one of the stones making up the wall of the fourth floor. It told me that before it was taken, its rough edges hewn, before they put it in this wall, it had been lying about in a field near where the hospital stood. The whole area was nothing but green fields, before they were paved over with asphalt, before the buildings were built. At that point when the stone was speaking, things in the place changed and I saw that stone abandoned near a railroad and telegraph posts, with open sky. The time was neither day nor night. I saw my father coming from the other end of the city. I saw that he was tired, the edges of his gallabiya covered with dust. He looked young. I couldn't guess how old he was nor what year I was being shown. I understood, however, that he was homeless, that this was during his earliest days in the capital, that he had not yet learned its streets, neighborhoods, alleys, and byways. In order to move from one place to another he had to ask, to seek, to ascertain, to show addresses that had been written for him. I realized that he was heading for one of the men from his village in the nearby suburb, that he had a long way to go and a long time before he would reach his destination. I saw him looking around. I saw confusion written all over his features. I saw his wretchedness and his misery. As he was walking, he suddenly stopped, looked around as if begging for help from an unknown, invisible quarter and cried, "Ah yabouy!"—calling a father who was not there. Then I saw him stretch out and lean his head on the stone. A moment later he placed his arm under his head against the stone, the very stone that spoke to me from its place in the hospital wall. I had a revelation within the epiphany. I went on a voyage within the voyage and departed to the point of departure as the stone kept repeating monotonously, "Your father used me as a pillow, your father used me as a pillow." I looked at my guide. He was silent. His silence gave me pause and tranquillity until the thought occurred to me: how did I see all that I've seen, but did not see his own moment?

Direction

Do not seek the master, al-Husayn, in the east or west.
Leave all others and come to me: his lasting abode is in my heart.

The Long Voyage

This is a difficult voyage. It suggests rather than states explicitly. It hints without divulging. It is the fifth day of the month of Shaaban of the fourth year of the Hijra. A woman I do not know is speaking to me. She tells me that Fatima al-Zahraa gave birth to him one year after the birth of his brother al-Hasan. The Prophet, pbuh, came to her and said, "Give me my son." She presented the baby, swaddled in white, to him. The Prophet, pbuh, was pleased and he made the call to the prayers in his right ear and declared the start of prayers in his left ear. Then he placed him on his lap and cried. So I said, "By my father and mother, O Messenger of God, why are you crying?" And he said, "I am crying for what will befall him after I am gone."

Voyages of Birth

I didn't inquire even though there were many serious matters and innumerable issues. I was afraid to bother him or to unintentionally disobey him. I followed him like his shadow as he traveled. After a short while, I witnessed the moment of birth of a red anemone. I saw the egg of a falcon crack open in a nest on a peak. I was present at the moment of death of an ancient whale. I saw the moment a cloud was born on high. I saw the cracking of a wheat kernel, the moment a palm tree was pollinated. I saw the birth of Gamal Abdel Nasser in a gray room in a small, out-of-the-way town. I witnessed the moment of the fertilization of an egg inside the womb of a woman in a gray city with white buildings at the far end of Syria. I saw the seed, then the clot, then the embryo, and the fetus in its various phases. I saw the father saying a few minutes after the birth, "Name her Laura." I turned to my master and guide in amazement. He answered me succinctly, "You'll cross paths with her in future epiphanies." I almost wondered out loud: how would I meet her when she was from faraway regions, when no opportunity presented itself? But I didn't ask.

I saw the formation of a distant planet and how it acquired its spherical shape. I witnessed the extinction of a star outside the galaxy. I saw the shooting star as it went down. I witnessed the moment the lightning was born, the bursting of the spark. I saw the germ of an ear of wheat, the birth of milk within the folds of the udder. I was there when the dew was born, the early formation of the wave. I saw the moment color acquired its color: red for the red, blue for the blue, and yellow for the yellow. I saw the birth of an idea, the arrival of a meaning. I witnessed the birth of separation and union, the tremor of loss. The visions came pouring in. I closed my eyes when the epiphanies glowed. I wasn't accustomed to that. I wished to run away from these voyages but he held my hand and waited. So I waited until that which had given me fright went away. At that point I held my breath and regained my composure and my calm. It was as if I were a drowning man who had just been saved, as if I had just been born. What reassured me was that he was standing by my side, giving me support. I saw him filling my visible horizon, giving me freely of himself. It occurred to me to ask forgiveness if I had erred unintentionally, but he calmed me down and I was safe from harm, so I resigned myself and kept myself in check. I let my mind think freely of all I had seen. Then I heard him say in a kindly manner, "Toughen up. There are long travels ahead of you."

A Poetic Diversion
I said, my friends, she is the sun.
Her light is near but she is out of reach.

The Epiphanies of Travels
Including the Voyages of Exile

A Fact
My destiny is to be always traveling
For I have no homeland to begin with.

A Tear
Oh God, we haven't cried for a long time
Except when we cry over what time has done.

The Book of Mutations
I saw my father as a child, crawling, then playing. When was that?
What day and what year? I didn't know and it was not revealed to
me nor did my intercessor and master deign to share it with me. I
made an estimate, a blind guess, but I couldn't pinpoint it. At the
age of three? Four?

Perhaps closer to five?

During these travels as I come face to face with my father and
people I love or people I do not love, I will experience several kinds
of situations: I will come face to face with someone in the sense
that I see them and at times they will see me. In other encounters I
will see them and they will not see me. At times I will find pleasure

in their company and at others they will find pleasure in my company and sometimes we will find pleasure in each other's company. Sometimes I will miss that person.

I saw my father sick, his mother worried. She hung a triangular amulet around his neck. She begged the sheikh of the mosque to recite prayers and incantations on his behalf. She kept looking at my father's pallid face, its color faded, fearing that the jinn may have substituted another child for him during the night when she left him alone, that they may have replaced him with another child that they had and given him the features of my father. Grandmother Najma, who was over a hundred years old, who already had her green teeth that humans at such an advanced age grew and who, in her youth, was married to a pious jinn—that was why she never married any mortal man—came to her. She advised her to carry my father to the abandoned waterwheel, to place him next to its dried-up well and its broken wheel and to stand in supplication, imploring those who had worked miracles and the masters of Sufi orders to help her recover her healthy child from the jinn and for the latter to take back their ill and sickly boy. If that proved to be impossible, Grandma Najma advised her to seek her recompense in God Almighty's munificence and let the jinn take back the changeling and keep it.

My grandmother, her heart filled with tears, went ahead and left my father all alone, unaware that he had been abandoned, engulfed in night and quiet. Around him reverberated the sounds of the forlorn and mysterious night. I was afraid for my father lest he be eaten by the wolf or snatched by some traveling gypsies who went from village to village, their eyes on little children and on light, expensive articles. I stood near his thin body, imploring my master to keep me company and he granted my prayer. I spent the whole night, but toward dawn, as the stars began to wane and the outlines of the palm trees to come into view, I became confused with respect to time. Visions began to blend into each other and my ability to experience epiphanies grew intense so I voyaged to several places at the same time, simultaneously arriving at cities that were far apart. I also traveled to various times: seeing the streets of a city at its inception and hearing the hubbub a century after it was built and the common sound of its daily existence: the creaking of a door, the cracking of a wall, the rippling of water, a man's shout, the bleating of a ewe, the lowing of a cow, the braying of a donkey, the clamor of a procession, and the roar of the crowds in times of trouble. I saw the hard times and the times of peace. I branched out, I split into different segments. I traveled away from myself in various directions, as if I had become several persons controlled by one mind, seeing beings with the same two eyes, and speaking with one tongue. That lasted for some time then I grew restless and pulled myself together. I was back after I had strayed away. I was aware of my going as I returned and of my return in my going, seeing that which had traveled away from me taking shelter in me and that which left me settle down in me until I was complete.

I opened my eyes to the morning in its full glory. My father was not in his place. I was frightened and shook uncontrollably. My father's mother came from her house. She saw his place empty. She slapped her face and screamed and rent her clothes. When she bent over to the ground, to pile up dust on her head, my father appeared. He came out of the cornfield. He was laughing and looked healthy, with rosy cheeks as if untouched by illness or disease. He was cured. My mother shouted at him, asking where he had been. She fell upon him, felt him, and carried him. Her heart was at ease, her worries subsided. She never disclosed to anyone how the jinn had granted her request and returned her healthy child to her. I, however, noticed something that she didn't. I saw a change in the way he walked. He was now lurching forward as he walked, with a light hint of a limp. That was something he didn't have before but which we seem to have inherited. It even showed in my son and daughter and later on in my grandchildren.

Then my father appeared to me in the courtyard of the house. His mother sat there, eyes open but she couldn't see. She was blind. When did that happen? I got no answer. My father looked to be six or seven years of age. I learned that he was fatherless, considered an orphan, and that he didn't remember the features of his father who had suddenly died, leaving behind his son at the age of three years and several months.

I traveled back in time to a distant night. My grandfather was pale, tired. He had come back from a long trip on foot. I didn't know why he had walked. He came in while the night was still young and the stars far away. He got up then sat down. He looked at the distant sky, to three stars that were in a straight line which, when they moved to the east, indicated that the time had come for the dawn prayer. But the three stars were not far from the center of the sky. My grandfather kept coming and going, refusing to go into the downstairs room where my grandmother slept with my father next to her. He sat in the open courtyard, coughing repeatedly until his whole body shook. His coughing was so loud it awakened my grandmother, who, startled from her sleep, spoke to him from inside. Worried, she asked him if he was all right, and beseeched him to come in from the cold night. He told her that he was awaiting dawn. My grandmother asked him, as his coughing grew worse and he grew more feeble, whether she should boil guava leaves for him. His coughing grew intermittent, as if something was getting stuck in his throat. I knew that her voice sounded to him as if it was coming from a distance, that a buzzing noise had begun, and that his innards were getting tender and slowly falling into a bottomless well, that he was not capable of replying, that with a heavy tongue he was saying, "It's over; it's over." I knew that the last image that came to his mind was that of his son, my father. My grandmother came out, rushed to my grandfather's side, screaming and wailing. I directed my gaze at my father. He was fast asleep, dreaming of the oven's firewood and the smell of the water skins swollen with water carried by the water carriers. He was very thirsty and his father was carrying him, getting ready to give him a drink of water when an unknown man started screaming in the distance, gathering many children. My father woke up in great fright.

I looked to my right and saw my master, gentle and translucent. I expressed a wish without speaking a word and he gave me permission. At that point began my miʻraj ascension to the house of dreams.

A Lightning Voyage

I traveled to a distant dream of my father's on a night unknown to me during his childhood. I didn't recognize the place in which he was stretched out. I was by myself but I was in contact with my intercessor. Colors and beings changed. My heart and all my senses came alive. I became aware of the letters forming words and I grasped essences and meanings. I saw myself. I was aware that I was the one standing in the field of my own vision. I saw what was above me and what was below me, and everything surrounding me. My face suddenly changed. It became that of my grandfather. I wasn't alarmed or frightened because I was aware that I was still me even though my features had changed. I didn't care whether my size increased or decreased or even whether my physical existence vanished. I was preoccupied with what I could see of the place: the plants were green, there was a nearby desert, there was a row of four-story houses close to each other. My father was in the third-floor balcony. His features were elusive: I saw him as a child, as a young man, then in his middle age. Then the different stages of his life crisscrossed. He asked me, "Who are you?"

"Your son, Gamal," I replied.

"Gamal who?" he asked.

"Gamal, who will grow out of your loins and who will be your son."

He looked puzzled, unable to understand. He turned his back to me after staring at me for some time. All of a sudden I saw him standing on the shore of a vast, endless sea, a sea of such uniform blueness that it looked like a mirror. He was holding an engraved metal bowl, filling it with salty seawater then tossing the water away. The water turned into a steam that seemed to rise to the farthest ends of the universe. The movement of his hands continued. I realized that many years had passed since he started emptying the water of the sea. I asked him, "What are you looking for?"

He turned to me, his hands not stopping or slowing down. "I'm looking for what I've lost."

I didn't know how much time had passed but I heard the fish, the whales, the shells, the coral reefs, and all sea creatures screaming for help against him. If he were to continue, the sea would dry up, the bottom would be left without a cover, and the creatures would become extinct. The sea sighed in resignation, throwing back to my father what he had lost. I hurried to find out what it was but I was prevented from seeing it.

After a while my father turned. His body had grown gaunt, showing the toil and dust of heavy days that could not be shaken off. I said, "When you depart you will go at the same hour as your father. You'll say the same words, but you will not address them to me for I will not be by your side." I realized I was speaking to him without words; just by looking at each other, we were having a conversation. Ordinarily, in any case, we didn't have conversations; our communication was by means of the eyes to begin with. When I looked at him I knew all that he wanted from me and when he looked at me he knew what I wanted from him. Thus a glance from me would be a question and a look from him an answer, or the other way around. Between the two of us were exchanged many emotions that all the words in all the languages and dialects in the world could not express. He said to me several times with his eyes, "But I don't know you!"

With sorrowful glances I replied, "You haven't begotten me yet."

He fell silent. My voyage was drawing to an end. I withdrew, backing away without steps. I was in the midst of thickening clouds gathering above, below, and around. It seemed my intrusion in his dream was heavy. He woke up short of breath and sad. I saw Imam al-Husayn next to me. My father was about thirty or thirty-five years of age, or so I estimated. He was sleeping in a house that was not his. I learned that he was a guest and that he would be leaving in the morning. Where to? That was hidden from me. I learned that it was the first time that I came face to face with my father before he begot me. I learned that at that time in the life of the world I was mere atoms, scattered, diverging into various elements, some of which had already become part of him and some others that were on their way, while still others had not yet found their way there. I learned that thousands of places had contained me and that part of me was still far away, out of reach and far from realization. I saw him, after he woke up, exerting an effort to remember my features, my form or name. But the details of the dream had evaporated from his mind, as had the name that I had told him. But the dream left him with a vague feeling bordering on malaise.

And thus ended my lightning voyage.

Inculcation

Since the world is shaped like a sphere, humans yearn to go back to the beginning. The end is connected to the beginning. There must be an end, otherwise there would be no beginning. The first beginning for a human is a small womb where there is no air, no letters, and no words. The end is a tomb where there is no shade and no visions or dreams. In the beginning we stretch on our backs, suckling. Toward the end we lie on our backs, impotent in old age. The first steps are shaky and hesitant. The last steps are shaky and timid. The infant's neck is made heavy by the head, shaking, saliva flowing. The neck of the old human shakes too and the saliva flows. In childhood, humans are surrounded by loneliness so they cry. In old age loneliness becomes unbearable so humans are sad but they don't cry. It all begins with a bent back and that is also how it ends. As a human comes into the world no one knows what the newborn thinks. When a human leaves the world, no one knows what goes on in the mind of the deceased nor what images they see, or what ideas occur to them. Thus the dots are connected, the circle closed, and symmetry with the round world is complete. So, observe and learn.

The Voyage of Beings

My travel continued in the company of my master through barriers and voids unknown to me. I marveled that the Diwan contained all that. I found out that I was connected to all living things. I heard the calls of the branches, the conversations of the stones, the whispering of the stars, the lisping of the dewdrops, the dialects of winds, the howling of the meteors, the supplications of the comets, the moaning of the atom at the moment of fission, and the echoes of the expansion of the far-flung universe. I understood what was said or expressed. They all sought to get close to my companion. They whispered to him; they called him; they tried to keep him entertained; they showed readiness to divulge their secrets, to speak.

The walls of the house where my father lived with his blind mother spoke to me. The eastern wall told me of his mother's repeated warnings to be wary of his paternal uncle, to be cautious with him because he wanted to do him harm. The southern wall told me about her worrying about him when he went out to get water or to barter anything with a vendor, such as exchanging a keddah of wheat for a handful of lupine seeds. The wheat silo, the oven, and the mastaba in front told me about my grandmother's loneliness, her nightly fears, her getting up and feeling her way to her son—my father—to smell him, to listen to his breathing, then feeling her way to the door to lock it and bolt it, her turning off the nightlight so that neither relative nor stranger would find their way to where they slept.

The door spoke to me about my father sitting in front of it watching the other kids playing. As he considered joining them he would remember his mother's warnings and stay away. As his eyes followed the brothers leaving together or fighting together against the other kids, he would wish his brothers had lived or that he could have another brother. He wished to go to the Qur'an school, to learn to read and write letters, to add and to subtract, to know how to write his name or the name of the palm tree and the clover blossom and that of the cotton plant, to learn what letters represented the chirping of the sparrows or the bleating of the sheep. He wished he could learn the letters of the Qur'an. He imagined himself in the faraway al-Azhar, standing before a venerable sheikh, reciting the Qur'an after memorizing it, sitting in front of huge tomes and volumes, leafing through them. It would be a long road that began with his going to the Qur'an school, but his mother refused: he might be kidnapped on his daily trip to school. My father lived in fear of his uncle. Whenever he saw him from a distance he would run, shaking with fear.

I saw my father running, running so fast I feared for his breath. I called out to him to slow down but he didn't hear me. It was impossible for him to hear me because I saw him but he didn't see me. I knew him but he didn't know me. I traveled to him but he didn't seek me out. I looked toward my master to apologize if I had erred by calling out to my father, but he was busy looking at my father, with his kind and gentle eyes.

A faraway star, out of the blue, began to speak to me from its right corner in the sky to tell me about Imam al-Husayn. I raised my head in amazement, unable to utter a single word; I became all ears. The remote star said that al-Husayn had stayed with his grandfather, the noblest of creation, Muhammad, the Messenger of God, pbuh, from his birth for six years, seven months and seven days, and stayed with his father, the Commander of the Faithful, thirty-seven years, and with his brother al-Hasan forty-seven years, and stayed in this world sixty-six years. The remote star said that it had seen the Prophet leaving the house of Aisha and passing by the house of his daughter Fatima, where he heard al-Husayn crying. The Prophet said to his daughter, "Don't you know that his crying hurts me?" The remote star, as its living, feeble light came closer, told me that al-Hasan and al-Husayn were at their grandfather's house when night fell. He told them to go to their mother, but they were afraid because the night was dark. It was then that lightning began to flash and they walked in its light until they reached their mother.

The remote star also told me that it had seen the Messenger of God prostrating during the last evening prayer. Al-Husayn, who was a child at the time, climbed upon his back and the Prophet, pbuh, prolonged his prostration until al-Husayn got off him. After the end of the prayer, one of those present said to him, "O Messenger of God, you prostrated in the middle of the prayer for such a long time that we thought something had happened or that you were receiving Revelation." He said that neither was the case but that, "My son wanted to ride on my back and I didn't want to hurry him until he fulfilled his wish."

The remote star spoke to me in a voice that traveled the vast, mysterious universe and told me that it had heard the Messenger of God crying and addressing al-Husayn, "The unjust party will kill you." The star asked me in a tearful light and sad flashes, "Do you know what era you're in?" At that point my ability to speak returned to me. I looked to my guide and he gave me his permission silently. I did not expect my voice to penetrate the galaxies and celestial space but I answered with a sad and hurt heart, "My worldly time is a bad one where things are upside down." The remote star said as its faint light moved away from me and as its echo faded, "Things are bound to change."

A silence decended as my eyes remained fixed in its direction, on the void leading to it until I realized that all contact was lost. A strange silence that I had no prior experience of enveloped all; it was a dark, glacial kind of silence, the source of which was hidden from me. It was as if the whole universe were responding to my plaint. In the midst of that oppressive silence a very tall, mature palm tree, resplendent with leafy fronds, whispered to me in a melodious voice full of kindness, neutrality, and a wondrous timelessness. It spoke to me about my father. I began to see what it was disclosing to me about him: I saw my father as a child. I estimated him to be two years of age. I didn't ask how old he was because I was certain that an answer was out of the question, as I had faced silence before when asking about such matters. My desire did not weaken though and I decided to address my curiosity to my intercessor and to the president of the Diwan, should an appropriate occasion present itself. Maybe something could come of it.

I saw my father merrily playing in front of my grandfather. At that point I requested moving suddenly in time. I saw my father as a just-born baby, his mother rocking him, playing with him, talking to him in baby talk, and showering him with words of love. I saw his tongue, small and delicate, his eyes slightly swollen, not yet over the constrictions of birth. My sorrow increased and my heart was assailed with chagrin: what a difference between what I was seeing and the face of my father as he departed this world! His face before the later journey was burdened with the weight of years and days, with wrinkles, with unsated longings and an unfulfilled heart and the exhaustion obvious even during his moments of happiness.

I blamed myself harshly because I lived with him for a long time and was familiar with his hard times and the sources of his pain but it never occurred to me that previously he had been a child, that he had been rocked, that someone had played with him and sung to him. I tried to find excuses for myself—the only thing someone like me could do, now that it was too late. My excuses got so heavy they overwhelmed me totally. My sleepy eyes began to well so I hid my tears deep down my throat. The palm tree took pity on me. It bent with its high fronds, touching me. Its tufts said to me, "Don't be sad. You'll learn the *number of years and the reckoning*." That consoled me somewhat and I took comfort after feeling so forlorn. I saw that the palm tree was towering but solid, shaking only during stormy nights. Our village was surrounded by a wall of palm trees. My eyes traveled to the spot where the head of the master of martyrs had been severed. I saw him bandaged with palm-tree fronds. My father's palm tree spoke to me: "You'll be back at Karbala."

My father's palm tree related to me my grandfather's death, how my father became an orphan, his paternal uncle's greed, how he leaned against its hefty trunk, drawing lines in the dust with a branch, thinking of the land that my father had inherited: one and a half feddans and twenty-four date-palm trees scattered all over the village.

Once again I was given permission to take a lightning trip. I saw myself walking with my maternal uncle at a bend in the road through the village that exuded the honey-sweet smell of figs at sunset, the silence broken by the rhythmic beats or music of the flour mill, muffled but in harmony with the strange quiet emptiness leading to the unknown. My uncle stopped and pointed to a palm tree in the middle of a grove of palm trees: "This is your father's palm tree."

I saw part of my past. My younger brother and I were accompanying my father on a walk in the streets of the village. My father's paternal uncle appeared. He was short and thin, wearing a large turban. We backed off, hiding behind my father. We did not extend our hands to shake his. When we visited the village we didn't go to my father's family or any of his folks because my father had stopped communicating with them some time before and because we had heard they wanted to do him harm. But what kind of harm and how? We didn't know.

I saw my father having just returned from our village. I looked carefully and I saw that I was about twelve years of age. My father told us the news of his trip. He paused before saying that he had sold the palm trees. My mother asked him, "Couldn't you just take out a mortgage on them?" He said, "No one wanted to give me one and soon it will be back-to-school time and the boys will have new expenses and new clothes. It wouldn't do for them to go to school wearing last year's clothes."

I went back, crushed with grief, to the lone towering palm tree. I approached it. It belonged to my father even though it was not longer his. He endured a lot of hardship to hold onto it, then he had to sell it to provide for us. I looked at it for a long time whereupon Imam al-Husayn looked at me. I was able to decipher his silent gaze. He was asking me not to rush things, to beware of haste. "For *Man*, according to the glorious Qur'an, *is given to haste*."

Once again I began to listen to the palm tree. It told me that it had seen my father from on high living with his blind mother, four or five years after the death of his father. His mother feared her husband's relatives and was also afraid of the coming days, so she saved what little money she had. When my father would say to her, "Get us some meat to eat," she would look where he was sitting and tell him, "I am working hard for you so that you wouldn't grow up penniless," whereupon my father would revert to silence. Grief-stricken I stared at him. I understood he was being robbed of his childhood at that early age, that he was burdened with worries at an age when others were concerned with playing and having a good time. I never saw him play when he should have been playing or running around, when he should be doing just that. I saw him facing the world in silence, spending most of his time peeling reeds and creating intricate shapes, passing near the mosque, listening to the children's voices as they repeated letters and words after the faqih. Then, feeling sad and wistful, he would move away. Once again the palm tree bent down from her towering height. My father's time was gone. I saw a dignified sheikh from a distance, walking toward me gingerly. I waited for what might happen.

O You Who Judge and Ordain

All around me there was a color unlike any other in the physical world. All of one degree without shades or waves, blue and yet not blue. The sheikh advanced through it, facing the master of martyrs. I heard no dialogue but I understood that he was getting permission. He turned to face me. I recognized him. In looking at each other our eyes embraced. I hadn't seen him face to face since he came in the company of the beloveds and masters, when we had embraced through our eyes and he had left without saying a word and I had turned away from him without speaking either, but I understood and acted. This time he spoke to me. Al-Sheikh al-Akbar Muhyiddin ibn Arabi said, "Know then that God Almighty, when He created Adam, pbuh, who was the first human body to be formed, and made him the model for all human forms, there remained of the clay from which He molded him a piece out of which he created the palm tree. So it is Adam's sister, our aunt."

I said, "This is a palm tree that belonged to my father and just as he has departed so will it, sooner or later. Every past is nothingness and every future has no existence. One day it will be sheared off, its frond will turn yellow then wither and dry. Its trunk will be sawed, part of which might be used in the roof of a house whose inhabitants we do not know. Perhaps part of it will be used in a wooden bridge straddling two close banks that may be traversed by someone we do not know."

Al-Sheikh al-Akbar said, "Caution will avail nothing against destiny." Then he fell silent but after a short while he added, "In the House of Permanence in the Diwan you will find a palm tree just like it, green and always bearing fruit. Among its miraculous qualities is that anything eaten from its fruit, anything that withers or falls off will be replaced immediately at the time it is eaten or picked. If you pick one of its dates another one will be formed right at the time it is picked. Thus it will suffer no decrease, ever."

I heard a mysterious voice exclaiming, "O You who judge but are never judged!"

Al-Sheikh al-Akbar then vanished.

True Prophecy

I saw Ali ibn Abi Talib pass by Karbala during one of his travels. Al-Husayn was still an adolescent, sheltered from the catastrophes and reversals of fortune. I saw his father stop without dismounting, his heart greatly perturbed, looking for a long time at the town surrounded by palm trees, at the Euphrates with it gushing water, at the sky suspended above without supports on the ground, then cry. Those with him asked him why he was crying but he gave no answer.

Prelude

The beloved palm tree started to talk to me again and I listened. It said that my father's paternal uncle started going around the village, visiting homes and talking to relatives, to strangers, to permanent residents and to those just passing through. He spoke to them about the blind widow whose husband had died, living with her a son who understood nothing of the affairs of this world. He told them that she was doing as she pleased, bringing shame to his deceased brother's memory and sullying his honor and that of his son afterward. I saw him sitting at waterwheels and near the southern well, in the open air clearing lit by the moon and the distant stars. He spoke with his tongue and his hands, for he stuttered and had a halting voice. He used his little finger to punctuate his words, saying, "If the woman's reputation is such then can the boy (meaning my father) be truly his father's son?" He spoke a lot, his eyes fixed on the one and a half feddans more than on anything else.

The Epiphany of Successive Faces

My palm tree paused. Its trunk was green, its fronds white; their swaying in the wind slowed down then all was still. A secret incantation started inside me. That which was near and that which was far became equal, and east and west became one. I started on a journey to the four cardinal points while standing in place. My travel was as fast as lightning, but the actual lightning around me was a mere spark. The melodies were mute. I passed through sleepy towns in a wan sunset light. My steps slowed down in suburbs whose inhabitants took shelter inside their homes, so there was no one to guide or give directions. My innermost thoughts and feelings flowed out and times intermingled before me. Echoes of fleeting and long-gone moments reverberated. I covered vast distances and saw multitudes of faces. I saw hands clutching handfuls of Karbala dust, carrying them wherever they went. I saw the moments at which the dust of that memorable spot boiled over mixed with the color of blood, thus foretelling what would happen to my master and guide. I saw a few faces of his small army and I saw faces from the army that I had known and that had known me and whose war I had witnessed before the bad times set in. I saw faces circling around me, like stray lanterns floating around. I saw thirsty faces. I saw faces kneeling down after crossing the canal to kiss the liberated sands. I saw pale faces, others still. I saw speaking faces, shouting faces. I saw and heard the source of the screams at the moment of engaging the enemy hand to hand. I saw absent faces and others who were present and accounted for. I saw puzzled faces and I saw a few proud faces. I saw faces burdened with being away from home, with loneliness and isolation. I saw cheerful, laughing faces. I saw faces that had just come into the world and others headed for a mysterious unknown. I saw faces striving and I saw humbled faces going nowhere. I saw faces within faces, sailing in the midst of flying shrapnel, sinking, floating, holding on to the sharp edges. There were features devoid of joy, while others were in pain, frowning. There were faces I knew and many I didn't. Visions and sights followed each other in succession, specters and twilight, intermingling and opening up, moving away then getting closer.

In the vast sea of faces I caught a glimpse of a face I had seen only once during the time of the bleeding wounds, the time of the defeat. I entreated my intercessor to permit me to stop by his side. I addressed him in searing pain, and with a very clear memory. I said to him, "You disappeared from my sight after I saw you for the first and last time, but you are still in my heart, and true permanence is in the heart. Like death it is never complete until it settles in the heart." I remembered, as pain gnawed at me, my visit to the widow of my friend the martyr, her indifference, the vanishing of his memory, the setting in of forgetfulness. I said to him, "You are living inside me as a friend and role model. I will not lie and I will not make false claims. Days may pass when I don't recall you, but you are always alive as the meaning of what you've been through comes to mind. You have seen the days of great loss, the beginning of the obliteration of a whole era and the beginning of the calamity. Those were the days I couldn't bear to go home, days I feared falling asleep or being by myself. I kept moving from one coffeehouse to the next, from street to street. The tired soldiers retreating from the second line of defense appeared on the scene. I remember one

of them, wearing shabby clothes, hair disheveled, features perturbed. Sinai was full of those who were thirsty and full of the dead.
Hyenas and wolves were overstuffed. I heard their languid howls
on the hot June nights as they went out in the wilderness seeking
some fresh air to be able to digest human flesh. One of the women
conscripts of the enemy that has become a friend said . . ."

A Short Interlude
I say, "I wonder at my own people: they triumph when they are
defeated and are defeated when they are victorious."

A Connection Within a Connection
The female conscript said, "Our armored vehicles sliced through
the bodies just like a knife slicing through butter."

I met him in a gray newspaper office. He was hoarse after going
around for a day and a night rallying people, beseeching Gamal
Abdel Nasser not to step down, not to carry out what he said he
would do when he appeared on television in great distress. A few
seconds before his appearance I was hoping for a surprise that he
might announce or for a development in the war news that might
alleviate my initial wounds. But when I saw features already in
mourning, my hopes were shattered and my days blown apart. In
the gray room the one with the pained face said, "Words are no use
anymore now. The first homeland has been lost and now part of the
second homeland is being taken away. The only solution is to fight."

We left, going our separate ways. In front of the building I asked
my friend who knew him who the pained man was. He said that he
was a Palestinian studying agriculture at Cairo University, and that
he was a poet. As for his name, it was Mazin Abu Ghazala. Heavy
days trudged on. I remembered him during the difficult and painful
days that followed. How much time passed before I read his name
on the front pages of newspapers? Maybe a month, maybe two.
In one of those mornings leading up to winter I saw his name on
the front page, back when news of the resistance and pictures of

martyrs were published on the front page. That was before things changed and values were turned upside down, before brethren became the archest of enemies, before getting in touch with them or sympathizing with them made one a spy or a traitor. So, Mazin Abu Ghazala was martyred—I say "martyred" without fear on my part—on the Toubas Heights. I still remember the spot where his blood was shed, the very last spot he saw on earth. I wonder what it looked like. I still remember where the news appeared on the page and how it was worded. I still remember Toubas, therefore my heart is alive.

A Flash
Yes, memory is for those who have hearts.

A Connection Within a Connection Within a Connection
I saw Mazin's face as the body collapsed. The shell hit him in the right side of his chest. His features were now fading out. I saw a tiny glimpse of Karbala: Abdullah ibn Muslim ibn Aqil was approaching Imam al-Husayn saying, "Will you permit me to fight?"

Al-Husayn said to him, "Haven't you and your family seen enough killing, my son?" To which he replied, "O Uncle, how would I look your grandfather, Muhammad, in the face if I abandon you? That won't do at all."

I saw Abdullah charging the enemy. A man shot him with an arrow that pierced the right side of his chest. He fell, crying in a rasping voice, "Woe is me! I am finished!"

Mazin's features loom in the far distance. I shouted, "O Mazin, you knew how to die and we didn't know how to live!"

I saw the face of a soldier about my age, standing in a trench surrounded by sandbags and sheets of corrugated iron. He was pointing to the other bank of the Suez Canal and saying, "In a short while they will change guards." I saw a face going around, floating like a lighted lantern suspended by an invisible thread. I didn't know to whom the face belonged.

I saw my father's face as he appeared in those days, which I didn't know were his last. I saw him tired, looking at me from inside his eyes. We were standing at a bus stop. Men and women were leaving, dispersing, going home at the end of the day. I saw my father's face going out early in the morning carrying our breakfast: a bowl of ful medammis and a pitcher of milk. I saw him whole, wearing the gallabiya, walking a route that I knew only too well, on a street that had its features imprinted on my mind, having walked in it as a child and as an adult, over and over. It was the road connecting al-Darb al-Asfar Alley and the entrance to the Mida'a Alley. The grocery store was still in its place, the primary school, the greengrocer's, the ancient mosque, the entrance of the small, narrow public bath, the chairs arranged in front of the coffeehouse. I saw all that, revealed to me bit by bit, but I only saw my father. The street was totally empty. The light was orange in color, a shade more cosmic than earthly. Then I suddenly saw myself. My father didn't seem to have noticed me or to have seen me. He kept walking while I walked backward, facing him with my chest and my features; he was advancing while I was backing up, unafraid of stumbling or falling. I could see from my back, facing him as he moved; our height was the same, each hair on my head right in front of a hair on his head, my eyes opposite his eyes, my nose opposite his nose, the expression on his face was the same on my face. I called out to him but I didn't hear my voice nor did he, but I imagined that he turned somewhere. Suddenly there were many faces pouring in. I saw the face of the winds, the face of the rain, the features of the dew, the face of the shade, the face of the night, the face of the day, the sunny day and the cloudy day. This was too much to be contained by my eyes, by my limited pupils. I couldn't bear it. I sought refuge with my beloved but he was preoccupied by looking in a direction that I couldn't pinpoint. It wasn't one of the four cardinal points or any of the intermediate ones. I looked toward where the towering palm tree had addressed me, but I couldn't see it. I realized that its time was coming to an end. Perhaps it would contact me again later. It disappeared from me and fell completely silent. I had no power to make it speak. I was sad but I wasn't afraid of sadness, for if sadness abandoned a heart completely, it would stop functioning.

Direction
That which is united by time is separated by time.

Lesson
Know then that this world of ours in which we are living now has an end because it is conceived and brought about in time and everything conceived in time must come to an end.

A Wish
If only the ignorant could know that which they don't know!

How the Confusion Began
My master, the light of my eye, disclosed to me some of the secrets of my journey. I found out that among my companions on the trip were sounds, smells, feelings, and the minutiae of the transitory and the everlasting. I found out that if I sincerely and wholeheartedly responded to the epiphanies, I would see and if I saw, I would hear and if I heard, I would feel and if I felt, I would pursue and if I pursued, I would understand and if I understood then I would know. Thus I rushed forth to that distant moment of that night hidden in the folds of time. I saw my grandmother asleep.

The extreme heat told me that everyone was fed up with it because of its long and burdensome stay. Some people said that they had not seen anything like it for years and years. People put on very light clothing and sought protection from prying eyes in the dark of the night. My father couldn't stand the oppressive heat, so he went up on the roof and lay down on the dry dung fuel cakes and the reeds stored there. He had on an old gallabiya. He lay on his back looking at the sky and the stars and a mysterious mist filling the gaps. At that moment a distant star told me that my father was about to experience a few moments that he would recall over and over again, in disparate places and at different times, while awake and during sleep. The venerable night told me that his features during that sleep looked tired, older than his real age, and that his sleep was quiet, that he made no sound and that his breathing was regular. That was also confirmed to me by the southern calm fraught with warnings. At that point my own heart went crazy. I wished I could shout or rouse him to warn him but I didn't because that would be impossible. Then silence spoke to me. I heard stillness saying that it was totally calm, disturbed only by the barking of a dog or distant echoes of unknown sources coming from the depths of the world, or the rustling of branches, or leaves as one animal or another passed through, or the prolonged howling of a crouching wolf. The reigning silence told me that the intruders were barefoot, that they climbed the northern mud-brick wall and climbed down into the inner courtyard. Then they went into the room. They fell upon my blind grandmother, pinning her down. There was a piercing scream of utmost terror by a human being, bringing about an irreversible end. Everything was sudden and blindness ruled everything. The scream talked to me saying it was the last sound my grandmother made before she was totally muzzled and before she was stabbed fourteen times. At that point the fright that came over my father spoke to me. It told me that my father did not wake up because of noise or a scream. He had been fast asleep, having no dreams during those moments, but something mysterious, inexplicable, made him get up, breathless. His heart was beating fast and he was sweating profusely. The fright that came over my father asserted to me that it did not wake him up, but that it took hold of his body and soul the moment he opened his eyes, that other mysterious things accompanied it when it possessed my father, and that all of that made him run through the roofs of adjacent houses.

The silence spoke to me again about the barking of the dogs that began, that long, ominous, and continuous nighttime barking. At that moment I saw the murderers inside the house, led by my father's paternal uncle, searching inside the silo, the store-room pantry, and above the oven. Then they climbed on the roof where reeds and dung fuel cakes broke under their feet. I saw the blade that cut the arteries and ended my grandmother's life. I was afraid that they might see my father or catch him. I saw his face filled with fear and terror in the dark. I heard him saying repeatedly, "Protect us, please God! Protect us, please! My mother! My mother!" He had not yet found out what happened to her. I found out before he did. I was aware of her in her last moments before he knew or even imagined that I would be his son.

I was now close to him and he was near me. The pores of his skin told me he was sweating profusely. I saw his shaking limbs, his tremulous steps. I saw the birth of that look that stayed with him even during his bright moments when his troubles seemed far away. It was a look of hardship and toil, exhaustion and confusion, the look of someone, seeking rest, if only for a short period of time. I listened to a thin, sorrowful voice whose source and nature were unknown to me, telling me that it was not just a look, but rather an ingrained feature and a significant sign. What I saw was the birth of confusion and fear of the invisible unknown. "But," that voice continued, "you'll never know the enormity of the yearning that exhausted your father throughout his life, that delicate pale sadness that at the same time was as sharp as a blade whenever he recalled that moment as he crouched in the darkest of nights, threatened and pursued by death and the certainty that he would never see his mother again, ever."

As my father recalled those moments he would be stopped in his tracks; his steps would become tremulous, his routines filled with anxiety, and he would suddenly break off in the middle of a conversation. Worry would insert itself into his moments of happiness and a blanket of incomprehension would be thrown over what he would be listening to. Nightmares were constant visitors in his sleep and he would exclaim in a loud voice, "Ah yabouy!"—again appealing to his deceased, non-existent father.

The voice moved away yet I saw several consecutive moments at different times in which my father would be sitting silently with us, then suddenly say, "Ah yabouy!" He would be sitting in the balcony in the last house where he lived, the house whose ceiling and walls were the last things he had seen, then he would lean his head on his hands and suddenly say, "Ah yabouy!" He would be eating, sitting with guests who had come to visit us from the village, talking and laughing then suddenly fall silent and, "Ah yabouy!" He would be eating, chewing, and swallowing then fall silent for a moment, then say, "Ah yabouy!" He would be coughing, crossing a crowded street downtown then would stop until the crowds passed him by on all sides, then he would say, "Ah yabouy!"

An Incident

On the night of October 28, 1980 CE, separating the sunset of Monday from the sunrise of Tuesday, I returned, after staying out late, to the house of my friend where I was spending some days in Paris. I opened the brown sofa bed whose cover had blue flowers. I washed my face and brushed my teeth and poured water in a glass that I always made sure was within reach for fear of a sudden thirst. Then I went to sleep. I don't know what I dreamed of or what I saw, but I awoke in a panic, breathless, my heart racing, sweating profusely, and shaking. I didn't know what dream I saw or what sound awakened me, if there had been a sound at all, but at the very center of what shook me was my father. I was afraid for him, anxious and full of feeling for him. I sat in bed repeating incessantly, without any pauses, "What's wrong, Father? What's wrong?"

Then I awoke. I looked around and began to get my bearings. This was not a room in my house. This house was not in my city. I was in a city far from my homeland. I was on a trip away from my father and my father was quite far from me. My worry abated somewhat. I looked at my watch. It was Tuesday, 3:20 a.m. Paris time, the same as Cairo time.

Explanation

Al-Sheikh al-Akbar Muhyiddin ibn Arabi made himself visible to me. And since I did not do anything or take any step without looking at my master al-Husayn then asking for his permission by words or glances, I looked at him and he gave me permission. Al-Sheikh al-Akbar started by saying that what happened to me in Paris was not out of the ordinary for some people, though not all, and that I should not think too much about it because several things were still inexplicable but someday they would be understood.

I noticed that he was speaking to me without getting close to me, that a distance I could not gauge was separating me from him. It seemed to me to be a short distance but his voice did not change, nor did his height or girth increase or decrease. He spoke to me in gentle signs and eloquent language, "I saw something similar in my father's case, may God have mercy on his soul. Fifteen days before he died he had told me of his death; that it would be on Wednesday. And so it was. On the day of his death—he had been gravely ill—he sat up, not leaning on anything or anyone. He told me, 'Son, today is departure day and also the day of the beginning of life everlasting.' I said to him, 'May God keep you safe on this trip, and make your reception blessed.' He was pleased with that and said to me, 'May God recompense you well for me. All that I heard you say which I did not know and of which perhaps I disapproved and sometimes rejected, I am witnessing myself today.' Then there appeared on his forehead a white shining patch without blemish, different from the color of the rest of his body. It emitted a sparkling light and my father felt it. Then that white shining color spread to his face and the rest of his body. I kissed him and bade him farewell and left his presence. As I was leaving I said, 'I am going to the mosque until news of your passing reaches me.' He said, 'Go and don't let anyone enter my chamber.' He gathered around him his family. At noon I got news of his passing so I went to him and found him as I had left him, seemingly between life and death; no one could say for sure. Then we buried him in that condition. So praise God who bestows his mercy on whom He pleases."

I said, "So, my father departed the same moment I woke up in panic?"

Al-Sheikh al-Akbar said, "Yes," then disappeared.

What If?

What if he had slept in the room, next to his mother? What if he had not awakened in a fright? What if he had not moved away? I wondered, so I saw him again, this time near his mother. The night was heavy and the silence oppressive. Silence did not talk to me nor did the distant star. Rather I saw the sudden appearance of the murderers, the knives going up and down. They got my father. At that point I was plunged in sheer blindness. I was scattered, splitting into invisible atoms, vanishing in the house of oblivion and not coming together: I was not a seed nor did I develop into a clot. I was nothing. I didn't speak. I didn't see. I didn't listen. I was obliterated and my consciousness dissolved into my unconsciousness. I cried for help. I screamed. My intercessor held me, ending that oppressive epiphany. I was shaking and he soothed me, calmed and consoled me kindly. He told me in confidence what happened when the blade sank into the back of his father Ali ibn Abi Talib. He said that he saw his father's killer with his own eyes but didn't lay a hand on him, didn't torture him as some historians who were really agents of Mu'awiya claimed. It was his father himself who enjoined that as he was taking his last breaths. He told him and his brother al-Hasan, "I adjure you, when you catch the man, if I die, kill him but don't mutilate his body." My companion and guide said to me that he had seen the killer of his father with his own two eyes. At that point I noticed the emotion in his voice, and I bowed my head in silence, at a loss for what to say. How could I console the one who was consoling the whole world? How could I alleviate the pain of one who was alleviating the pain of martyrs? Who am I to address the one so familiar with and experienced in the wounds of the world? It was as if he realized what I was going through so he let me go back to my father, or returned my father to me.

Salute

Peace be upon the bygone days. Peace be upon expired lives. Peace be upon transitory joy, the kindly smile, the moaning groan, and the moment that can never be recovered. Peace be on the days of struggle, the earth that has contained, and the generous shade. Peace be upon what is yet to come. Peace be upon time that takes lives away, that restores life, and that upholds traditions. Peace be upon the drizzle and the dew. Peace! Peace be upon manna and quail.

Voyage to the Beginning and the Ends

I traveled in the company of my imam to those days of the life of my father. Beings were drawn to me after a long separation and I drew near them after a peculiar exile. Successive nights told me about the beginning of my father's flight and his wanderings. His footsteps told me about his tired steps, his labor and his toil, how he sat down and how he got up, how he stretched out near abandoned waterwheels and dried up wells, at sugar cane fields. They told me how he ran away from his paternal uncle who took over the house and lived in it and began to search for him to kill him so he could seize the land and the palm trees. The evening lulls spoke to me and sunset silence disclosed to me his fear, his caution, his missing the sheltering roof, the soft bedding, the closed door, and the smell of food cooking in the earthenware pot on the wood stove, the smell of loaves of bread the moment they came out of the oven. They told me how he recited the Fatiha to keep away the devils and the evil spirits at large and the ghosts of murdered people roaming the streets. They told me about the spirits appearing to people in different forms, in human form metamorphosing into forms of animals and demons, growing and shrinking and emitting flames.

An unfinished moon casting a little light told me about my father when he hid among the palm trees in the depression extending below the village houses and how he saw a strange apparition darting across the entangled fronds, jumping, dangling, turning upside down and throwing round stones off into the distance. My father didn't know where he got the stones or where he kept them. My father recited the Fatiha and a short chapter of the Qur'an. The apparition disappeared. Later on my father found out that that apparition was a highway ifrit and that he appeared on dimly lit nights and threw stones toward the unknown.

Successive nights told me of my father's fear and trembling, his praying that the dark be over and for the daylight to come quickly. They told me of his fear of wolves and hyenas, especially hyenas. He heard that they pursued humans patiently and relentlessly until the quarry got tired. At that point the hyena would jump on the victim and deal them a single blow, felling them, whereupon it would begin licking certain parts of the victim's body, around the anus and the bottom of the feet until all resistance was broken, then it would begin devouring them voraciously.

A verdant palm tree laden with dates spoke to me. It told me that it owed its very existence, its gentle swaying in the breeze and its blooming fronds, to my father. It would not have been possible for it to come into being had he not buried a pit after he had eaten a small, yellow, oblong date. He had been living for days on dates and other fruits that had fallen off their trees. He had looked at that yellow date with his sleep-deprived eyes and dusted it off. After eating it, his thoughts drifted and he remembered his mother. He prayed loudly to God to have mercy on her soul, then he started crying. As he was crying he buried the hard pit in the soil. On that very spot several tears flowed from his eyes. So it was his tears that had watered the beginning. The palm tree told me that ever since it came into being and at that same moment every year it had been shedding two tears. It said that its very core came from my father's old tears and that it wouldn't die unless it was cut off or uprooted. I was amazed and touched. I said to it, "So, my father's tears have watered you and you have been saving those tears in your well-protected womb?"

"Had it not been for your father I would never have been, nor would my fronds be swaying in the wind or bearing so much fruit and enjoying being so fertile," it said.

I was about to request talking to the moments the two tears were shed, but my guide, the one who eased my pain, held my hand gently but firmly. He led me to where I saw a tomb surrounded by soft smooth sands of uniform color as if existing in an everlasting late afternoon. Around that spot several pale green bushes that I was not familiar with and whose names I didn't know appeared. Al-Husayn pointed to them saying, "Here is the resting place of my father, the Commander of the Faithful. These bushes are of us and we are of them." Then he led me to another spot. There I saw Gamal Abdel Nasser's marble tomb. There were no guards or visitors. The time was ahead of my own, unknown to me. I found out that the tomb did not contain Abdel Nasser's remains. I was about to inquire when he pointed to little flowers with red petals; in the middle of each was a small blue circle and right in the center was a white dot. He said that these flowers were of him and he of them. I had a question but I didn't ask it nor did I set a time for doing so.

Al-Husayn accompanied me on another visitation, this time to unmarked, unattended graves unknown to anyone, with no visitors at that time or on holidays and sacred occasions. There were no vendors of dark yellow flowers, the flowers of death. At those graves also there were no Qur'an reciters. I came to understand that those were the graves of soldiers who died in successive wars. I saw Sinai and the bank of the Suez Canal and several other scattered places in the Nile Valley. I saw trenches whose features had disappeared under the sand and the demolished foundations of structures of reinforced concrete.

Suddenly I saw a face that I had forgotten. I had seen it before only for a passing moment. It was a Saidi construction laborer whose name I didn't know, carried on a stretcher. His right leg had been amputated after an air raid by the enemy—the "enemy" in the language of my old days. He had left his faraway village seeking to make a living. He had come with his traveling crew to the front. I remembered where I had seen him: it was in the military section of a hospital that was overflowing with casualties. He had not been assigned a bed yet and his head hardly touched the stretcher. His eyes were full of sorrow and fear, a fear of difficult days ahead, disabled, without a leg to carry him and help him. That worry, the dark features, the shape of the face were not unfamiliar to me. For a moment I imagined that my father's features cast a shadow. I was gripped with pity and fear that my father's leg had been amputated one day even though both his legs were intact and even though my father had already departed on that final journey from which there was no return. But his departure did not prevent me from being frightened or worried when I thought it possible that some calamity or another would befall him. I saw papers with smudged contents, spent ammunition, wires of battlefield telephones laid out in the midst of danger and fear and various other feelings. I saw scattered debris and a dog tag with a soldier's number. I saw paths in the wilderness, traces of cautious glances, and souls floating up high. My master made a circular gesture with his finger and said, "These are some of your people; he is one of them and they are of him."

Then my master accompanied me to another vision, to my father's tomb. My heart started beating very fast. I didn't find the tomb but rather I saw a very high building, white, massive with blocked windows, a strange structure whose contents were unknown to me. I saw small butterflies, ivory in color, thus invisible in ordinary daylight. Al-Husayn said, "These are of your father and your father is of them." I said in anguish, "Do they know that I am I and that they are they?" This time he was silent.

I went back to my father as he was being pursued by his paternal uncle. I returned so my beginning was in my end and my end in my beginning. A small, soft white cloud appeared to me floating above very high peaks, above mountains far away from my homeland, to which my father never went and which he had never even heard of. I saw thin lines above the undulating uneven mountaintops and upon close inspection and thinking I realized they were waters resulting from the melting of the snow, that they formed the headwaters of rivers. These thin lines would meet other lines and form bigger lines that would furrow a deeper course. The one course would join another and the headwaters would flow into the outlet and the outlet into the source. Beginnings and ends would unite with one another. Thus the big rivers would flow into the seas and oceans and, with evaporation, back to the heights. It would be impossible for someone seeing the feeble beginnings to imagine the tumultuous ends.

I noticed that the cloud was whispering to me, trying to draw my attention. I was surprised: I was seeing the clouds on high for the first time, wandering in their midst and through them, stepping and bending toward them. I could even lean on them if I wanted to. The cloud, as the sky peered through it, said to me, "I contain your father. I am of your father and your father is of me." I asked, "How could that be?" It said as the good wind was tossing it, pushing it to a place unknown to me, that at that time it was water, then it became vapor then cloud, fog, and dew, then went back to what it had been in the first place. In one of its transformations, it was part of the water of an irrigation canal that ran through my father's village. It was one of those canals that were filled with the excess water coming with the flood that inundated those parts. The cloud said that it touched my father's body. I asked, "How?" It said, "Your father was homeless and afraid to appear in the streets of the village. He had nothing but a gallabiya, a skullcap, and a pair of underpants. The gallabiya was frayed and torn in several places. He would sometimes wash it and leave it for the sun to dry and if someone passed by he would cover himself by getting into the water. Thus he got into the water to cover his nakedness as four camel drivers passed by, driving their camels laden with hay, firewood, and palm fronds. He spent a considerable amount of time in the canal because three men came and stopped. They squatted and began a conversation and talked and talked. When they left he got out, tired. I was drops of water wetting his body and its pores. He lay in the sun and that was my time to be transformed. I left your father's body as invisible vapor and ascended on high but I left him with a legacy that surfaced only when he was quite advanced in age."

I said, "That is true, O Cloud whose origins and course are unknown to me!"

I told it about pains that came over my father during December days when he had trouble walking and, gnashing his teeth, muffling his groans, his features twisted with pain but he didn't complain. He had difficulty climbing stairs one at a time. I said my father didn't go to doctors of his own accord. On winter nights coughing would overcome him and my mother would ask him to go to see a doctor. After the fit subsided a little he would say that he'd go to Qasr al-Aini Hospital in the morning. The morning would come but he wouldn't go. Sometimes he came back bringing some guava tree leaves, which he boiled, saying that the drink cured coughing. He would ask me for an old newspaper, which he would fold and place on his chest—a folk remedy—but the coughing would not abate. This was repeated throughout the winter. After each fit of coughing he would say, "Ah yabouy!" He didn't see a doctor. If only he had!

True, everything is decreed. True, lifetimes have limits. Everything has limits but for everything in this world there are causes, intersecting, parallel to each other and impenetrable—but if only he had seen a doctor!

I expressed the utmost regret but the cloud told me, "You are talking to me about things I do not know. What I know is the birth of that pain that ran its course to the bitter end and which started at the coccyx."

I said that was a spot of which we had not been told, but it said, "You're either forgetting or pretending to forget."

I was dismayed at what it said. I saw my father leaning on my shoulder when I was between thirteen and fourteen years of age. We were standing inside a public hospital. There was a young doctor wearing a white coat telling another doctor, "Chronic spinal pain and chronic cough." My father seemed resigned, silent as if he didn't care what was being said or what was happening around him. That was how he was during his illness, something to which I had gotten quite used: quiet acceptance and patience. I saw a man advising him to go to a Bedouin in the desert near the Pyramids who performed cauterization treatments, but he never went. The cloud told me it had gone through endless space and touched boulders that no human had ever seen, that it was a prisoner for a time inside glaciers until it was liberated by a rare transitory warmth, that it stuck to iron bars in the windows of sleepy houses and high bars in prison cells and in small windows in houses of worship. It told me that it had stretched on glass panes, landed on cold chimneys and wires, that it got suspended in space during certain mornings, sunsets, and nights until the sun's rays dispersed it to high peaks. The cloud's plaintive confidence was winding down and it was getting farther away. I felt I was departing for stretches that were not encompassed by sight, that were not in the realm of the eyes.

I knew that I was getting close to the House of Persistent Sounds where everything that was ever spoken was still alive. As I entered that house, I heard sentences that had been said in calm, peaceful evening gatherings when warm and intimate exchanges were made, together with words accompanying gestures and moments of sudden realization. There were sentences said at the beginnings of roads leading somewhere, words said at the beginning of a voyage or deploring an absence, inquiring about arrival, estimation of distances, and casual greetings. I strained my ears as I passed. I heard shouts of border guards, calls at night demanding identification, a march played by brass wind instruments. I was touched and shaken; that one was of me, taps followed by reveille. How could I miss or forget those rituals? The moment my friend was interred, in full military uniform, after they had removed his boots and stretched him out, lifeless, and one of his troops had exclaimed, "Look, he is content, calm!" The kindly, anguished cry from a fellow officer who had known him and served with him in the war: "Please say hello to my brother! Please don't forget!"

I heard my father's voice and my hair stood on end and I trembled all over. It was my father's voice, the voice that was growing faint in my memory. My father was answering for me. When? I didn't know. Stopping was impossible. I was compelled to go on and on. As for my attempts to see more, that was not possible and my wish to stay here or there was not granted in any case. I heard the rush of the waves as each wave overtook another wave. Then I heard the applause, applause then the shouts. Gamal Abdel Nasser was giving a speech. I was amazed: was the process of identification complete? The voice was that of my father, but I realized it belonged to Gamal Abdel Nasser. The words had been spoken by Abdel Nasser earlier when he nationalized the Suez Canal, when he related the long history: "We will fight; we will fight; we will fight," as he said in his speech from the pulpit of al-Azhar Mosque. He said he would not leave Egypt, that he and his children were in Egypt, that they hadn't gone anywhere. The voice was fresh as if the words had just been spoken. When he said what he did I was breathing the air of this world, aware of sunrise and the succession of nights, the feast days, the time of sadness and the settling of sorrow in one's soul. My father was walking the earth, we were under one roof in one house. I heard his voice in the morning and at nightfall. I recalled with my mind's eye that Friday noon, al-Husayn Square in an autumnal November foreshadowing winter. There were rows upon rows of popular resistance volunteers, holding rifles, a collective shout rising, one that I won't ever forget. There was a man wearing a gallabiya and a short jacket; perhaps it was a leather jacket. I wasn't sure.

Newspaper headlines declared: "Port Said Has Paid the Tax in Blood." I walked, full of enthusiasm and a vague desire to take part. I smiled when I heard my voice at school telling my schoolmates— I was lying—that one of our close relatives was now fighting in Sinai. I heard my voice in the alley calling my younger brother, telling him that I had seen an enemy plane on fire. I was lying. Those were bygone days, their sounds remained, but they were snatches

79

that were not heard in chronological order. The voices and sounds were floating everywhere. Some were clearly audible so I could understand them. The rest were scattered here and there, so I wasn't able to fathom them; they recaptured some of the flavor and the fragrance, but the days themselves were elusive, you could say they were lost. It occurred to me that what was lost could not be regained, but I dismissed the thought—for if that were so, why the quest then? And how would my master respond?

There were the sounds of those days. We were sitting in the small living room: the intermittent air raid siren indicating danger; the long, continuous sound indicating respite from danger; distant explosions; a voice from the street shouting, firmly demanding that someone turn out the light.

I heard my father's voice but I was aware that it was really that of Abdel Nasser. Gamal Abdel Nasser was speaking in my father's voice: his whispering conversation when he visited the frontline villages of Ismailiya, when danger in Port Said was only a stone's throw away. I was now listening to the winds; I knew they were the winds that blew that particular day. I heard my father's voice again but the speaker was not my father. He was talking to a soldier during one of his trips to the front: asking about meals and whether they were sufficient, about bathing times, the range of surface artillery. The voice was reverberating in a closed room. It was a meeting attended by some commanders of missile battalions. What was the possibility of intercepting and shooting down marauding Israeli planes by means of well-concealed gun emplacements? How to go about it when the missile defense shield had not been completely finished yet?

Then I heard the voice of my father speaking his own words, saying prayers for me and my brothers and sister and praying for me and my wife and my son who wouldn't remember the picture or the features of his grandfather. My son, when my father passed, was three years and five-and-a-half months old. I heard my father's steps circumambulating al-Husayn's mausoleum. I heard his voice telling me in tired tones—this was three years before his final departure, before he ascended the light and got lost among the scattering stars—"You know, Gamal, I feel my days are numbered." I cried, "Don't say that, Father. You'll live a long time, with God's permission." But my optimism was misguided and my hopes dashed. I heard the moans of a man coming from the countryside to the city in Mamluk times. For one reason or another he was arrested and crucified. An old question came back to me: why are people unjustly put to death? Why end someone's life prematurely? I heard shouts of, "Give us total independence or give us death." The voice of my imam came to me from a very distant past, "I speak for those who are afraid. I give voice to those who cannot speak. I haven't come out to corrupt or to commit unjust acts. I have come seeking reform in my grandfather's nation. I want to enjoin what is good and enjoin against what's evil. If you accept me by accepting what is right, God will reward you. If you deny this call of mine, I will patiently wait for God's arbitration between me and the people, for God is the best of arbiters." I heard Umayya ibn Abi Sufyan guffawing sarcastically when he heard news of al-Hasan's death by poison, that same Umayya, son of Hind, the woman who devoured the liver of Hamza, uncle of the Prophet, pbuh. I heard him saying, "God has soldiers made of honey!" I heard a muttering, a murmur, a cry of sorrow, a murmur of surprise, a woman screaming for help, a woman whose labor contractions were irregular, a woman entreating someone not to leave her alone in the world. I didn't know from what era it came, but I heard funereal chanting in an obscure, extinct language whose meanings and symbolism were not revealed to me, but which left me with a sharp, piercing grief. I heard water flowing in a rocky region. I heard a roaring waterfall and a wave receding from the shore. I heard the water dripping from a faucet that had not been shut firmly. I heard successive raindrops hitting hard soil, others falling on soft, grass-covered ground, and yet others on thick-leaved plants. I heard the rain slapping against the large glass windowpanes of a coffeehouse. I heard the water filling my father's palms as he performed his ablutions on a

Friday morning. I heard the sound of a bird that had just landed on a coast after a journey of migration whose length no one knew. I heard the calls of birds flocking in a northern sky as autumn's chill was advancing, preparing to fly south. I heard a night curlew passing. I heard the sounds of huge extinct birds. I heard a turtledove standing on an old antenna attached to the roof railing. It was noon and my playtime had come to an end. I was waiting to hear my father's footsteps on the stairs on his return from work, wearing his light khaki uniform, carrying food or a bag of fruit. I heard the silence of a hot midday as the turtledove kept cooing intermittently, a sound that was sad, like the invisible rhythm of time, distant, very far. I listened, but the sounds of my father's return had not started yet. There was a beautiful voice reciting, but it was gone before I could make out what was being chanted. I heard the beginning of a song extolling the days of struggle with which I was not familiar. A brass trumpet. Intimate talk of women, puzzlement. A girl saying she didn't know what she should do. A woman talking about being jilted in a cruel manner. The cry of the first moment of orgasm. A gentle, kind voice asking, "What do you want from me?" I was on the point of responding, as that was a question I had been asked and which I answered, but it went away.

All the sounds in the house were repetitions of old sounds: echoes, the sound of knees clacking. A rattling sound, whispers, my father speaking to my mother late at night, telling her about gifts he would be taking with him back to the village: rice, soap, fabrics, and so on. Tender music, intermingled voices in a small restaurant. Unfamiliar language. Silverware hitting plates. The rim of one glass clicking that of another. The piston of a kerosene stove pushed repeatedly, the flame irregular before settling into a pleasant hum. That was my mother in front of the stove on which our food was cooking. The legs of the low table set on the floor with us gathered around it. My father, mother, brothers, and sister. My father doles out our portions, especially the meat. The sound of my father sipping his tea. "Make me some tea." Mysterious whistling, continuous at times, intermittent at others. Sound coming from a great distance. The sound of camel hooves on desert sand. The sound of grains of sand scattered by the steps. Al-Husayn riding camels? Maybe.

I heard the sound of bushes striking roots in desert soil. I heard the echo of a shot. My ear could tell the difference between one explosion and another: that one was muffled, which meant that it hit its target. Who was it? Where? How many casualties? An explosion ringing out and followed by an echo meant it had missed the mark. Another explosion: that was a cannon shot, that one was from a tank, that was a rocket, but this was a landmine. I was standing among those who would cross the canal, showing them my utmost affection; in a few moments they were going to their fate, to danger, to an enemy who would later on turn into a friend, as they said and claimed. I heard the sounds of my accompanying them the first time: I could hear my own heartbeats, marks of my fear. I wouldn't lie or claim things that happened to me in spite of the passage of time, year after year. I was afraid but I made a point of appearing tough as I responded to my friend's quiet, piercing eyes looking deep inside me. I heard the swaying of the rubber boat when I got on board. I heard the boat moving across the water with us in it, with the stars above us and the night providing cover, how we moved in the water away from our place in the camp. As we got closer to the enemy, human closeness also increased. I had a sense of security. I heard wireless signals, cautious, others that were not so cautious, and some that were somewhere in between. I heard sure-footed steps, staggering steps, and careful first steps, exploring, tentative and soft, and last, shaking and weak steps. I heard sudden shots, shouts of attack, and screams of defense when men went back to their beastly roots. I heard the sound of surprise at its most essential level, where it came from and where it went before dissipating. I heard the echo, cosmic vibrations, and signals of an unknown source. I heard dried-up bushes beseeching me to stop, to listen to them. I requested that and permission was granted.

The bushes asked in a voice coming from the House of Questions, "Why death in war when what happened has happened? Why the opposite results? Why when our murderers were now strolling arrogantly in the very cities that had been impossible for them to breach? Have you not seen them in the old neighborhoods where your father lived and left part of himself in each part of them? They are there now, asking questions, investigating. Why?"

At that point I realized I was leaving the House of Sounds, that I might come across it again but I didn't know when or how. I saw a patch of ground, which spoke and said to me, "Your friend, the one you are carrying in your heart everywhere you come or go, has stepped on me. Do you remember your visit to his wife and your experience, what the passage of human time can make humans forget?" I nodded. The patch of land said, "Three have recently stepped on me: one of them is the one who aimed the main gun of the tower, the one who pulled the trigger that shot the round that broke into shrapnel, some of which pierced the right side of the heart and was lodged there."

Hearing that, I felt a sudden pain and asked, "Did the killer of my friend come here?" It was then that my friend appeared to me. I saw him walking as he stood and standing as he walked, his wound still fresh, bleeding, still bleeding. His blood wetted his khaki shirt, exactly at his heart. He spoke to me, thanking me for fulfilling his wish when he came to me in a dream and asked me to visit his family. He looked worried, displaying an anguish that I had never seen him display when he was alive. In a moment I saw what I had been late to discover: his face was still his face, but his features were those of Gamal Abdel Nasser, and when he spoke, I heard my father's voice. He said, "Were you asking about my killer? He was the first to visit you." I answered sharply and in friendly rebuke, "None of them visited me, Ibrahim." He repeated, ignoring my calling him by his first name, "He was the first to visit you." I interrupted him, my vexation getting the better of me, "What do I have to . . . ?" He interrupted me calmly in his usual way of taking one by surprise, "The first one to visit you, the living." He looked sad and I heard him saying, in my father's voice, "My whole life was nothing but a dream!" I didn't know what to do: should I answer my father or talk with my martyred friend? Or stare at Gamal Abdel Nasser? I remained silent. He said, "What happened? Was it the long sleep or has obliteration set in or is it forgetfulness?" Then he departed; they all did. An intense anguish took hold of me. I responded in confusion, "Where did they go? What's the use?"

I came to and noticed that my supreme guide and guardian was looking at me and regarding what I was saying somewhat disapprovingly. I cried, "Please forgive me, master of all martyrs. I wonder what's come over us?" He didn't respond, so I said, my voice shaking, "By your mausoleum to which I have entrusted the security of my childhood and all my early life and my father's fragrance, and which I have made the be all and end all, the ultimate refuge for my troubled life. You know what I don't know." I was not sure his frown had dissipated, so I said, "You are my solid support!" He turned to me kindly and I cried out, reassured, "Now I have reason to be afraid!"

A Verse
It is God who created you in a state of weakness, then gave you strength after weakness. Then, after strength, gave you weakness and gray hair.

A Fact
Human souls have been fashioned with timorousness and fear as essential traits to begin with. Timorousness in humans is stronger than it is in animals. As for courage, it is incidental. Have you not seen an infant of one or two months shaking in alarm upon hearing a sudden sound?

Succession of Visions
I saw my master al-Husayn in his own, original time, his first life, sitting at home, bearing a heavy burden. He could sense the slowly

advancing future, the beginning of the turn, the change in fortunes. What he was seeing was horrific even though the signs were not totally visible yet. But he could see and was beginning to understand, ever since his older brother was poisoned. There was a lingering sadness clouding his beautiful face. He would scratch the dust with his finger, his gaze traveling beyond what others could see. He was cautious and wary, for himself and those around him: Mu'awiya was targeting him, sending his spies and secret operatives to Medina. Every morning the wali of Medina would send a report to Damascus detailing al-Husayn's movements. Mu'awiya did not deem that sufficient. He sent one of his veteran and most trusted secret policemen to track al-Husayn's comings and goings, his visits to the mosque, staying close to the tomb of his grandfather, al-Mustafa, pbuh, the stops on his way, his conversations with people, and his kindness to strangers and the poor. He sent another secret policeman, of Greek origin, and a third and a fourth and a fifth, each of them ignorant of the others, not knowing that someone else was doing the same work at the very same moment. In Damascus, Mu'awiya read and compared notes. I saw al-Husayn, calm, his face sad. He did not publicly display his enmity against Mu'awiya, not breaking the pledge that he had taken on himself. I got close to him as conditions and circumstances were raging around him.

The wealthy were surrounding Mu'awiya, those with old money and those with new money. Interests were taking hold and consolidating. New interests were coming into being, new posts were being created and ambitions were growing. Conquests were increasing, captured big cities were expanding and so was greed. Promises were made right and left, methods of intimidation and terror greatly enhanced. I saw the days of my pure beloved and moved about, witnessing much. I also entered the palace of Mu'awiya. I was surprised, horrified by the conspicuous displays of wealth: the gold and silver, the silk and brocade, Mu'awiya's fancy clothes and his perfume. I saw his intelligence and deviousness, and his chameleon-like appearance change several times in one sitting, his unsurpassed ability to show the opposite of what he secretly believed or thought. The days of Muhammad, pbuh, were not that far in the past. His flight from Mecca was only about thirty-three years or so earlier. Those who knew him, saw him, or talked with him, those who had sat with him or fought under his command were still alive. As for Abu Bakr's humility and Umar's ascetic ways, they were even more recent. I heard with my two ears what Mu'awiya told his boon companions on a night when he was feeling good, "The influence of the people of the House of the Prophet will be erased. Taking shots at the master of creatures is difficult and getting into it will be hard, but those related to him . . . ."

I heard worse and couldn't stand it, so I left. I made my way to Mu'awiya's police headquarters. I saw the special attention he paid to the secret police and how he deployed untold numbers of them in the midst of the population. I saw his reliance on old women who could penetrate the most secret of places by listening and writing down, secretly poisoning this one or conspiring against that one, spreading rumors and making up stories. I saw district captains, walis, aspiring courtiers and approval seekers, those trying to advance their careers, and the scribes in government offices. I saw poets and storytellers and crafters of proverbs talking to people about the merits of Mu'awiya, his sagacity and piety, and his generosity—especially his generosity. I also saw them bad-mouthing Imam al-Hasan and al-Husayn and anyone loyal to them. I saw things that confirmed for me through an era other than my own that what the mind imagined to be far-fetched and impossible was actually possible, that everything could change.

I would not forget anything of what I had seen as I continued to travel through the time of my most faithful beloved in the House of Visions. I passed by unfamiliar stations. I saw my father standing, gentle and serene. I was about to call out to him, to tell him that he was in Medina, close to the tomb of his beloved, al-Mustafa, the Prophet, pbuh, to which he wanted to make the pilgrimage, though he departed before his wish was fulfilled, before we could fulfill it for him now that we were able to. But we didn't. I saw him as a young man during al-Husayn's time. I was at a loss. I shouted, but I was moving away from him as if I were a mount dashing far away from where it had started. He kept shrinking in size until he became a mere dot, then just an abstraction. It was then that I saw my friend, the martyr, assuming the pose that I was familiar with. I saw his blood wet where he was injured. He came to al-Husayn's time bleeding. He saw me. I was about to call out to him but either he moved away or I just kept moving. Then I saw many soldiers, each showing a fresh, unhealed wound, wearing the khaki shirts, gray helmets, and dusty boots, some of which were filled with water from the Suez Canal. I was able to count the white hairs on the head or chest of each of them despite the high speed at which I was passing through. They were getting ready to shout, but before I could hear them I was already too far away.

I saw my father, thin and emaciated, with tired steps, his head having turned completely gray, something that had not happened while he was still alive, as he departed before his hair had so completely turned gray. What era was that? I was engulfed in yearning and exhausted by sadness. I wished to stop but had to continue traversing the House of Visions. I hovered in the void, covering the expansive wilderness until I ended up in my venerable master's domain with a lump in my throat. I was recalling my father's tired features, aware that he was near yet far, that he had not lived in that era in the distant past. I didn't know his roots or his early forefathers and yet I carried his difficult days with me and I cried for him before their sunrise and I lamented him before their stars appeared in the sky or their moons set or their winds blew, before their cold and their heat. I lamented those days while still far away in the past, even before they were in the womb of the unknown. They gave me pain even though they were a future that was yet to come. I advanced far into those bygone days. I stopped at the beloved's door. I was surprised by the fragrance of his mausoleum in my old Cairo, that mysterious perfume: the incense, the musk residue, and the spent fragrances, the rosewater, the old rugs, the sandalwood, the cool marble, the red shades of the hanging chandeliers, the engraved ceramic, the ivory inlaid in the pulpit's wood, the pages of the ancient volumes of the Qur'an, the sparkle of the niches, the perfumes of longings, and the supplications of the wounded. I turned my face toward him but I couldn't see him. I was overcome with a feeling of loss even though he had told me when I entered the Diwan that he would accompany me most of the time but not all of it.

I felt alone and my whole being welled with tears for my loss and my being orphaned. I was so afraid I almost cried but my humiliation did not last long. He revealed himself to me in his own worldly epoch. I saw him sitting at home in an unsecured house. Mu'awiya had died and his son Yazid was pressuring him to pledge allegiance to him. What was going on around my master was passing strange. Things were upside down, changing from one extreme to the opposite extreme. People were pledging allegiance to Yazid. A lot of money was involved, and posts and intimidation and sweetened deals of persuasion, the caliphate turning into a monarchy, bequeathed. I saw al-Husayn thinking of the fickleness, change, transformations, people hiding what they really thought, moving away from the message of Islam and trading what was permanent for what was transient. The fruits of labor were now concentrated in the hands of a few people in the form of gold, silver, and precious and semi-precious stones. Evil was personified in Yazid, the dissolute, wine-drinking, fat, pock-faced, ugly-inside-and-out Yazid. There he was, occupying the highest post, successor to Muhammad, Prophet of God, pbuh. Time was turning and eyes were watching, and hearts noticing, both corrupted hearts and those in between. Right was as clear as sunshine and facts were glaringly obvious and the evidence straightforward. But people did not come out openly in support of what was right; fingers were not pointed at what was clearly crooked. Delegations were following each other in great numbers to Yazid's palace in Damascus. The rule of oppression was becoming rock solid and the means of oppression were reinforced. Meanings were turned upside down and values debased. Exception became the rule. What was happening to people? The Prophet's flight to Medina was barely sixty years ago; how then were the faces showing the opposite of what was in the hearts? How were the tongues uttering the opposite of the minds and the conscience? How did the faces betray people's true feelings? How were the facts ignored and the constant changed? In the offices, in the police stations and secret police headquarters suggestions were openly and publicly made to kill al-Husayn if he did not take the pledge of allegiance to Yazid. Many were calling for an open season on his pure, pious head. One person was rebuking the wali of Medina for not killing al-Husayn when he was in the wali's house because he had not supported Yazid. Al-Husayn appeared to me, worried, thinking of the poor people in the world, those he knew and those he didn't know and there were many of them, both in his time and other times. He was thinking of the future in which mercy would be shown, fear and worrying would disappear, and piety and the fear of God's judgment would prevail. He was not concerned with his own affairs or his own person. He was not presenting himself to the people as the son of the daughter of the Prophet, pbuh, but as someone keeping alive his grandfather's vision and message. Al-Husayn was now bowing his head, remembering seeing Medina's poor, led by a secret policeman, shouting and demonstrating in support of Yazid. What pained him was their enthusiasm for something that would bring harm to all of them, since they did not know what tomorrow would bring them.

I got closer to al-Husayn and my sympathy for him increased. He did not talk to me about what I was observing and watching. Rather he let me just accompany him back to those days filled with hardships to see for myself and draw my own lessons. My heart was filled with sadness. I approached him, addressing him even though I was separated from him by an invisible barrier. I spilled my heart out to him not knowing whether he heard me or not. "Why are you so sad, burdened heavily, yet the tears in your eyes are frozen in place? And your eyes so full of worry and sadness beyond compare? You are thinking long and hard on fickle times as I have done many years after you. You are kept awake at night as you see ideals and values trampled underfoot. In the very heart of the Diwan, I complained to you about my perplexity and alienation and here I am facing your own perplexity. I wish I had lived my days in your world or spent them in your days to console you and ward evil away from you."

At that point I felt his luminous presence by my side. I saw him beside me and at the same time I saw him in front of me. I saw him looking at me and I didn't know whom I should address: my master who was accompanying me and who was so kind to me or my master in front of me getting ready to confront calamities, preparing for a dark era just around the corner? I blurted out with the best of intentions and all innocence that that which was puzzling him would in future days puzzle me, that that which was keeping him awake at night would keep me awake too. In his time they turned on him and changed and in my time they would turn and change too, even though the differences between the two eras were huge, for what was my time compared to his? I said to him, "You've taught me, my intercessor, that all things, even those we thought wouldn't be, are subject to change."

He answered, "Remember that the worst changed to the better, just as the best changes to the worst, otherwise there would be no change to begin with."

I said, "My imam, you lived through your bad times toward the end of your life on earth. As for my life, it is going from very bad to much worse. Please allow me to tell you about some of what happened in my time."

My master nodded. I said in a broken voice, "Do you know, green of heart and pure of soul, that the first thing I became aware of was that a whole country was stolen from its own people and that they suffered exile and dispersion?"

He motioned to me to continue, so I did, with new courage pouring in my veins, "The liberation of Palestine! All lessons focused on that meaning and goal, as did songs, books, lectures, scholarly theses and dissertations, movies and plays. Weapons were selected, troops were paraded in the summer and the heat, on land with uneven terrain, on flat plains, green and yellow. Night ambushes were set. More important, blood was shed and people were killed, dear ones departed. As time went by, the spot from which your grandfather, al-Mustafa, ascended to heaven was captured. There were cries and slogans were shouted: "Palestine is wounded! Palestine is our fire! Palestine is our shame! Return to the 1948 borders! Return to the 1967 borders! Return to the 1973 borders!" But they came, my imam, to my very home, to me who has lived through the war, heard their thundering planes in the sky, appearing like hovering white dots that came from the east, then the whole earth exploded. I saw the bombs as their shrapnel pierced the bodies. I saw with my two eyes the death of loved ones, the forced migrations of masses from their homes. In a square close to the sea in the city of Port Said, a man wearing khaki clothes, most likely a government employee, knelt down and kissed the soil, source and destination of forefathers and offspring. I didn't know him personally but I couldn't forget his face. I didn't know whether he returned with those who had come back or was forever lost. I saw the trees stop pollinating and bearing flowers or fruit after being scared by the bombs, after their many wounds, for, like humans, trees are subject to fear."

My imam said, "I know."

I said, my heart throbbing and my pulse racing, "I saw the plans and the exerting of concerted efforts and the mobilization." Then after a slight pause I went on, "We fought and were not afraid. So how, now that we were capable, did everything change overnight? Their flag is now flying next to our flag. We are receiving their radio and television broadcasts and seeing their enemy uniforms and their rifles in salute. Now the cowardly, hypocritical reporters and writers who rush to eat at all tables are describing the warm and cordial meetings. Posters have been hung and huge masses have been recruited to go and applaud, not knowing the present danger or the danger soon to follow. Now their flags have become part of our daily reality. That which was impossible to imagine has actually taken place."

He motioned and I went on, "Then they poured into our old streets and ancient districts, winking and making fun of us, examining and inspecting. They love nothing better than to sit near your mausoleum, where your head is resting."

My master said, "Listen, Gamal. There is nothing that is created in any way, shape, or form, be it a star or a tree, a ruined relic, or a sagacious mind, that is not subject to change."

His words consoled me, especially that he called me by name, which meant that he bestowed a double favor on me in addition to accompanying me. It was then that I saw Gamal Abdel Nasser standing deep in thought yet looking at me. He seemed both distant and nearby. Then I saw my father standing near where the sun was setting. I wished I could reach him. He was by himself and very far from me but my eye was able to see an expression on his face that I knew quite well. It was the expression his face had when he came home, carrying our breakfast or lunch or our new clothes for the Eid. I saw him looking at the far end of the universe.

I turned and saw Muslim ibn Aqil in his time, listening. Al-Husayn was asking him to proceed to Kufa, to its people who had written to him, asking him to go there, to hurry to establish justice, to set the crooked time right, to erase injustice and to replace it with a just government. I heard Muslim say that that was an inauspicious country in which al-Husayn's brother was killed and his father wounded. But al-Husayn insisted: he had received their messengers and Muslim should head there to see matters more clearly, for condoning an injustice was like committing injustice. Muslim proceeded. Al-Husayn looked at Abdel Nasser and my father. I saw my mother at the time that we were all together. I saw my brothers and sister, my wife and children and my grandchildren and my friends, those I disagreed with and those who remained by my side. I saw the women I loved. I saw all my neighbors and my traveling companions. I saw everyone I had ever seen, everyone on whom I had ever laid eyes, everyone my eyes had followed. I was seeing them all at the same time. My heart was content and I was filled with hope.

A Short Pause
Being together is a joy and a delight. Being apart and alone spells undoing and ruin. With that begins hateful perplexity that leads to no comfort. That is followed by a weakness that is not followed by strength. If only gathering together would last so that simple human dreams might come true!

An Even Shorter Pause
Be patient, for the unknown has revealed things to you that you have missed.

What Was and What Will Be
I bade farewell to Muslim ibn Aqil, cousin of my master al-Husayn, as he left Mecca. I had been revealed to him as one of his friends. I accompanied him part of the unpaved way over rough terrain. Then my master prevented me from continuing with him. I learned later on, after more than a thousand and three hundred years, that Muslim's two guides died of heat and thirst and that he had expressed pessimism, but the light of my eye, the one who brought me solace after hardship, asked him to continue. I was the messenger who conveyed that order to him. I went to him in the guise of one of al-Husayn's companions, informed him of my master's command, then left him on his way and returned to Mecca. At the outskirts of the city, three of Yazid's policemen hovered around me. I was frightened, so I took precautions and moved away from them quickly. I traveled to my father's time and caught up with him at a very difficult time that was hard for me to bear. I reached him when he was a young boy staying with his mother's family, not spending time in any one place, without a bed of his own or a roof over his

head. He had no plate of his own to eat off. He seemed to me to be quiet, a stranger, for as I learned much later when I lost my father, every orphan is a stranger. I saw that he was not picking quarrels with boys his age or older. He was always silent, worried about shelter and food, not mixing with children his age, always standing at a distance from them. He had a feeling that he was superior and hoped for a mysterious future awaiting him, a time when he would be somebody, thinking of the big world and those distant cities, the roads leading to them, their extensions where the sun set. He thought often of al-Azhar where the secrets of learning and skills were disclosed. If only he had not been orphaned! But he would close his eyes and see a moment when he could read what was written and write that which he read. He did not think that was far-fetched or far off in the future.

I saw my father sleeping under the roof of a water carrier. An old piece of hide, originally covering the belly of a goat, but which was now part of a leather bucket hanging above an old well where few stopped to drink, spoke to me. It said it had touched my father's back when it was part of a water skin filled with water for the thirsty. He used to carry water to numerous homes. I saw him walking slowly, holding the water skin by its mouth with his small hand. He panted when he climbed higher ground. He would knock on the door of a big house, enter, empty the contents of the water skin into the big earthen water jar, never looking around: that was the code by which water carriers worked even if they were young. He was now drying his sweat. I walked around; I saw his eyes. He wished to sleep. I got closer to him and was able to smell his clothes and his hair and, wonder of wonders, it was the same smell that my nose caught when I was a child. I would wait for his return at midday and run and hang on to his neck. He would embrace me if his hands were free and would bend so I could embrace him if he was carrying a bag of hot falafel or vegetables or meat or fruit. He never held back from me. I could smell his smell, which blended with the smell of his khaki suit, the very smell that grew weaker as time went by because we rarely embraced and stayed mostly apart. It was the very same smell, my father's very own, special smell that was now gone from me forever, with no way to recapture it. Maybe its fragrance has lingered on in his clothes, which I put away in a suitcase and which I didn't have the heart to open. I realized that my master has done me a special and kind favor by allowing me to recapture that paternal fragrance that I wished would never end.

I got so carried away as he was standing that I became oblivious to him. When I came to, I found that he had fallen asleep, tired. I wished I could carry the water skin for him or help him in any way but I realized that that was impossible and of little use, so I inserted myself into his dreams. He saw me on a platform at a railway station. I was departing and he was seeing me off. He said to me, "Travel safely." Then he got closer to me and asked me, "But who are you?"

"I am the man who will be your son," I said.

His face lit up and he appeared to me as a handsome young man, then said, "With you, my estrangement ends."

I nodded but his face clouded over suddenly, saying as if talking to himself, "But I'll go back to what I was in the beginning: a stranger who's cut off."

At that point, he looked tired, old, and emaciated as he appeared in his last days. He raised his eyes toward me and said, "You will hear of me and remember me, but when you seek me out, you won't find me."

I was dismayed. I shouted as the train started moving away, "Forgive me, Father."

He stood on the platform, his hands stretched downward. The train increased its speed. I was getting farther as gloom loomed. My father woke up. I left his passing dream. I saw him in the house of one of his other relatives. I didn't know how close a relative he was and I didn't see the moment when he moved out of the water carrier's house. This man was a date harvester. I saw my father tie a rope around his waist, climbing palm trees picking dates. At night he slept on a bed of straw, his body bruised, tossing and turning. He would remember his mother and his eyes would well up with secret tears, for he hated anyone to see him crying. And despite his hard life, his hunger and his lack of stability, he felt that all of that was something passing, temporary, that other days lay in wait for him, that such days were not far off.

In that man's house, my father was not comfortable. The man had many children, who did not leave my father alone. The youngest sat on the mastaba and asked my father to give him the pitcher so he could have a drink of water. The woman asked him to bring her some dung fuel cakes from the roof and my father brought them. She asked him to light the oven and he did. Then I saw my father working in a flour mill, filling sacks with flour, as the tiny white specks covered his face and arms. I saw him picking boll weevils under a very harsh sun. I saw him herding goats toward the irrigation canal. One man shouted at him, so he pulled up his gallabiya and carried a kid into the brackish water. I also saw him carrying across the water a boy several years younger than him whose name was Abdel Latif. I saw him weaving palm leaves into small geometrical shapes, harvesting figs that smelled like honey, stacking sacks of wheat, tying dry reeds together, carrying racks of dough. I saw him listening to old men sitting in the expansive clearing. Among the things I knew about him was that he never forgot a name or a title or a dialogue or a face or a bend in a road. He knew everyone in the village, lineages, known relations, and little-known matrilineal ties. He investigated and inquired to know. He was wary of his paternal uncle and tracked his news. If he found out that that uncle had left the village on a short trip or that he was sick, he felt somewhat relieved and was able to move more freely in a larger circle. I saw him sitting by himself behind a mud-brick wall, resting, thinking, planning. I saw him alone and my sadness grew and I was shaken by a cruel distant past.

The light suddenly grew strange. I lost my bearing and had many questions. I longed for a voice that hadn't survived, not even in the form of an echo or a trace. I found myself in unfamiliar surroundings, hearing mysterious tunes. I followed my father walking along a road unknown to me, with the closed doors of strange houses on both sides. I followed him more closely: he quickened his steps and I quickened mine. I called out to him, but he didn't turn. I got close to him. I extended my hand. I suddenly noticed his clothes that were unfamiliar to me. He turned toward me. I was taken by surprise. I stopped. I saw in front of me Muslim ibn Aqil, al-Husayn's envoy to the people of Kufa. I didn't see my father's features. I was in an era different from his and different from mine.

Poetic Interlude
When love smiled and we rejoiced,
Thinking we were safe from parting,
Discord in secret sent its envoys,
Scattering all that we had joined.

Poetic Interlude
You were the blackness in the pupil of my eye,
Causing those who looked on you to weep.
If anyone wishes for another after you, let him die,
For I have kept you and watched you well.

Poetic Interlude
I seek the gift of your breeze from the wind,
When it is stirred toward you,
And I ask it to take you my greeting;
Please answer, if it takes my message to you.

A Tune
When I was certain I couldn't see you,
I closed my eyes and I saw no one.

Absence

The lamp of our union was glowing
Then separation sent its wind, and it went out.

Epiphany of Union

Union is the opposite of separation. Union is life, separation death. Union is the rule, separation the exception. All existence is based on union and continuity. Continuing breathing means staying alive; if breathing, one breath after the other, is interrupted, a person dies. As for embryos, they are not started, formed, or given a pulse except after a union.

Moving and Traveling

I saw my father's features in Gamal Abdel Nasser's body. He was wearing a red tarboosh and a green woolen gallabiya. It was my father but it was also Abdel Nasser, but their presence did not belong to the familiar world, nor did their movement or steps. I saw him walking on a road covered with fine dust, stopping at a rural coffeehouse where travelers gathered. I saw myself sitting in a far corner. I could see what was happening inside and outside at the same time. The coffeehouse was in Kufa, amazingly at a time when coffee, as a drink, had not yet come into being. And in Kufa, how? My father asked those at the coffeehouse in Gamal Abdel Nasser's voice, "Is my son, Gamal, here?"

The patrons fell silent. Why don't I answer him? Why am I silent? I was about to answer, but my tongue was tied and my voice frozen and words did not make their way in my throat. Why didn't I get up? Why didn't I accompany him? A voice that I did not recognize answered me, "Your time has not yet come."

My father got up and moved away, alone, distressed. The way he walked was his, the way he stooped a little while he walked was that of Abdel Nasser. A short man wearing the garb of Kufans during al-Husayn's time whispered, "The one wearing the green and the red, is he your father?"

I said, "Yes."

"This is the garb of Paradise," he said. Then his voice got weaker as he said, "Don't be disturbed by what you'll see." I almost asked him what he meant but when I looked, the coffeehouse was empty. The walls had become longer, the space was narrower, and the air had grown stuffier.

I saw two stools, about two meters apart. In the space between them was a desk without drawers, dirty with dried ink stains, lines, and fingerprints of unknown origin. It was a cell in a prison, a prison belonging to the wali of Kufa, Ibn Ziyad. An officer, wearing civilian clothes of my own era, entered, drying his sweat with perfumed facial tissue. His features were not unfamiliar to me. But when? Where? I hadn't learned yet. He looked at the tips of his shoes and moved them several times. There was a noise, steps, the sounds of slapping, spitting, and kicking. I saw them pushing Gamal Abdel Nasser, blindfolded, hands tied, wearing the clothes I had seen him wearing when he made his first appearance: the loose-fitting shirt and baggy pants. They made him stand against the wall. He seemed intent on keeping his head up. I saw only him and the officer in front of him, just the two of them. I didn't see those who were pushing, but I could hear the sound of their shoes scraping and other sounds of their presence and movement. I knew that they belonged to the brutal secret police . I found out that they were the first three who had been sent to Kufa to scare people against taking al-Husayn's side or supporting him. At that moment a flash of lightning lit in my mind and I figured out the identity of the officer: it was none other than the officer who had beaten me and slapped me and threatened me and called my mother and father names. It was the very one who had shown me kindness and gentleness then pounced on me trying to gouge my eyes when I was detained in October in the year nineteen hundred and sixty-six when Gamal Abdel Nasser was at the peak of his power, revered and strong, majestic and cruel to those who hated him and some of those who loved him. That officer was an arrogant young man, proud of his rank of major, whose name was Munir. I felt nauseated and a heavy, thick melancholy came over me as I remembered. I focused my gaze on his two hands that had slapped my face and his two fists that had punched my chest. I relived the moment when I came out of detention, obsessed with seeing the one who had slapped me and called me names. My distress grew and I wished to leave that cell.

At that moment, I sensed and then heard calm, gentle breathing nearby. I turned and my heart was filled with tranquillity. My intercessor was standing nearby. I felt at ease, at peace and in harmony. I traveled immediately to the city of Kufa itself. I saw Muslim ibn Aqil who appeared to me wrapped in a shade of reddish color associated with the soft glow of the hues making up the Diwan. I looked at the light of my eye, al-Husayn, whose face was redolent with compassion and beautiful gentleness. I was drawn to his radiant face and I wished I could just keep looking at its wonderful features. I knew that that primordial longing filled him as he faced his cousin. There he was, Muslim, appearing to me at the moment the pessimism dwindled, the pessimism that had gripped him ever since his two guides died. Forty thousand Kufans swore the pledge of allegiance to him. He wrote to al-Husayn, "Come. The people are with you." The police reported it to the wali of Kufa, alerting him to the gravity of what was happening. The wali went to the mosque, ascended the minbar and, after praising God, called on the people not to rush to sedition and divisiveness. One of Yazid's men shouted, "This is the way the timorous think." To which he answered, "I'd much rather be timid and obey God than be strong and disobey Him."

I saw reports being written in invisible ink in police precincts and places frequented by the secret police, who were everywhere; I saw the reports being reviewed and augmented by that officer whose features were always haunting me. The reports were sent to Damascus, warning headquarters against the wali of Kufa, al-Nu'man, pointing out his piety and integrity and, worst of all, his sympathy for al-Husayn. The officer had never seen Yazid, but he knew exactly what was required. He counseled that the governor of Kufa be replaced by someone capable of handling the situation before it was too late. The officer actually had his own undeclared purpose: to be given a higher post, maybe in Damascus itself, a post that would enable him to amass a considerable fortune, to lay his hands on some land. After all, others lesser than him had seized farms and bought beautiful slave women. He imagined himself roaming the desert or traveling in the cities, meeting al-Husayn by chance, grabbing him, stabbing him, cutting off his head and going to Yazid and telling him, "I've killed the one who claimed to be more entitled than you. I slaughtered the one who dared to refuse to swear allegiance to you," then receiving rewards and gifts.

Yazid appeared to me in Damascus. When I saw his features I was taken aback. Those were features familiar to me, features that repulsed me when I saw them up close. They were the features of someone I had come to despise. How had he come here? I didn't want to get lost in my astonishment so I kept it to myself. Yazid appeared to me while perturbed by what al-Husayn represented. That which al-Husayn was saying was passé, the talk of ascetics about values that had become irrelevant, obsolete. Yazid was now seeking out the worst and lowest of men, giving them governorships and other high posts. He didn't trust those with proven integrity. Nor did he favor those known for piety and God fearing. He was about to embark on moments of transformation and those moments did not favor those who dilly-dallied. What mattered now was: whom should he appoint as amir of Kufa? Which one?

Yazid reviewed the files, listened to various advisors, and examined characters and qualifications. It didn't take him long. He found the one he was looking for: a godless, cruel man with no regard for kinship and no mercy for the poor, a brute who showed kindness to no one. It was Ubayd Allah ibn Ziyad, amir of Basra. There was no time to spare, so he ordered the appointment of Ibn Ziyad, who was to head for Kufa immediately.

Ubayd Allah ibn Ziyad appeared to me. A short while before leaving Basra, he had a chance to publicly prove his allegiance. When they informed him that they had arrested al-Husayn's messenger to Basra, he ordered that he be brought to the main square. There he unsheathed his sword and beheaded him. Thus I was enabled to see the killing of the first messenger in Islam. Then Ibn Ziyad sheathed his sword without wiping off the blood and gave a speech. He said that Yazid had appointed him as wali of Kufa, that he intended to proceed to it, and that he was appointing his brother Uthman ibn Ziyad as his successor in the governorship of Basra. He warned the people, threatened and intimidated them, swearing to punish those close at hand for the infractions of those who were far and to punish the innocent for what the guilty have done.

I saw Ibn Ziyad summon the officer from my era, telling him to send his spies to Kufa, to mix surreptitiously with people there, to speak about his brutality and hard-heartedness but also his generosity toward those that followed and obeyed him. Then he asked that same officer about al-Husayn, his garb, his habits, his routines, when he went to sleep, when he woke up, the manner of his worship, what he was like in company, what food he ate, when he ate, and how many hours he slept. The officer promised to submit to him detailed reports. One evening Ibn Ziyad left Basra wearing a white cloak and a black turban. Halfway on the road to Kufa, he put on a veil. According to news that he had collected, Kufa was rallied around Muslim ibn Aqil and forty thousand men had sworn allegiance to al-Husayn. So, precautions were necessary and prudent. I saw Ibn Ziyad entering Kufa disguised as al-Husayn. Some people saw him and thought the imam had come and shouted, "Welcome, son of the daughter of the Messenger of God! Your coming here is the greatest of blessings!"

At that point, not leaving my place, I traveled back to that cell. I saw that very same officer with his features and his chubby figure, wearing the same clothes I had seen him wearing the first time, going around the desk, standing in front of a blindfolded Gamal

Abdel Nasser and asking in a different voice, "Why did you come here now?"

A minute passed.

The officer's hand, fingers extended, was raised. It landed on the face that had often shone kindly and been watched with admiration. The officer paused to gauge the impact of the first slap, just as he had done with me. Strangely enough I felt the pain as if I were the one who had been slapped and tortured. Two minutes passed. The hand was raised again, one slap after another. I didn't hear a single moan or groan. The cheeks turned red, as did the officer's palm. I was afraid that a cry might escape my lips. I identified with him. My heart experienced unusual feelings and its beats had an unfamiliar significance; before me was Gamal Abdel Nasser, but the presence was that of my father, his smell, the smell of his clothes when he came home every day, that smell that I could never mistake and which would never be repeated: the fragrance of the time I felt most secure, contrasted with my own ephemeral smell. Days and nights with the moon in its fullness, with clear skies, pleasant shade, and sweet dew passed in quick succession. Their hours fed me on hope and made me long for that which I loved and cherished. Then when I felt whole, the days thought that was too much for me. They envied me and strove to bring dispersion to togetherness, dissension to unity, bitterness to sweetness, subtraction to addition, thus eclipsing my bright delight, overburdening my bloom with separation. They sapped the trunk of my union and brought barrenness to my greenery. We were dispersed after being together in the same time frame, in the same land, under the same sky, united by nights, materially poor but rich in contentment. We proudly reacted against an enemy that sought to humiliate us, to divide us even though at one time we were but different organs in one body, operating smoothly in harmony. And here I was watching my father being humiliated and slapped. My days were threatened, the significance of all I was about was dissipating, and that fragrance that was so dear to me was evaporating. My heart was burning but I didn't tell my vision to anyone. I took refuge in looking at my protector and companion. He looked distressed: an old grief had settled in his face like old tears in the eyes. My eyes did not make a mistake, nor have they grown tired. My perception and understanding have not failed me.

The officer shouted suddenly after taking three steps back, "How dare you strike him?"

I was stunned. The language was foreign. One I had not learned as a child or been taught how to spell. My whole body was shaking. My Arabic language was not used. It was forbidden to speak it or exchange greetings in it or use it to call a beloved or a relative or to enunciate feelings or express love, gentleness, companionability, to tell biting jokes, or for communication in offices or to teach it to children opening their eyes to a strange new world. In what black times had I landed and in what accursed days had my travels taken me? My weakened heart was shaken to its foundations. The officer removed the blindfold from Abdel Nasser's eyes and undid his handcuffs. He pointed to the short stool and sat at the desk, taking out a green pack of cigarettes, the same pack he offered me, but which I declined because I didn't smoke. Abdel Nasser shook his head. I almost jumped: it was exactly the way my father shook his head. I could never mistake the way my father shook his head when he hid his irritation or vexation. The officer feigned friendliness and the desire to get close to Abdel Nasser, saying, "You know that I have witnessed part of your era. I belong to a generation that is named after you. I saw you several times, but not up close, for the likes of me could not dream of meeting you. I've been touched by your words and enjoyed the songs that mentioned you. You've survived. The fact that you are here is a mere misunderstanding. You were not arrested for embezzlement, even though they accused you after you died. You were not arrested for taking bribes; even though they tried to tarnish your name, we did not believe them. True, you are now in front of me, but please forgive me. It is not in my hands. I am just performing the duties of my post. Don't forget

I protected you from them. Those who beat you up had not heard of you. Your name has not been mentioned for a long time. Your pictures are no longer published and your statues were destroyed. You were a threat even in your tomb. Don't forget, I stood between them and you. Don't forget, you are at a time that is not your time. Abdel Nasser, why did you come? Why?"

I heard a murmur. I went to Ibn Ziyad again. "Welcome! Welcome! Your coming here is the greatest of blessings!"

Ibn Ziyad did not speak with those who thought he was Imam al-Husayn. He didn't look left or right. He arrived at the palace, showed his credentials, and summoned the officer. He ordered him to expel all strangers from the city and to gather a group of Bedouin scum, make promises to them, tell them they would get a lot of barley if they walked the streets of Kufa shouting slogans supporting Yazid and cursing al-Husayn. He ordered him to have policemen wear plainclothes and do the shouting themselves, so that things would not get out of hand. He ordered that the city be searched to find Muslim ibn Aqil and catch him, dead or alive, that that was a pressing task. He ordered a number of vagrants beheaded before the largest possible number of people while calling them al-Husayn's men.

The officer showed great enthusiasm and promised things that pleased Ibn Ziyad immensely. Ibn Ziyad said he wanted detailed and precise maps of all Kufa's exits, entryways and roads, a precise, comprehensive listing of its houses and their owners. He wanted a comprehensive survey of all roads, those in common use and those deserted, up to a distance of three nights' travel. He also wanted drawings of all the places where it was easy to get close to the Euphrates River to draw water, places where there were sparse palm tree orchards and other vegetation and where those were abundant. He ordered lists of villages and hamlets so undercover personnel could be deployed in each of them. If some of the villages and hamlets were deserted, then some secret policemen should be dispatched to live there. The officer listened. That was the bowing of his head I knew, the features that preceded his staring at me and suddenly calling my father and mother names. I heard him wishing that praise of him would be expressed and perhaps his news would reach Yazid in Damascus, who would then promote him. Perhaps his wishes would come true. If only that were to happen!

His officers and men were deployed, each showing zeal to please the chief of police, each fearing unknown eyes spying on him. Some of these plainclothesmen went through the roads of the town, shouting, calling al-Husayn names with additional zeal, tightening their features like those feigning it to show excessive emotions, thinking that that might convince others. I saw the soldiers arresting three strangers, just ordinary homeless wayfarers who had not been proved to have committed any crime. Nobody even knew their names. They were beheaded in front of the palace to frighten and terrorize the population. I caught a rare moment of change, the moment the scale tipped in favor of one group, a moment when positions were reversed. I heard a saying being repeated, "Why should we care about al-Husayn?" The way the question was pronounced, the secret stress on some letters, the way it was phrased, were all things that were repeated across languages, dialects, and across ears, when insight turned a blind eye. Many did not bother to wait, publicly announcing their enthusiastic support for Yazid to Ibn Ziyad. They reversed themselves totally and shouted the opposite of what they had declared earlier. They knit their brows and pursed their lips as if they had been misguided but now knew better. I looked around me, searching. Where was Muslim ibn Aqil? Where?

I saw the officer facing Gamal Abdel Nasser, frowning, bombarding him with question after question, "Why have you come here? Why did you appear now? Who did you speak to in Dokki Square? Were you sent by a foreign country? Is some group or another supporting you?"

He was unleashing his questions in a fast tempo, as if deliberately trying to catch him off guard. I realized that methods did not change from one era to another. That was how the officer interrogated me. I observed Abdel Nasser's silence, his big eyes that were still piercing. The officer secretly averted his gaze for a few seconds, to escape their influence for a moment or two. The silence, apparently, was troublesome to him. He started asking again, "Why did people gather around you? Why did they encircle you? Who told them of your coming?"

The silent refusal continued. The tone of the questions grew more tense. The officer made a signal with his hand. Three men entered the cell. Abdel Nasser didn't see them but sensed their presence, although he did not show any reaction. He didn't display what I did when two plainclothesmen who specialized in flogging and torture to make suspects confess entered. Their standing behind the prisoner created anxiety and psychological confusion as blows would be expected at any moment and unseen blows would be more painful. I turned around but the officer ordered me not to. In a quick glance I was able to see the features of a brown, thin young man wearing a shirt and pants: a striped white shirt and gray pants. The shirt had short sleeves and the pants were baggy. He was holding a bamboo stick. I didn't catch his name and I didn't hear anyone calling him by name. The officer chided me and called me names. I found out that they were anxious that the victims not recognize their tormentors or the ones whipping them. That was why they used other names, and walked carefully outside among people. At that moment I got confused, my attention divided between facing the officer and answering his questions and anticipating the blow. Waiting for the blows was harder than the actual blows when they started. Abdel Nasser did not turn around or bat an eyelash. That was amazing and it hadn't happened that anyone who sat before the officer throughout his years of service had kept such grip on themselves.

"Why did you attack our friends? And why did you agitate for the lowering of their flags?"

Abdel Nasser did not hide his amazement but he said nothing. He turned slowly, his gaze fixed where my master stood. Did he see him? Did he see me? His eyes kept looking to where al-Husayn's fragrance was spreading. There seemed to be a silent dialogue between the two of them that I could not understand. I've always had this dilemma when I faced my father's calm, sad gaze, when his silence lasted a long time and I felt his deepening loneliness as he looked at me weaving interpretations, questions, and inaccessible explanations. The last time I had such an experience was from the house balcony before my departure, when he stared at me, showering me with his kindness even after he stopped talking and I just looked at him looking at me. But I did not understand and I did not know that only eleven days, no more and no less, were what remained of his life. If only I had reciprocated! A glance for a glance and longing for longing! If only that were so! Would he have gotten his fill of my features before his long travel? I wish I knew. I couldn't be certain. Yet these gazes of his have a place and a station that I couldn't get into now.

I could see Muslim ibn Aqil saying to Hani ibn Urwa, "I've come to you as a guest and I seek protection."

Hani said, "You are asking a lot of me. Had you not entered my house and trusted me, I would have preferred that you leave and take care of your own affairs. But now I am under an obligation. Come in. Come in."

I saw Ibn Ziyad heading for Hani's house, ostensibly to visit him while he was under the weather, but in reality to win him over, for Hani had influence and great support among the locals. I saw the servant telling Hani that Ibn Ziyad was at the door. Hani called Muslim, gave him a sword, and asked him to stand behind the curtain. He would arrange for Ibn Ziyad to sit with his back to the curtains. Hani taking off his turban would be the signal to fall upon him, to finish him off. Muslim stood and hid. Ibn Ziyad entered, accompanied by his chamberlain. Muslim was in his hiding place, frowning. I looked very closely at him and saw my father's cheeks, the pursing of his lips, his knit brow and his eyes, especially the anxiety in his eyes when he was perplexed or thinking or contemplating doing something that he didn't want to do or that was repulsive to him. I saw Hani lifting his turban, but Muslim did not move, did not take that step. It seemed to me that he was not going to do anything. I was astonished. I was afraid. I felt consternation and anger. Hani raised his turban for the second time. I got very impatient. What was happening to Ibn Aqil? At that moment I spoke and he heard me even if he didn't see me. He alone and no one else heard me. I said, urging him, "Go ahead."

He looked around, his innocent face wrestling with a dilemma: "Treacherously kill a Muslim?"

My voice rose in exasperation: "Ibn Ziyad is a murderer. You'll kill a criminal. Ibn Ziyad will kill you. He will mutilate your body. He will throw your head over the wall of the palace. He will deny water to my master al-Husayn. He will order him killed and decapitated. He will parade the head in the streets of Kufa. He will take al-Husayn's women into captivity. He will almost kill his son. Kill him. Perhaps killing him will change things from worse to better. Go ahead. Do it."

He said, "'He who kills a Muslim is not one of the faithful.' That's what I heard the Messenger of God say. I will not kill him treacherously, never."

I saw Ibn Ziyad getting ready to leave. I got very agitated and totally disoriented and confused. I extended my hand, trying to grab the sword, but my hand plunged into the handle, as if I were grasping the air or clutching the fog. I was empty inside too. Ibn Aqil heard my tired, faint voice: "Why? In a few hours he will kill Hani who is extending his hospitality and protection to you. Ibn Ziyad will send one of his most brutal officers, who will disguise himself and look for you and use trickery to find you. He will be an officer whom you don't know, whom the people of Kufa do not know, but whom I know and whose features are indelible in my mind. Why didn't you do it? It would have been possible for time to have changed."

Ibn Aqil asked in amazement and wonderment, "But whose voice are you?"

I was called from an unknown corner, "Gamal, this does not belong to you and you do not belong to it."

I went out tracking Ibn Ziyad. What concerned him the most was: where was Muslim hiding? If he arrested him and mutilated him publicly, that would end the reluctance of those afraid to announce openly their enmity to al-Husayn. As for those wavering, the majority to which he should be devoting his greatest effort, they would settle the matter for themselves. But, first and foremost, where was Muslim ibn Aqil?

I saw that officer dressed in the garb of those days. I watched him closely, playing his role so perfectly I almost believed him even after what he had done to me. When someone told him that he would take him to Ibn Aqil, I shouted warnings but my voice could not penetrate the barriers, could not travel the distance from my time, which at that moment enclosed me as a placenta would an embryo. I saw Ibn Ziyad summon Hani, confronting him. I got closer, apprehensive. Hani responded, "I would never deliver him to you. You want me to deliver my guest so you can kill him?"

Ibn Ziyad struck him in the face with his club, not hesitating for a moment, even given Hani's status and his old age. Ibn Ziyad realized at that point that the most dangerous thing facing him would be a sentence that might get repeated and gain currency. That would be more dangerous than a tremendous army. I ran out of the palace, terrified, running in the streets of Kufa, my shouting voice reverberating, heard by some, unheard by others. I didn't know why that was the case and decided to inquire about it some other time. I shouted the news of Hani's murder, thus being the first to let the Kufans know. I ran to Muslim to urge him to carry on. I saw him on the way, his sword unsheathed, and I thanked God for that. A considerable crowd had gathered around him, so he had the men and the arms. How many did I see? Maybe three or four thousand, heading for the palace. The policemen retreated, evacuating the roads, the squares, and the street corners. The officer was hesitant: what if the tables were turned? What if things went the other way?

He decided to stay out of sight temporarily and get himself pre-occupied with something else until he found out which way the wind would blow. Ibn Ziyad was besieged. He had thirty police-men and twenty notables with him. He ordered the policemen to sneak outside. They infiltrated the crowds. They scared the people about the consequences of fighting. I saw a reddish light envelop-ing the houses of Kufa and the tops of its palm trees. There were many policemen, each promising generous bonuses: money, wheat, barley, a higher post, a kindly look from the higher-ups. They sneaked, infiltrated, spread, whispered, persuaded, warned, sowed defeatism, promised the obedient members of the public rewards, and encouraged greed. I watched them spreading, sometimes whis-pering and at other times saying things out loud. I saw the officer whispering and making secret suggestions. I was just one person and there were many policemen. My voice was not allowed to breach the barriers except at unpredictable times. I was incapable and they were capable. I felt great pain because of my inability to match their power: one man facing a whole era and a worse one yet to come. What made matters worse and more difficult was seeing people growing enthusiastic for what was against their own inter-ests, shouting and vying for that which would harm them. That was rough and talking about it could be dangerous. I experienced some of it in my own time when I saw some of my own people shouting for and hailing conciliation with the enemies, welcom-ing a peace which was not peace at all, raising their hands to greet their murderers. I've already alluded to that when I said, "I wonder at my own people: they triumph when they are defeated and are defeated when they are victorious." But there were other themes and difficult topics that I would get into when permitted to do so, that being a matter left to God Almighty. As for now, I would close this door out of fear and for self-protection.

I saw defeatism creeping in and weakness sapping men's vigor. I heard one man tell another, "You should leave. It is very danger-ous." I heard a strong and healthy young man whispering, "One only lives once!" I heard a woman saying to her man, "Tomorrow the men from Syria will come. So what are you going to do in the war? Stay alive, for your kids." I saw a man retreating, then two men. I saw a whole group move away. I saw people closing their houses after going inside, defeatism turning into dispersal, then retreat, then running away. The day was coming to an end. Ibn Aqil was surrounding the palace with a thousand men. He realized that the numbers of men and arms had dwindled. So he retreated to downtown. Ibn Aqil now had five hundred followers. He went through a side street and came out with three hundred. A hundred went into the mosque with him. When prayer time came, thirty lined up behind him. At the end of the prayer he gave the peace greeting to his right then to his left. Now he was all by himself, not a single follower, friend, or ally.

Muslim ibn Aqil left the mosque after nightfall to deserted streets. I saw the officer somewhere in Kufa with some policemen, showing signs of enthusiasm. Ibn Aqil was a stranger: no one pointed him in the direction of a house to offer him shelter. He moved away from the mosque as the stillness around him deepened, as people disappeared and supporters became rare, as companions departed and men hid behind house walls. Ibn Aqil moved from one quarter to another. He felt wounded and was afraid, but most of all he was sad for being thwarted and afraid for his imam, al-Husayn. How would he tell him what happened? How could he persuade him not to come? How would he contact him now? Who would carry the message and where were the mounts? A heavy anguish had him in its grip: how did that change come about? How did everyone go back on their word? Abandonment taking refuge in disappointment? He turned around to look, but he was mistaken. There was nobody behind him. He couldn't see me or hear my footsteps but he sensed my presence. He was dismayed and perplexed by how easy it was for his massive support to have evaporated. The world seemed mysterious and human souls inscrutable. I looked at al-Husayn. I wished I could beg him to enable me to console Ibn Aqil. I was held back

113

by the kindness and compassion filling his face. I went back to Ibn Aqil. I tried. If only I could warn him against seeking refuge in that woman's house. I wished I could tell him that it was her son who would lead Ibn Ziyad's soldiers to him. How could I know and not speak out? But the Diwan had not permitted me, had not lifted the barriers between me and him. My human nature, nonetheless, overcame me so I ran crying, "Beware, Ibn Aqil!"

He didn't turn around.

"Ibn Aqil, be careful!"

I stopped. He began to turn to take a position to face me but soon I was thrown into the clutches of confusion. I was hurled into the house of surprise and fear. In front of me was my father. I saw him tired, a stranger with the load of heavy days on his shoulders. His clothes were dusty and his face looked like his face during the year that I didn't know would be his last, the year his body shrank and he grew pale and his eyes got narrower; his laugh had also grown weaker, his movements slower and his cough stronger. After my astonishment wore off somewhat, I said, "What are you doing in Kufa, Father?"

He didn't answer. I went on, "Father, you are in a land you've never set foot in, a stranger like me!"

His silence continued. Suddenly a feeling of desolation and utter loneliness began assailing me. I felt cold inside and melancholic. I saw myself with my own two eyes. I saw myself a stranger in a strange country in which I had arrived on a gloomy afternoon, a country in which I knew no one and no one was waiting for me. I had not come to see anyone in particular and I had no idea where I would spend the night, or where I'd find shelter. Everyone around me was hurrying. The windows were closed and lights behind some of them suggested an evening gathering, warmth and the smell of food, thereby doubling my sense of deprivation and the depth of my loneliness. I saw my father as worries ganged up on him: that was his face when he complained to me how lonely he felt, how no one talked with him, how everyone was busy and preoccupied with themselves. I said, "I have frittered away the life I had been given with you. Let me accompany you now." He extended his hand, making a gesture as if to keep me from going on. So, he heard me. When was I heard and when not? When did the barriers descend into place and when were they lifted? I didn't know. When the time came I would ask the Diwan. My father pointed at me, indicating a distance between what was nearby and what was far off. His gesture was quite decisive: I saw where the twilight began, near him, then expanded to herald the moments of sunset. On the opposite side I saw my closest companion and realized he was preoccupied with something else. It was a very dark night, but I was able to pierce the darkness with my eye as if it were a clear, sunny day. I could see the waterwheels, the dovecote, the bridges, and the just-irrigated fields covered with water, the field mice and the palm tree and the minute details of the crickets. I was able to count the lines in the spider webs. I could see what was in front of me and what was behind me, unobstructed by any barriers. I was able to see two different things from two different eras. I listened and was able to hear the moaning of the dust and the plant roots feeling constricted by a rough soil. Then I saw a shadow running. I saw the houses of Kufa overlooking the roads of Juhayna, my village. As for the thick palm groves, they were in Basra, the dry air from Hijaz, the stars from the Gulf of Aden, the smell from the entryways to Tulkarem in Palestine. The fast gushing of the canal waters was from Fez in Morocco, but the waters themselves were from springs in Yemen.

I saw my father. He was now a frightened boy, almost breathless, his heart beating fast. I saw my father's paternal uncle running after him. I saw them both, even though neither of them saw the other. They were separated by a winding road; his uncle was giving chase after he caught a glimpse of him. He wanted to strangle him, to get rid of him, and grab the house, the land, and the palm trees all for himself. My father kept running. No help was in sight. I shouted to tell him where his uncle was, but

I didn't know whether my voice reached him or not. I saw him jump over the fence of an old barn and dig a place for himself in a pile of hay. I heard a voice that exuded ageless authority. It was the distant star. It said that what I'd seen and what I was seeing would leave a deep mark on my father, that it would come over him again and again, in sleep and wakefulness and would visit him in the last hour while sleeping, before his final departure. I asked the star, "Will this be the last image of this world that will stay with him?"

The distant star did not answer, so I asked, "What date was that? Which moment in calculable time?"

But the conversation was cut off. I heard moans. My father's uncle, who should have been like a grandfather to me, moved away. I saw my father shivering like a wet little bird. At dawn a man entered. He sensed my father's presence and asked, "Who's there? Human or jinn?" My father's fear subsided. He told the man what happened and the latter took him inside the house and offered him hot milk, a loaf of bread, and some cheese. My father said in the voice I was familiar with in his last years, "I swear I haven't eaten anything in two days." The man patted him on the shoulder. His hunger, his fear and sadness and suffering pained me, so I opened my hand and placed it before my eyes and said in sorrow, "That's enough."

Clarification

My maternal uncle told me after my father's passing, after my heart was dealt that treacherous blow, that he remembered a man named Abdel Karim Zaydan for whom the beloved deceased had great affection. Every time my father went back to the village he remembered to bring him a gift: a gallabiya, a parasol, fragrant sandalwood prayer beads that he made sure to buy in the vicinity of al-Husayn's mausoleum, a tin of halva, or a cotton shawl from Ghuriya. Two months before Abdel Karim Zaydan passed away my father went to the village and visited him. That time he brought him a small box containing sugar, tea, and fine bars of perfumed soap.

Epiphany of Voyaging

My voyaging is constant with my intercessor by my side. Deserts don't scare me and unforeseen assailants don't daunt me. I wear everything I am entitled to: a robe of eagerness, a shirt of love, a vest of passion, or a jacket of yearning. Blossoms are revealed to me and newborn stars sparkle to me from afar. My eyes can see the unseen. My comprehension is vast and my understanding far-reaching. As for my sadness, it is fragile. My disposition changes with every breath I take. My traveling is a permanent state and it is impossible for me to settle down in one place. I travel as I stand and I stand as I travel. I am susceptible to neither *slumber nor sleep*. No hardship or negligence can overwhelm me. My memory is intact and no isolation or loneliness can threaten me, nor can any ill touch me while in the company of my beloved. Thus it is: a turn for a turn, a look for a look, and longing for longing. For is there a reward for good but good?

A Tidbit

I will love you for as long as I live.
When I die, my decaying bones will go on loving you.

A Connection Within a Connection

Gamal Abdel Nasser remained silent. He did not reply to the officer's questions. With a nod from the officer's head the three guards made a clicking sound with their boots, giving an inkling of the cruelty about to be unleashed. I felt the majestic presence of Abdel Nasser, his towering stature, much taller than his physical height, his gray temples, and that gentle affection that his presence inspired. I had seen his processions in their full regalia, before any hint of an eclipse, back when he was still an unfinished melody. I remembered his presence at the dawning of eids and our waiting for his arrival. He was and I was and my father was. We were an intact group and those days, on the surface, were blossoming and full of promise. But those same times were also hiding things, not divulging or giving any intimation of what was to come, of that which was still hidden in the obscure folds of the unknown. I saw with sorrow his flabby skin, his bent back, and his fatigue as he faced that officer coming from the Houses of Harm and Tribulation. He was clean-shaven, his skin tanned, and he had the same smell that assailed my nostrils when I was blindfolded, totally helpless. I saw how young he was compared to latent old age, how tiny against an all-encompassing vastness, in chains versus free movement, brackish, stagnant, and foul-smelling water versus flowing fragrant water. The officer shook, not hiding his rage, breaking all the rules he had been taught, "So, you don't answer! You don't know what awaits you."

The officer stood up suddenly, looking at the entrance of the interrogation cell. I saw a few faces peering: some Israeli, some American, representatives from the Mossad, military intelligence, and the director of the CIA. The officer disappeared from my field of vision. Some shadows got longer. Accusations came in quick succession to Abdel Nasser: "You are charged with being hostile to those who hold power in the world."

"You built the High Dam."

"You were the enemy of the masters in the White House, the Pentagon, and the Senate."

"You were partial to the poor and opposed the rich."

"You looked to the future."

The voices multiplied and grew indistinguishable from one another. I could hardly make out his voice when he was younger and more vigorous, his days full of promise. He was announcing the nationalization of the Suez Canal. People were applauding and their cheers were thundering. Where have they gone? Where were they now? His mere name spelled defiance. It brought back the glory of days past, and filled hearts with determination. We didn't have a radio at the time. I went out of our room on the roof and stood on tiptoe, holding on to the edge of the railing, and some chipped paint wetted by the moisture stuck to my skin. His voice was coming from the first floor through the wind shaft, rising in the early evening. As I raised my head I saw far away on the horizon a large neon sign lighting the sky in red and blue. I sat on the roof wearing a brown gallabiya. My father stood in the corner next to the wooden mast, holding our neighbor's radio antenna. We stared at the sky as three planes flew over at low altitude followed by three other planes. Sitt Rawhiya came up to the roof and joined us. My father asked her what was happening and she said that it was the army, that the king was over and done with. She said people were saying the army would reduce prices and make things cheap, that people would ride public transportation for free.

The following morning I went out. I crossed the street from the entrance to our alley, passing the stores of al-Bagoury the grocer, Muhammad the greengrocer, and Galal the falafel vendor. I stopped at Amm Muhammad's newsstand and bought *al-Ahram*. In the middle of the front page there was a large photograph of the leader of the revolution, General Muhammad Naguib, and a smaller picture of Nasser in profile. He looked thin, with a big nose and a radiant face. There were other photographs of equal size. My father stretched out on the roof on his back, leaning his head to the wall as I read him the names. We didn't pause at his name in particular.

It was my father's custom to take my brother and me with him when he went out, and he took us to a stadium in the Darrasa desert. There were wooden bleachers and spectators in suits and gallabiyas. There were posters from the neighborhood merchants welcoming the free leaders. I heard that the police would mount a show. I saw inflated balloons on the field, which was covered with dark yellow sand. From the far end of the playground came horses with horsemen wearing embroidered clothes, who galloped and burst the balloons to the cheering of the spectators. Then came the boy scouts marching. I saw the green kerchiefs around their necks, the white cords with the whistles at the end, and the leather belts with daggers. They stood around a corner of the platform, raising their hands. Gamal Abdel Nasser was standing there. I didn't see him, but I heard his voice and it was resounding, his speech punctuated with pauses. That was the first time I heard him. Then we left. My father bought us some sugarcane juice. I heard his voice again after many years had passed. He was troubled as he announced the crushing blow and the loss of the troops. That was the beginning of the eclipse and the first signal of the sunset that weighed so heavily on us and darkened our early youth, the end of something; but it did not do irreparable damage to that late afternoon when I heard him for the first time nor to my father's steps when he walked with us. The damage was not done even though all of that had passed and I didn't go out of my way to see it except within this voyage of mine. In the material world, however, grasping that would be difficult if not impossible, even though I had given to those moments a measure of my existence.

I heard the noise of kicking and slapping but I didn't hear any moans or screams begging for mercy, even though he was over fifty and weighed down with the pain of diabetes and heart disease. Things got heated and there was a cacophony of different voices and sounds. I was able to make out the sounds of shortness of breath, the reopening of wounds, and frayed nerves. Voices, noises, and images multiplied around me. The shrapnel of our shared time flew hither and yon. I wished I could ask for explanations. I was shaken by pain and grief and wounds. This became too much for me so I hurried away. I heard ancient crying. I looked and I wished I had not looked. Muslim ibn Aqil, his face kicked in, teeth smashed, jaw dangling, feeling extreme thirst. His eyes were full of tears now that he was a prisoner, impotent, surrounded on all sides, his sword taken away after he had fought valiantly. Someone standing said, "Someone seeking what you ask and suffering what you suffer should not cry." Ibn Aqil said, "I swear by God I am not crying for myself or bemoaning my death. I cry for my family on its way. I cry for al-Husayn and his house." I heard a tremor. I turned and saw my master grieving. I saw his radiant brow knit. I held myself back and averted my eyes.

I stopped being inquisitive. It pained me to see my beloved suffer pain, even if only for a moment. I had forgotten he was a normal human being. But that did not last for very long. My sun began to wane slowly and my world turned yellow and my night drew near. I began to see in my horizon my first scattering stars. My nostrils were filled with the smell of the dust of our village and the old well whose walls were covered with green moss, and the waterwheel scoops. All of these smells covered those long distances to my father's lungs and haunted him in sleep. I saw house lights in Kufa and a black ant weeping in the blackest of the night on a massive rock. My striving continued even though I had not yet reached completion. When human beings reach completion they depart, just as a carrier is loaded and departs once the load is complete by sailing or taking off and then returning. Humans alone reach completion then depart without return. I implore you: deliver me! Deliver me!

A Passing Thought
Death comes in two forms: the greater death and the lesser death. The greater death consists in condoning injustice, turning a blind eye to falsehood, deadening one's conscience, disregarding the unjust usurpation of a right, and getting preoccupied with seeking fleeting posts or hoarded treasure. It also consists in accepting the status quo and avoiding trying to change it by neglecting to fight for what is right. As for the lesser death, it is the cessation of the senses, ceasing to breathe, cardiac arrest, and coldness of the body when the soul departs and the limbs stiffen.

Striking Out
It was a sunrise moment, but there was no sunrise: red, yellow, blue, all in the distance, and mysterious diaphanousness. In the kind, gentle light sat the president of the Diwan, the pure Lady Zeinab, resplendent, sweet, serene, and majestic, filling the four corners, and there was our master, al-Hasan, in charge of all points to the

right of existence. As for the other presence, that was the heart of radiance, the dispeller of all darkness, the master of martyrs, my intercessor, my guide, and my security against fear. I didn't know exactly where I was or on which side. The brilliant light unveiled a village with sandy roads and buildings near and far. That was the moment of al-Husayn's departure from Mecca, accompanied by his family and companions, their camels trudging forward on the rough terrain. They were all heading for Kufa. He had been advised to take a side road but he refused. He was proceeding along a well-traveled route, unafraid of Yazid's spies planted along that road. His heart was heavy, the signals were murky, but he believed that hardship must be followed by ease and what was tight had to be relaxed, and that accepting injustice in silence spelled certain perdition.

Before setting out al-Husayn toured Mecca, remembering first places where he tarried, those where he stayed, and those where longings stirred in him their shadow, those that witnessed his early days when his father was young and full of vitality and his noble grandfather filled the world. He recalled his carefree moments during his childhood in the city, playing surrounded by those hills. He wished he could take a look that he knew might be the last at those places. He remembered the breezes that sneaked through the desert heat. With his eyes he kissed the Kaaba. He drank of the water of Zamzam and took a tour of the nooks and crannies where he had left many reminders of his past. A thought occurred to him, cruel in its tenderness, sharp in its fragility, telling him that he would never see any of those places again. He tried to get rid of the thought and proceeded to distribute things he didn't need among the poor and the sick. In one fleeting moment his face took on an expression that never left thereafter. He bade Mecca goodbye and went out on the road and there he met the poet al-Farazdaq. He asked him how the people were. Al-Farazdaq said sadly that their hearts were with him but their swords were against him. So, his heart was not lying to him: an exit but no return. His expected fate was being revealed to him at every step. Time was turning; he was now drinking from the fount in the House of Harm and Tribulation. After another stage on his way he was met by the messenger of Ibn Aqil, who conveyed to him the grave news of his death. So, the destiny was no longer unknown. Here was al-Husayn among his troops, radiant, determined, his heart overflowing, his intentions sincere, riding, risking his life to confront those that would take the people backward, all the way back to the original days of ignorance, to that which would burden man's limited life with misery. In a remote part of his wounded heart he still had hopes of confronting people, debating with them, trying to dissuade them from their inaction, from their fear of transitory power. But premonitions told him what was going to happen and how his blood would be shed. So, his days were numbered; let that be so, but his being killed at their hands would turn into a huge conflagration that would start from a mere spark. He almost saw with his own eyes what was going to happen.

At that point I looked toward the center of the Diwan where its members and pillars were watching and listening. My master al-Husayn was now watching his own journey. In my mind thoughts and worlds abounded but there was no way I could speak. I was only able to be a recipient, calm and not frustrated.

I saw al-Husayn going out to Karbala. The Diwan recalled those grave moments and I saw him. After him I saw the formation of the dew, the flowers coming out of their cups, a wave coming out of the womb of another wave, a moment coming out of another moment. I saw the gaze going out to the object of the gaze, the moment the day came out of the night, the star coming out of the depths of the universe, the impetuous tear coming from the eye. I saw what Gamal Abdel Nasser's emergence in that strange time caused. People were talking about his coming. Those who witnessed the incident in Dokki Square affirmed that it was him; same features, same physical traits as in the old pictures. A tired man asserted that he could never mistake his face for someone else's. A young woman who had not lived during his life on earth swore that his shouting voice was the very same voice to which she had listened for a long time on secretly circulated recordings. A peasant from the deep countryside said that Gamal Abdel Nasser had come to answer the calls of the powerless and the forlorn, that he had come because this country was under the protection of the members of the Prophet's house, for it had al-Husayn, Sayyida Zeinab, president of the Diwan, Sidi Zayn al-Abidin, Sayyida Fatima, Sayyida Sukayna, Sayyida Ruqayya, and Sayyida Nafisa, may God have mercy on all of them. A young journalist asserted that Gamal Abdel Nasser had escaped from his prison, his forehead bandaged and limping lightly, that he was seen in a taxi with three persons whom he didn't know. He said his escape had been meticulously arranged.

I saw all the protective measures. I saw foreign soldiers standing at the intersections, displaying strange-looking weapons, scrutinizing passersby, examining features and identity cards and other papers. I saw CIA men stopping trains and cars, overturning loads, and taking control of access points.

I was certain that something was afoot but I couldn't fully comprehend it. I almost asked, but I traveled to a moment in the past and saw Gamal Abdel Nasser wearing his military uniform, the moment he came out to announce the revolution. Then the vision changed and I saw that he was in a remote desert, planning something. He had only a few men with him and I knew that what he was destined to be would come to pass.

I saw a heartbeat coming out of another heartbeat, the blood pumped by the heart flowing in its cycle and that *man can have only what he strives for.* Glory be to thee, God.

The rhythms of my breathing changed and I saw my father's departure from his village, the first place he had known and where he had spent his early years. I saw him walking with a man his age named Umar. They were walking toward the bridge. My father was turning his back to the houses, bidding farewell to one world and welcoming another, the former well known to him, the latter unknown. He stopped, turned around. The houses were hidden behind palm trees, doum trees, and various kinds of acacia trees.

His eyes were now full of tears: it was hard for him to leave the village for a land that he hadn't seen or set foot on. It was hard for him to leave Juhayna even though he had suffered immensely in it, his uncle tormenting him, turning his days and nights into a living hell. He was even about to finish him off. One night he tied him up and took him toward the canal, intending to weigh him down with stones. He would've been drowned had it not been for the coincidence that sent his way a good, kind-hearted man, the master sergeant of the village police station, Ahmad Husayn, and had it not been for the precinct officer, Abu Hashish, each of whom had his own stories and situations that would be related when their time came and permission was granted by the pillars of the Diwan. May God enable me always to seek their proximity, to cross their thresholds humbly.

I saw my father's eyes well up with tears at the bridge as the houses disappeared even though he had only seen and been at these houses' thresholds. I saw his tears because he knew that what used to be would be no more, that when he returned to the village one day, sooner or later, he would find that what he knew had changed one way or another. That was what my father realized at a young age, something that I could fathom only after a long, painful experience in which I suffered many wounds.

It took my father two years to prepare himself for departing the village after his life there had become unbearably difficult. One night the idea struck him but he was afraid to even think it through. A kind-hearted man named Muhammad Ali encouraged him and put his fears at ease. My father inquired about Cairo, life there, what the houses looked like, how to make a living, how to go about making a living, about shelter and relatives' addresses. He memorized the addresses and repeated them aloud to himself. He made up his mind to go, then changed it, then made it up again. The circle of time turned and I saw my father as I knew him when he made plans to visit one of the saints' shrines or when he went back to visit Ahmad Husayn, the policeman who saved his life. I saw him as he came and went asking about train schedules, which trains were fast and which were slow, then his buying the gifts, how he would get a large empty basket made of braided palm leaves, arranging wrapped gifts in it then taking them out again, making sure not to place the tea next to the bars of soap, then wrapping the packaged gifts in old newspapers, then rearranging everything. The night before his departure he would toss and turn and arrive at the railroad station several hours before his scheduled departure. That was the level of my father's anxiety as I had known him even though those were short trips from which he returned. What agony, what anxiety and anguish he must have felt those few nights before leaving the village!

On the appointed day he started out with nothing but a wrapped bundle containing a new gallabiya, an undershirt, and two plain calico underpants. Next to his chest he held on to ten Egyptian pounds, his savings over many years from the income of the one feddan and a half. I looked at my master and beloved al-Husayn. He figured out what was going through my mind and I got the answer. I found out that my father had gotten so fed up with his life that the whole world felt as if it were narrower than the eye of a needle, but that he was still curious and hopeful: He would give the ten pounds to an acquaintance in Cairo and beg him to enroll him as a student in al-Azhar. There he would receive an education. He would be able to learn the alphabet, understand words, read the Qur'an, the Hadith, and the exegeses. He would recite and write and become a learned man. He would get to know the world, for ignorance was like blindness. He would try to learn the location of the stars, the cycles of the sun and the moon, the names of flowers and the histories and biographies of great men. My father was fond of genealogy and learning who had been born to what village, and the deeds of men in bygone eras. He had such a sharp memory that once he heard a name he never forgot it and if he experienced a cloudy winter day, the memory of its gray light never left him. When he sat in a group he remembered where each one was sitting and the color

126

of their clothes dozens of years later. He remembered the days of heavy rain or unusually hot temperature. That was a memory that never failed until the night of the twenty-eighth of October, the night I was far away from him, following the steps that were completed when he left the village to go to Cairo.

Cairo, he thought to himself, was a big city with many opportunities for a livelihood and it wouldn't be difficult for him to find a source of income that would make it possible to get an education, to read and write and to know things that were more than just idle hearsay and word of mouth. There he was, having covered a long portion of the road to Tahta, the first city on his way. At that point what I had been wishing for was granted to me. The whole Diwan gave me permission to appear to my father.

I appeared to him on the road. I was twenty years old, wearing a white gallabiya and a woolen skullcap, and holding a bamboo cane. I didn't know whether I had my own features or not. My father approached me. I watched him walking even though I had not yet come into this world. He passed me then came back to me, asking me about the distance remaining until Tahta. He asked me while his traveling companion was some distance from us on a mild and beautiful day. I had the chance to study his face and recognize the zones of sadness and longing around his eyes and his mouth, all the time aware of that mysterious line of sadness linking me to him and him to me. I gave him directions, mentioning a bend in the road in the midst of the palm trees, a drainage canal that he had to cross at the village of Tulayhat, a wet, muddy part of the road that he had to avoid, and a rich man's house surrounded by dogs that he should be cautious about when approaching. I also mentioned to him that the sun would be quite intense at midday and therefore he should not take shortcuts in the cornfields and the passageways in them but stick to the main road where the trees would provide him with shade. He thanked me and wished me God's protection. He almost asked me who I was but was too shy. He turned and I cried out to him and he turned again in surprise, "Do you know me, friend?" My mouth smiled and I extended my hand with the cane, saying, "Go in safety. It seems you have a long travel ahead of you. Take this to scare off dogs." He prayed for my safety again and turned, holding the cane. That was a cane he kept throughout his life; even on those days that he was upset and left the house, he never let it out of his hand. I didn't know where that cane came from. The first time I had seen it was during that encounter but I didn't know its origin or which bamboo plant it had been taken from, who leaned against it, and to what use it had been put or what sheep or other animals it shooed away or what other form it had taken. That was something I was not informed of.

My father moved away, hastening to catch up with his companion. I could see the two of them talking. I wished him safety and turned to the president of the Diwan to extend her care to him on this jouney of his. I was missing my existence, which was completed before I even began. I faded out even before I ever came into being. I asked what year that was and the answer came: it was the one thousand, nine hundred, and twenty-third year since the birth of Christ. But I was not given the day or the month, even though several curious tidbits of information were revealed to me. The moment he left the boundaries of the village, a migrating dove landed on a patch of land adjacent to old cemeteries south of Fustat and the sun rose over desert sands east of Abbasiya, a man named Rimali counted a sum of money, and a law school student named Muhammad Khalaf received a gift from Naples, a box of candy with an almond filling. Between the moment of my father's departure from the village and his final departure from our world fifty-seven years passed; between his departure from the village and my mother's birth, two days; and my birth, twenty-two years; and his marriage to my mother, sixteen years. Between his departure and al-Husayn's departure for Karbala there were one thousand, two hundred, and forty-three years, and between his departure from the village and Gamal Abdel Nasser's final departure there were forty-seven years. Between his departure from the village and the Israelis' coming to Egypt there were fifty-four years and between their coming and his final departure, three years. His stay in this world was eighty years, according to my mother, ninety according to my maternal aunt, and more than a hundred years as one of his relatives who himself enjoyed a long life asserted. According to the official registers, however, he lived sixty-two years. I tried in vain to find out the truth from my master and from the president of the Diwan, but that information was not made available to me.

I returned to my father and hovered over him as he rode a slow freight train heading for Cairo with his companion. I walked slowly with the caravan carrying al-Husayn to Kufa. It was confirmed that Abdel Nasser had indeed escaped from prison. I kept moving around and my visions kept coming vividly. Al-Husayn returned to my side. My apologies: I returned to his side and he kindly comforted me, gave me strength, and supported me. I said, "My feeling that I am lost has grown after all these epiphanies."

"All created things and beings have to return to where they have been. This is certain," he said. The longing in my father's eyes came over me again. I felt my heart burdened: Gamal Abdel Nasser's features as he faced the officer, the pain and suffering of Ibn Aqil.

I said, "I fear what is awaiting me."

"If only the ignorant being knew what he doesn't know," he said.

I said, "Please enlighten me more."

He said, "Don't you have faith?"

"Yes, but my heart needs reassurance," I said.

At that point I saw that he had gone to a far corner of the Diwan. I was frightened and I couldn't hide what I was thinking. I asked, "What territories are we traveling to? In what womb is forgetfulness carried? What heavy placenta is wrapped around memory? What hiding place keeps days and nights hidden?"

I saw that al-Husayn was angry. He confronted me, "Haven't I told you?"

I was crestfallen. I felt devastated and had a bitter taste in my mouth. I said nothing. He said, "Have I not warned you about the one thing you should never ask about?"

My heartbeats raced in regret and sorrow. He disappeared from in front of me, but I saw him in his place at the Diwan. I didn't know if I had gone back to where I began or whether I was in the right place, for me.

A Doleful Lament
I have encountered trials and tribulation in these travels of mine.

The Stations

The Station of Getting Ready
It is the sun, except that the sun sets
And the one that we have in mind never sets.

He caused me to stay in the Station of Getting Ready then he
left me, deserting me and going far away from me, so I became a
stranger in a desolate place after being in pleasant company. I ended
up forlorn after being in a union of affection and mercy. I ended
up a stranger in my alienation, distant in my distantness, away in
my being away, but I was like someone mustering all his strength to
prepare for a great journeying. I was able to see what was in front of
and what was behind me, what was above me and below me without moving my eyes or my head. I became all vision as if I were the
one looking and the one looked at, the seer and the seen.

I saw a marvelous bird unlike any bird in the whole world that I
knew of, its body fashioned of the spectrum of light, its feathers containing all colors of the world. As for its head, it was human, and so
was its face. My heart told me that I knew the features but I couldn't
quite focus because of the intense glow so I knew that the time for
my recognizing it had not yet come. I saw it hovering in the sky of
the Diwan but because that sky surrounded the Diwan the way the
white of the egg surrounds its yolk, the marvelous bird seemed to

me to be flying both upward and downward, its ascent a descent and its descent an ascent. To my surprise it spoke and ordered me to get ready. I acquiesced right away without saying a word even though I was astonished because my master, who had been my companion and my guide, had abandoned me. I was silent because I knew that any thought occurring to me and any feeling stirring my heart was well known to the masters of the Diwan, my masters.

At a specific point I saw two men standing in the midst of what looked like a fog. My heart told me that the fragrance of their days was very close to me. They told me silently that they had received the same order as me. They stated that our destination was Karbala at a distant point in time. So we headed for Karbala. I knew that I was at the beginning of the station, that it was a station of ease: of colors, it was gray; of days of the week, it was Sunday; of the hours of the day, that preceding sunrise; of heat, the beginning of its intensity; of the states of the eye, the moment just before the shedding of tears; and of the heart, its racing beat upon receiving heavy forebodings.

Our journey began and we passed through many colors: pitch black like black marble or black velvet, and pure blue like the color of turquoise at its birth. Then we saw a thin, piercing light penetrating the Diwan from end to end. Then there appeared various strange-looking bodies like comets or meteors and others that were totally unfamiliar to us. They came at us and we thought they would go through us, devastate us, but they passed us and we passed them and no harm came to us. Old planets and new planets intermingled just like sparks of fire; they were perpendicular then gathered in a straight line, then chased each other but without crashing, each floating in its orbit.

Sights followed each other in quick succession as swiftly as one thought followed another. I said to myself that that could only be for a matter of great moment. Different colors succeeded one another, colors that were new to me and for which I had no names or descriptions. From time to time the shadow of the radiant bird of light that gave me the order passed in front of me so I figured out it was our companion on this journey of ours.

132

I did not think of my two companions because of all we had been through, but I realized that the time for getting closer was drawing near. I noticed that the closer I got, the farther they got. When my travel ended and my night almost turned into day they both totally disappeared from my presence. Thereupon that sharp thought, like a well-aimed arrow, hit my whole consciousness: how did I not recognize them? How did I not decipher the concealed features on the whole and in detail? How could that have happened when I have known them both all my life, my father so close and Gamal Abdel Nasser from afar though closely on my part? How did I not address each of them by name? How did I travel in the company of my father as if we were strangers? How did I not get close to him even though I was distracted by the planets and the visions? A question sank into my very essence: was it the beginning of forgetfulness?

I remembered an older friend of mine at a time when I was immersed in a grief so fresh it felt like soft, hot, liquid tar. My friend said, "You need a whole year to forget." I didn't reply. I didn't agree with what he said. I asked myself: how could he even think that I might forget one day, no matter how far off that day might be or seem? It was as if he realized what was going through my mind, so he said to console me, "All things are born small then they grow bigger, except grief which is born big then it grows smaller." I was upset by what he said then, and I was upset to remember it in my present situation. But the breaking dawn on that day, so remote from my earthly time and the breath I took on that morning that I have never lived took me away from those thoughts. I found myself far away from my era, in Karbala. In front of me was the camp of my master al-Husayn, his tents set up; only his family and his closest companions remained with him. As for the day, it was the third of al-Husayn's thirst. He had been prevented from reaching the water. On the opposite side were Yazid's soldiers. It was the sixty-fifth year since the migration of our intercessor, Muhammad the Messenger of God. It was the tenth of Muharram, a Friday.

I embraced my master with my eyes and wrapped his infant baby al-Qasim within the folds of my heart. My eyes ceased casting about when I saw my two traveling companions already through the Station of Getting Ready. I saw them, or so I thought: my father and Gamal Abdel Nasser, wearing the clothes of the period and holding weapons of that era, standing in the midst of the companions of al-Husayn who had remained steadfastly with him and gotten ready for thirst and lack of provisions or reinforcement. The two of them stayed with him, with those closest to him. I was filled with wonderment. I joined the ranks of the dearest beloved, the pure mirror of truth, the dissipater of mystery, the eye of fate, and the perfume of my days that were yet to come. I could see but no one could see me. When my throat was dry and my thirst grew most intense, I knew that I was suffering what he and his cohorts were suffering. I realized that the Station of Getting Ready was over, that fate had been decreed and that it had to be carried out.

The Station of Thirst
They are in doubt and confusion concerning a new creation.

I found myself among al-Husayn's family and companions, besieged like them, tired like them, but unlike all of them I was granted the ability to move back and forth from their set-upon position and the positions of those standing between them and the cool refreshing water of the Euphrates River. I didn't know how I'd end up, whether I would die or not. If I died, did that mean that I'd be totally obliterated and not come into being in the distant future from which I had come?

I pushed away the questions that revolved around my own ego and was overcome with a strong desire to seek out my father who had left me, who had died condemning me to spend my remaining days in the world deprived of seeing his face, of listening to his coughing fits on winter nights, or to his feet as he climbed the stairs quickly, then slowly when he got older and weaker. I could hear him before waiting for his knocks on the door of our house, of which he was the pillar and guard against unforeseen emergencies and unwelcome surprises. Father was the bright light in our life. I was now spending the rest of my life without feeling his presence there, somewhere where I could go and see him and shake his hand and sit with him, embracing him with my eyes even if I was not looking directly at him, talking to him and he talking to me. What was left of my time was now devoid of expecting to meet him suddenly somewhere. What was that day in the distant past? I was on the train coming from the suburbs when I saw him waiting to cross the railroad crossing. It must have been winter, since my father was wearing the only old overcoat he had. What was that day? Which day of the week?

I looked around. I was in a strange land, a land not my own and a time not my own: dry sand and burning sun and faraway water. There were thirsty mouths including my own and slim hope of any kind of help. Here was my master's son, al-Qasim, the infant, shot through the neck by an arrow. He hadn't been interred yet. His father al-Husayn came out, carrying him in his arms, asking heaven to witness what was happening to the grandchildren of his noble Messenger and his family and their valiant supporters. I saw that with my very own eyes and even though I was no warrior, I had never shot an arrow or hurled a spear, I wished I could be one versed in such arts to aim them at the murderers. I knew I was facing hearts that had been hardened and blinded to what was right, that none of their hearts would be softened or made any kinder. In my experience, once a heart got used to cruelty, it never got any softer. I saw my master feeling the enormity of the calamity yet he was not afraid of getting closer to the inevitable end. What really pained him was that horrendous thirst suffered by those closest to him.

I didn't know what to do. I saw my father heading for the river. That was his gait. I ran after him scattering the sand with my heels. "Father!"

He didn't turn toward me. I hurried until I caught up with him, then went ahead of him and turned my face to see his face, to have my fill and to make sure.

135

"Come to the river." Silently he ordered me. I was glad that he had recognized me and that I had my fill of his face, his features. I estimated that he was fifty or sixty years old. To be precise, it was my father as I saw his face during my preparatory school days in my early youth when he was at the peak of his health, waking up on cold winter mornings. One could hear the tapping of his wooden clogs on the bare tiles. He would open the door and close it very gently, then go down the stairs. I would hear his footsteps close and strong in the beginning, then diminishing as he hit the cobblestones of the alley until they vanished completely, whereupon I would gradually sink back into deep sleep. My father went far away, alas.

There he was next to me in a land he had never talked to me about, hurrying toward the river, holding a brown leather water skin, its leather dried and hardened as it had not been filled with water, nor even touched a drop of water, for a long time. I figured out it was the water skin that he carried on his back or, to be more precise, the water skin that he would carry in his coming boyhood when he would work as a water carrier for those who would give him shelter for a while. What I was seeing belonged to a remote era that hadn't come yet, the animals whose skins would be flayed to make the water skin I was seeing now had not even been born yet. It was a tough spot to be in and the heart was filled with worries about what would be and what would not be. It was puzzling: if I was so bold as to ask, maybe my boldness would bring displeasure toward me, which would lead to resentment, which could result in alienation, and alienation would banish me from the Diwan, and banishment meant deprivation. Therefore I remained silent.

Waking up from these reflections I realized that my father's voice was not his own, that the voice belonged to Gamal Abdel Nasser and that his swift running was that of Mazin and the way he bowed his head in silent thought was that of Ibrahim al-Rifai. It seemed he had so identified with them and they with him that he contained them just as they contained him. He became the point where all the beloveds who had departed prematurely met. I had loved many, near and far, and now the many were one. He was the one and they aggregated in him. Things could change, however, and my father could be divided among them. That was a fate of which I had no knowledge, as many thick and dark veils, difficult to penetrate, stood between me and any comprehension.

I continued running next to him, I who had never run with him in my earthly life. I didn't run as a child because he was kind to me and took me by the hand. I didn't run after I had reached maturity because there was a distance between us. With respect to that I admit that it was I who had been responsible for that distance, therefore I deserved the distress that I had suffered. That was certain and indisputable.

With every step I took, my thirst increased. I experienced the painful thirst that al-Husayn and his family and close supporters suffered, and the thirst of my father and all those who became one with him. I also suffered another strange kind of thirst, one not perceived by the five senses, a painful thirst that caused me to be restless, uncomfortable, and unable to sleep; a thirst that caused me bruising pain, one whose source I did not know and which all the rivers in the world and all rain could not quench. That was the worst and toughest thirst that grew and became sharp, leading to three paths in which steps would lose their way, where even the sand grouse would get lost. One of those paths led to my father, the second to my master, and the third to one of those I had loved.

On this day of Ashura, water was denied to the ones I loved, dryness was increasing, and all possibilities of help cut off. It pained me that I had to take the rough road to my father and my thirst for our first days intensified, for moments that I had not been and would not be conscious of, for his face and the expressions he had on it when he held me in his arms for the first time, when I was still a lump of soft flesh aware only of its hunger and urine and stool without being able to name them. My father would wear a flannel gallabiya in the winter and one of lightweight cloth or poplin in the summer and a jacket that someone had given him. The few times he came to visit my house after I got married he wouldn't stay for long. Those visits would be dealt with some other time when the Diwan had given me its permission and when epiphanies would allow.

What I recalled in the midst of my confusion was how he sat there, calm, shy, and humble, and how he looked at Muhammad, my son, and played carefully with him for fear of making one mistake or another. That was what I thought and remembered. I asked him, "Does Muhammad look like me when I was a baby?" and he motioned with his head, bowed with the burdens of loneliness, his head which had grown smaller in the last years of his life, "Yes, he looks like you." Then he would repeat that every time he visited us when Muhammad would come rushing at him and stand before him for a few moments. Thereupon my father would embrace him for a short while then look at me, as if remembering my question, as if the question had been awaiting an answer, as if he were pleasing me by breaking the silence, saying, "He looks like you when you were a child."

My father did not experience his role as a grandfather properly. He did not spend enough time with his grandson, the only son of his son, out of the grandchildren born before he departed, or my daughter, who was younger, and came seven months minus ten days before his final departure. Talking about my father and his grandson, my son, would, however, be a long topic not suitable for this station because of the painful details involved that would cause me to lose sleep and wound me in my remaining days. Were I to open the door to such talk it would be like aiming Yazid's army's arrows at my heart and that I could not bear.

My thirst grew for my father's smell that I used to smell in my early years, which have a station of their own, that of security. Ever since those years passed and were gone, my sense of safety departed and my hopes diminished and I felt like one pursued. These factors would be too long to explain here but I could open a little window to that beautiful station from which I would see my father coming home at midday, his steps quick and in his hand our food and daily sustenance. Then I could hear his breathing at night and feel his hand holding mine in a crowded street then that smell, his very own smell.

That thirst for him brought to mind my own thirst and that of al-Husayn and his family: no one was kind to them, just as no force was kind to me or brought me closer to that old moment that would die and be buried with me. Nothing would remain of it except fragments and echoes in the house of lingering visions. If I were to tell their contents to anyone, they would make fun of me and mock me. For what would it mean to others that my father came home at midday on one of my childhood days? What would those moments mean to you, my beloveds? And who could fathom the depth and reality of my thirst? I was just offering what I could of my memory that was now full of people, cities, faraway streets, street corners, coffeehouses, mountains, and valleys of which I had no knowledge, full of hatred, love, and longing, of visions and imaginings. I would push all that aside to get to a distant moment: the day of the Palestine War. I was three years old. We were living in a single room on the roof of a five-story building. The ceiling in that room was high, supported by seventeen wooden pillars. My father would often lie down on his back during his moments of rest or relaxation or when he felt secure about coming days, and he would count them out loud, recalling specific days and associating each day with one of the pillars. He would also remember specific personalities that he knew and would give each pillar a name.

During those days in which I lived physically and in spirit, which my heartbeats, breaths, and the blood in my veins witnessed, the air-raid sirens sounded loudly and Cairo's dark skies were temporarily penetrated by sharp light beams coming from the ground searching for circling planes and by the lights dropped by the invading planes to illuminate the city covered by the thick blanket of night. That night the bombing intensified and my father said, "Let's go downstairs to Sitt Wajida on the first floor." From the alley several voices rose asking those in the higher floors to go to the lower floors and to turn off the lights completely. My mother was pregnant and in her womb my brother, who later on would be named Ismail, was forming. We went downstairs to Sitt Wajida and then we split up. My mother went to a room where all the women of the house had gathered. I stayed in the living room. The men talked about the bombs that traveled long distances and severed heads. They talked about Shaarawi, son of Master Sergeant Abu Ahmad who lived on the third floor. He had volunteered to fight on the side of the resistance forces. His father spoke of a tank called "Tiger" that the enemy had. It was armored, but the resistance forces shot it with a special kind of missile and split it in two. I listened and clung even more closely to my father. That gave me security and allayed my fears and kept bad things from happening to me. From a distance we could hear successive explosions. Someone said they were bombing Abbasiya. There was silence for a few moments. Someone said, "O God, protect us with Your mercy!"

The air raid was over and the all-clear sounded and lights were turned back on. My mother took her time climbing the stairs. That night I slept close to my father and from time to time woke up to make sure he was still nearby. That night the siege of Gamal Abdel Nasser and his men in Falluja began. The enemy tightened its stranglehold on them. Much blood was shed in other places. In Karbala attacks on al-Husayn's encampment intensified. I could see in all directions and absorb what I saw in such a way that what I saw in front of me did not interfere with or affect that which I saw behind me. I was anxious to quench my physical as well as my spiritual thirst. The water was getting closer to us and we were getting closer to it, the water of the Euphrates River, gray mixed with a pale red color, coming from faraway headwaters and ending someplace I didn't know.

I saw al-Hurr who had come to fight against al-Husayn then elected to fight on his side. I heard him shouting at Yazid's soldiers, "You invited him and when he accepted your invitation and came here, you gave him assurances of protection and claimed that you would protect him with your lives. Then you turned against him to kill him. You encircled him and put him under a vise-like siege. You prevented him from going freely in God's vast country and he ended up a prisoner who can't do himself any good or fend off any harm. You denied him the running water of the Euphrates in which the pigs and dogs of Iraq are wallowing and now he and his family are dying of thirst. You have done the worst to Muhammad's progeny. May God deny you a drink of water on the Day of the Great Thirst if you don't repent and cease what you are doing! May God deny you a drink of water on the Day of the Thirst!"

I saw Umar ibn Saad get up and take an arrow and shoot it saying, "Be my witnesses: I was the first to shoot!" I shouted at him, "What witness are you requesting, you fool?" But my voice was lost and dissipated. People didn't listen and they did not hear. They began their onslaught on al-Husayn and his companions. His was a small group and the others were in great numbers and well-armed. My father got close to the water of the Euphrates. The intolerable thirst assailed me anew. I was thirsty for another moment, one at the beginning—for which I longed the way a stranger under siege, cut off from his allies and reinforcements would long—a moment lost in the womb of days to which I came out, alone, with my one and only guide and imam al-Husayn, until I landed on that sad day to witness what I witnessed. I went out on this voyage of mine with no recourse to anything, having abandoned everything at hand. I relied on no one but him because I hadn't consulted anyone. Rather, I was led to the Diwan by my torment and because I was lost from myself. I went out of my days to my other days the way a dead person leaves behind his family and his possessions. I didn't know that my thirst would be tied to my longing for my beginning, to moments that no one else would remember, moments that were hidden among my most secret memories.

That was in our single room after it had been whitewashed one day whose name and place among the days I did not know. My mother was wearing a white gallabiya. She was young and healthy, not yet affected by time. She was helping my father set up an iron bed with black posts, each of which was topped by a yellow brass finial. In the corner of the room, on a piece of colored cloth my brother Ismail, a few months (maybe even a few weeks old, I didn't know) was lying. I could see his round white face and his eyes gazing at the ceiling, looking for something mysterious that little ones search for, for a long time. He was swaddled in a black gallabiya. After his birth the wife of Qasim the merchant came to my mother. After she left, my brother Ismail's temperature rose and he started shaking. My mother got a piece of alum and threw it down on a hot tin. The piece took several forms then settled on a face very much like Sitt Fathiya's face. Then my mother brought a paper doll and began to pierce it with a needle repeating all that time, "In your eye, Fathiya." And it so happened that my brother recovered. He stopped shaking and the chill was gone. My mother decided to wear black and to keep him away from the eyes of strangers.

I had an overpowering thirst for that remote, lost moment, hidden in the second half of a day of unknown name that I witnessed in Karbala hundreds of years before its time. The thirst was getting the best of me as the arrows kept following each other in quick succession in the direction of my master. My father followed me to the lowest point sloping toward the river. That was my father's gait, the frame of his physical existence, when he was anxious to do something in a hurry. He went down, taking the whole water skin with him, and it was filled in one fell swoop. He snatched it out of the river, completely full of water and dripping. The ascent was hard and he struggled to carry his heavy load as I descended to the river to fill the bag that belonged to me. When I touched the cold water my thirst grew greater and I longed for a shaded green area, a garden where we awaited my father's return after work. He would take us from time to time to visit the Agriculture Museum adjacent to the Ministry of Agriculture. He would enter through the old wide door with us behind him, greeting those standing at the entrance and they would return the greeting with a better one. One of them would say, "Welcome, Amm Ahmad!" Another would say, "How are you, Ahmad?" He would precede us into the museum, while my little heart filled with pride. My father is well-known here and doesn't pay the entrance fee!

My father knew everyone in the museum: the employees and his fellow messengers. We would make the rounds of the glass showcases containing grain and seeds of all kinds, different kinds of bread, agricultural implements and plows, replicas of ancient inscriptions on pharaonic temple walls. Then we would stand for a long time in front of statues of wax or plaster of Paris. My father would point to the statue of the village headman, saying to my mother, "Doesn't he look like Sheikh Haridi?" Then we admired the howdah on top of two camels with a beautiful doll inside. My father didn't hurry us; rather he told us to look and enjoy. He would choose for us a shaded spot in the big garden and tell us that he was going to go to the ministry to get the mail and deliver it. That was his job for many years. He would leave us and we would stay until he returned. We would await his return and look forward to his arrival from a distance. When he was late we would be worried and afraid. But that did not last for us. That feeling was gone once we grew up and grew apart. That was the beginning of my father's sunset. He would appear, coming toward us in quick, swaying steps—the same kind of steps he was taking toward al-Husayn and his family now. I bent over the Euphrates, and started to moisten my lips, to have a drink to quench my parched throat, but I remembered that my father had filled his water skin without touching a single drop of water with his tongue. I was ashamed of what I had started to do. So I carried my bag, saying to myself: I hope my father would be pleased with me, pleased with me after it was too late, as I have angered him innumerable times. It was as if he had read my mind and known what was doubling my wounds and sorrows, so he shouted, alerting me to the station I was in: "The thirst of those we love is tough to take!"

I followed my father up the slope. I saw the whole place as if I were looking at it from a point suspended in space, as if I were hovering or circling, watching what was happening below. I saw everyone, including myself, as someone seeing himself in a dream. I was also able to feel what was going on inside me. In addition, in this station I was granted something that was exclusive to me, something I hadn't known before, in my own experience or that of others who had taken similar routes, and that was my ability to experience my father's feelings as if I were him and as if he were me. Then to that was added the ability to feel the pain the moment it started for my master and guide, al-Husayn. Then that expanded and I was able to feel the pain of Zayn al-Abidin, his brother al-Qasim, and the sons of Muslim ibn Aqil. Then that which applied to me expanded: it was no longer limited to physical pain but extended to passing thoughts and feelings.

Everything that I experienced in this station was horribly painful and the least painful was sad. Among those experiences was what al-Hurr ibn Yazid went through, from the moment his hesitation started to the moment he joined the forces of al-Husayn. I became al-Hurr ibn Yazid, one of the soldiers of Ibn Ziyad, wali of Kufa. Mission: fighting al-Husayn and preventing him from reaching the water of the Euphrates. His determination was my determination and his intent was my intent. Then his doubts became my doubts and his reluctance my reluctance. Then I was overtaken by his pain, which was now my pain: what was I going to do and how would I face My Lord on the Day of Judgment? He was afraid and I was afraid. He was regretful and I was regretful. Then he chose and I chose: to stand by my master's side. Then I ended up being what I was: every single arrow hitting one of al-Husayn's cohorts hit me as well, in the same spot of the wound. My body became the receptacle of all the pains of that fateful day. From sunrise and until the moment that al-Husayn's head was severed, I bled as much as they all did combined. I experienced the pain and agony felt by those hit by the slingshots and sharp arrows, the thirst of an infant baby still suckling, and the sheer panic and horror of a woman seeing her loved ones killed in front of her eyes and her own fear of being violated by force. Thirst parched my throat so badly I almost felt I was coming apart. My staying in this station must have been for a grave, a severe punishment that I deserved, or for a mysterious reason that I couldn't comprehend. Despite all my torment, my father remained at the very core of my consciousness and the light of my eye. As for my master al-Husayn, he was my sacred destination and the object of my migration.

My father cried, "Ah Yabouy! Woe is me! They've killed me!"

His scream shook me to my very foundation. That was the highest degree of manly pain in the Said of our country, so far away from Karbala in both time and place. When a man screamed like that, calling for his father, it meant that a great calamity had befallen him and that he was helpless, that spoken words could not encompass it or that the usual forms of communication could not convey it. I looked from my all-encompassing vantage point and saw that the water that my father had succeeded in filling his water skin with had spilled and was now seeping through the sand. The water skin had been hit by an arrow and at that very moment, the water poured from my bag. I saw my father's shock and his harrowing pain and I felt it. I saw my father, who had lived all his life without quarreling with anyone or slapping or punching anyone, my father, who had hated fighting, actually loathed it, brandishing a sharp and shiny Yemeni sword and walking in the manner I still remembered. I realized that those he had contained in himself had separated from him. I looked more closely at them as if seeing them through a fog. I recognized Gamal Abdel Nasser, and Ibrahim, then Mazin. There was a fourth whom I didn't recognize at all. I couldn't see the distinctive facial features of any of them or their manner of dress. My father was now standing before my master. He was now speaking in his voice, which is also my voice, "Will you give me your permission to fight, Master?"

My father's condition was my condition. My soul was on the brink of tears and had grown so light, delicate, and dry, that this being and all it contained became a flowery fragrance. My father,

145

filled with sadness, dissolved, and I with him. My father who knew nothing about al-Husayn except circumambulating his mausoleum, kissing its door, and taking refuge in it at times of hardship, was now standing in front of him centuries before he was born, seeing him face to face, his breaths mixing with his, and, if he could, he would bear the burning heat of the sun in his place and would thirst and suffer pain instead of him. In my mind I rebuked the historians who were yet to come: Abu Mikhnaf, Ibn Kathir, al-Daynuri, Tabari, and the anonymous chroniclers because they did not and would not mention my father and his companions and their coming to Karbala.

"Will you give me your permission to fight, Master?" My father asked again as the luminous, sweet intercessor looked on. I didn't know what the answer was.

Some Secrets of This Station

Know then, may God grant you success and make you see what I have been made to see—I who was astray and whom He led to the straight path, who was distant and whom He brought near, who was lost and whom He guided, who was confused and whom He gave clarity of mind, who was wounded and whose wounds He dressed—know then, bright, intelligent one, that grief can only be for something in the past and thirst can only be for that which is missing, that longing can only be for that which is not present and the same is true of yearning. Know also that thirst is of two kinds: physical and mental.

Physical thirst is present when there is an absence of water, even though that is not necessarily an essential condition. For a person may gulp down water only to have greater thirst. This is well known in certain pathological cases. Or such a person may be close to a body of water or even sail in one, that is, that body is full of water but that water would not help that thirsty person quench his thirst.

As for mental thirst, it is of infinite variety. It covers such things as longing for that which has been lost, for time not at hand, for seeing an absent beloved whose presence and comings and goings are beyond our perception, for a remote moment which alone has been preserved from many years ago, for a fragrance that has crossed paths with our senses sometime in the distant past, for a brief sojourn at a forgotten street corner that lasted only a few seconds, for the whistle of a train that passed from and to places we do not know but which elicit sorrow and take us back to distant memories of beloveds. Such mental thirst can be longing for the rustling of a dress, for the taste of a dish whose cook we had gotten used to and who then departed, for a walkway in a garden, for the shadow of a minaret, for the smell of an ancient carpet, maybe for an intimate meeting fraught with an affection that has since died.

Thirst can also be for learning the truth and the mysterious, elusive essence, for uncovering the secrets of things and the mysteries of beings, for the past, for the vanished, for that which has slipped through our fingers. Thirst is a condition and a state of multiple facets. Knowing it does not require being aware of it because it is part and parcel of the process of growing up for humans: a newborn baby cries when it feels thirsty. We've said that nostalgia is one of its degrees, but so are yearning and passion, both of which intensify if their subject is absent.

All types of thirst are allayed by a meeting or finding of one sort or another. The heart throbs for an absent one then calms down when the absence ends, just as a stream of water calms the thirsty. Longing and yearning do not apply if their object is present. The object has to be absent. That is accepted by all. But what happened to me in Karbala was strange. I saw my father and it would have been possible for my longing to subside, it would have been possible for me to cross the bridge of loss, but what happened was wondrous: the more I looked, the more I longed. Every glance uniting me with the one I love, gave me loss. Things got too much for me; I was aware that what I was seeing was a fantasy even if it were real, that I was a spectator, and that I was dreaming. It didn't take long contemplation for me to realize that rather than a blessing, it was a strange form of torture of which I had not been forewarned and which had not occurred to a human before. I realized that that was my fate in all the stations; that whenever I got close to having my thirst slaked, my situation changed and my thirst was renewed. God Almighty commanded his Prophet to say, *"Lord, increase me in knowledge."* In the meantime, a person seeking increase would always be thirsty and would know no limit or end. Thus, my longing for my beloveds remained forever present. I ended up like someone drinking seawater: the more I drank the thirstier I became. I made a mental note to myself to ask about this, for that was new to me since I began my journey in the company of my master. I didn't know exactly what crime I had committed. This would require a lengthy investigation and the pursuit of various clues that I am afraid to lay out explicitly, therefore I will stop here. Please forgive me!

The Station of Nostalgia
Nostalgia has reached its highest point. I was in a station of great moment: from it the past peeked, coupled with a sadness great in its essence and tragic in the lessons learned. For nostalgia, dear sirs, is the first degree of forgetfulness. Nostalgia doesn't come with the same force every time it blows. At the beginning it is strong and vigorous, then it diminishes and then weakens to negligible proportions. This is followed by forgetfulness, which enfolds and engulfs it. Nostalgia, like time, is not visible. Of the daytime it has twilight; of night its early hours; of seasons the beginnings of autumn, of the phases of heat, its humidity; of times, the moment the sun is hidden behind clouds on a winter's day; of treasured memories, their sweetest and most cherished; of heart conditions, tired beats; of roses, their lingering smell; and of branches of knowledge, the knowledge of what was.

I was stationed in a far corner of Karbala as I was kept away from the fighting. All I could do was watch. I saw my father and those who had come with him fighting with al-Husayn. I was frightened, for there were only a few of them facing a much larger army. In the old days my father used to say that in war numbers were more important than courage. I was besieged by nostalgia and in this case my nostalgia was an unusual one: I was nostalgic for a past and a future at the same time. That was my state and I was in a time long before mine, seeing my birth before my mother became pregnant with me, seeing my going before my coming, my nothingness before my being, my absence before my presence, my yesterday before my today and my tomorrow. I was nostalgic for moments that were gone while being aware that they hadn't come yet. I was seeing what would happen in them, that I would catch up with them and that I would cry over them after it was too late, that no one else would remember them, for their life was tied to my life. No one would know them and seek them out in the Diwan. They were there somewhere or another and it was my master's will and the will of the president of the Diwan that I witness them from an era earlier than mine, from a station in which I witnessed my father as a warrior on my master's side.

At the beginning of the station nostalgia overwhelmed me. My heart longed for very distant mornings, on Friday, my father's weekly day off. He would not wear his khaki work suit and would not go to the ministry where he worked, but would head for al-Husayn's mausoleum and mosque, where he would perform the dawn prayers and come back to us with the first light of the day. In his right hand would be a plateful of ful and in his left a large glass full of milk. The ful was from a famous man originally from Aleppo who only sold his ful before sunrise and only to al-Husayn's patrons. At sunrise he would stop selling and leave. I could still taste the ful beans in my mouth even though several coming eras would separate me from him and several bygone eras have distanced him from me. I could still remember, too, the taste of the creamy milk.

My father would bring the *al-Masri* newspaper, whose name was written on top of a raised green flag with a white crescent and three stars. My mother would light the kerosene stove, pushing the piston several times then placing the copper pot with some ghee on it.

When the ghee melted completely she would spread the dough and wait for the fetira to be done, then take it out and sprinkle sugar on it. After the meal my father would sit down, leaning his back against the wall, and start pointing at the letters. I would sit next to him, following his finger's slow movement. From him I learned how to read before going to school. I learned the shapes of the letters from him even though he never went to school, never received a formal education, even though his old dreams had come to naught and he now entered al-Azhar only to pray after hoping at one time to enter it as a student seeking learning and the Qur'an. Sometimes he got carried away by a whim or a sense of humor and read a made-up news item, such as his meetings with his Excellency the prime minister and other officials. Another news item was about his submitting his resignation to the minister of agriculture because of his poor health, and another news item about the minister not accepting his resignation.

As Friday morning got a little older, slowly, he would perform his ablutions then accompany us, me and my brother, to al-Husayn's mosque and mausoleum. The mosque could not accommodate all the worshipers, so they spilled over on to mats and newspapers on the adjoining sidewalks. After the prayers I would still feel the imprint of the old carpet or mat on my forehead and my nose would retain the smells, primarily the smell of the shady, cool mosque, which would stay deep inside me until the end of my days. Then they will take my body to the mosque of my master and my beloved and my guide, al-Husayn, to perform the prayer for the dead for me there. This is my will, exactly as the intercessor's mosque was the last place my father's body entered, after which he went out for the last time, covered with a cover that would not be removed. This is my will, my beloveds and guardians of my affection. I beseech you by God not to forget.

I would hang on to my father's right hand and my brother to his left. We would go around the silver bars of the mausoleum and stand in awe of the green turban on top of the tomb marker. In our noses a mixture of several fragrances would compete. Permanent shadows had their own smell, so did the lingering perfumes, the breaths of those crouching in the corners. Marble had its own smell, so did the red cloth shades for chandeliers. The colored glass through which the sun entered the mosque casting blue, green, and orange hues had its own smell, as did the space inside the mausoleum. Old copies of the Qur'an had their own smell, as did those worshipers kneeling and prostrating themselves.

We would go out after the day had passed its midpoint and as the light's intensity had subsided somewhat. We would stand in front of a small store, very small, where my father would buy for us carob juice, which the vendor would serve in copper cups. We would take our time savoring the fresh, sweet drink. That weekly stop made me a confirmed lover of the carob drink. It has left an indelible physical imprint on me that is still unattainable. If I wanted to elaborate on that, it would take innumerable pages. However, not wishing to be excessive, I could only ask: where has the old taste gone? Where? I didn't know that the aroma of that dark-colored drink would stay with me until the end of my days, or that the memory of its cool refreshing taste would bring a tremor to my heart, or bring my whole being to the brink of tears, enabling me to withstand the tender longing.

After the carob drink we would proceed to an old hotel near the beloved's mausoleum. Men from our old village would come there and my father would sit with them, inquiring about news of the village, those who had died and those who were still living. My eyes would scan the place: I could see a printing press at the end of the vast courtyard. Vast? How come it was no longer vast but rather small and cluttered now that I had grown up? Why did it seem so confined and depressing after being the playground of my childhood, the place where I had a lot of fun? Tea would come in small glasses, narrow in the middle. Faces changed and features were replaced by other features, but every time we saw Hajj Abdu, the manager of the hotel, a Nubian who wore a gallabiya and a Turkish fez, and Abdel Maqsud Effendi, the fat hotel clerk, wearing a woolen three-piece suit that he never changed, winter or summer. He would sit in a glass enclosure, answering the telephone, and keeping track of the drinks ordered from the coffeehouse by the hotel guests. From time to time he would raise his hand in greeting. On a leather sofa at the center of the lobby would sit a Moroccan man, wearing a white woolen cloak, with a huge beard and green eyes. I would look at him from a distance. He told my father that he had left his faraway country on foot, that he crossed seas and deserts and that he went as far away as India, that he had spent all his life looking for a place where he could lie down in peace and tranquillity and after all his travels, during which he married several times, he couldn't find a place similar to that place close to al-Husayn's mausoleum in Cairo. Since making that discovery, he had lived in the hotel, the old al-Club al-Asri Hotel, and since then had never left it except to perform prayers in the mosque and circumambulate the resting place of the noble head. We also saw the black servant Umar with his big eyes and quiet way of walking and his brief greetings to my father, and the iron gate leading to the courtyard.

I was nostalgic also for another place, the traditional tailor's shop located in a narrow corridor facing my beloved's mosque. The wooden floor of the shop rose about half a yard above the street level and the three walls were lined with glass cases in which fabrics were displayed. My father would take off his shoes and sit cross-legged before Hajj al-Sawi who wore prescription glasses with a metal frame that slid to the tip of his nose. On the middle finger of his right hand he wore a thimble to protect it from pinpricks. He would spread the fabric—cloth for caftans, gallabiyas, and abayas—on his knees. I was nostalgic for his face, his skullcap, and the edge of the vest that peeked from his caftan, for the old Afghani rug underfoot. I saw that rug but I couldn't make out its colors as I used to see them in the old days; they were mysterious shadows concealing its patterns from my eyes.

My heart pounded hard when I looked at my father's gallabiya. I was aware, by looking and feeling and through nostalgia, that the man sitting there was my father. I knew the contours of his body, his posture as he sat, his head bowed in silence. But what alarmed me and caused me great anguish was that his features at that age escaped me, were absent. My weary eyesight did not come to my aid at once and my nostalgia for those features tormented me. What were they like? How did he laugh then fall silent? What was he like when he started talking? What were the gestures of his hands like? How? How? I lost his features as if he were moving in total darkness or as if thick clouds were hiding his face from me or as if my eyes could not see any more. I was terrified, so I screamed, "My master and imam, this is the beginning of forgetfulness!"

He did not answer. The feeling that I was an orphan that I first experienced when my father departed assailed me anew, doubly. But I sensed that those in charge of the Diwan had heard me. I wished they would bring me closer, but they did not show me any kindness, so I said with tears preceding my words, "I am afraid."

There was silence, then I heard the paragon of purity, the president of the Diwan quoting the Qur'an, *"Be not among those who despair."*

I looked again and nostalgia overcame me anew and I saw my father but I didn't see the features of his face. I was seeing him and not seeing him. I said, *"The sight did not deviate nor did it overshoot its mark."*

Continuing to quote the Qur'an, she said, *"Have we not given you a life long enough for those who want to reflect to do so?"*

I said, "Eyesight can be deceptive."

She said, "Have patience. You have reached an era you couldn't have reached without great effort."

The voice, wrought from the fragrance of cherished wishes and the essence of nostalgia, words like ancient rubies and the secret of the glance, comforted me. Nostalgia, however, overcame me, mixed with a feeling of forlornness, so I said, sobbing as if I had returned to my childhood, "That's the beginning of forgetfulness!"

A voice, soft and mysterious as if it were woven out of a rainbow, came to me: "You have forgotten and today you will be forgotten!"

I said tearfully, my heart shaken, "That's the beginning of forgetfulness!"

They all were silent. The president of the Diwan stopped talking to my master and me and did not look in on me. I almost asked why I was going through these unusual events. Why was I seeing my father now, taking in his smell, being aware of the color of light in the distant day, the store signs, the features of some passersby, the color of the overcoat of the old furniture merchant whom my father used to greet; why was I seeing all of that but not my father's features? Why did I imagine that the pangs of separation were easier to take? Why was I aware that he had been gone for a long time when he was still in front of me? Why didn't I experience that on my voyages of separation when I was accompanied by my master who didn't desert me? I was on the point of expressing these questions out loud had not that secret, mysterious voice warned me, "It is not given to you to ask about that of which you have no knowledge. Didn't Imam al-Husayn tell you that?"

I held my breath and once again stared at my father, trying to hold on to the moment to which I was clinging. That was one of the wonders of the Station of Nostalgia. I realized I could hold my longing or feeling in check in such a way that if I saw or felt nostalgia for a faraway moment, I could hold it in place for a time. If I were going through an overpowering grief then someone to whom I did not want to show that grief came to me, I would suspend my grief or sorrow or joy, but then, when I was alone again, I would release it anew and resume it. I looked again but was certain that, for this moment, I had lost my father's features. Of that I was sure. Thick shadows engulfed me, but I didn't know whether they were material shadows or mental shadows.

When I felt overwhelmed and my fear increased, I changed, I turned into someone else: I became that tailor, the owner of that shop, sitting cross-legged after Friday noon prayers, basting a garment slowly and cutting cloth with the solid, big old scissors the likes of which could not be found today. I thanked God who had given me the ability, at this advanced age, to insert the thread in the eye of the needle and to remember the measurements of my clients. I praised God because he enabled me to stay in touch with and to keep my clients, most of whom were good, well-off men: Azhar sheikhs, big merchants, and men from good families who came from faraway towns. May God have mercy on Sheikh Hashim who used to come to Cairo twice a year from his village, Juhayna, in the deepest Said and stay at the Parliament Hotel in Ataba Square. He came for two purposes only: to perform all the five prayers of the day in the mosque of our master and beloved, and to have me tailor his outfits. He was a venerable man, from the beautiful old time, the time when I left my shop open and went and did my business and came back to find that everything was as I had left it. Even the coffeehouse boy did not dare collect the empty cups and glasses until I had come back. May God have mercy on that beautiful time. Ahmad al-Ghitani would look at me, waiting for the arrival of Khalaf Bey, his benefactor who had helped him stand on his feet, get a job, get married, and start a family. His two sons would come and sit quietly and politely even though they may have been bored; perhaps they would rather have run about and played. Ahmad had never gone anywhere without them ever since Gamal was able to walk and the other one too. Ahmad was one of the few good men remaining. He never left the side of Sheikh Hashim but accompanied him from the hotel to the mosque, to the members of the House of the Prophet. He would pass by him in the early morning before he went to work at the ministry. After the departure of Sheikh Hashim, may God have mercy on his soul, Ahmad didn't stop coming to my shop. He was always inquiring after visitors from Juhayna. He would accompany them, show them around, spend time with them. If he wanted, he could've become a big merchant. His companion, the one who left Juhayna with him, Umar al-Makhut, was now a wealthy merchant in the Ataba market. He would come to al-Husayn district in a carriage drawn by two elegant horses, a big fish merchant. It was Ahmad who introduced me to him when he pointed him out one late afternoon and ran to him and invited him to have a glass of tea in my shop, but Makhut apologized, saying he was too busy. As he left, Ahmad pointed at the fancy carriage and said to me, "Would you believe that we left the village together and came to Cairo in a hearse?"

I told him that if he wanted, he could be like him. He told me it was a matter of luck: "What is important is to raise my children now and spare them all the hardship I've suffered."

Poor Ahmad! He spent all his time keeping people company, being a friend, performing social duties, offering condolences here, attending a wedding there, or visiting the sick. If my time came he would be the first to take part in my funeral; he would be one of the pallbearers and would pray to God to have mercy on me and would remember me every time he passed my shop. He might even come to my tomb on days of Eid or other religious occasions, and would sit silently and shyly. Were he to talk, his stories would never end. He is smart and remembers the smallest details and is well-versed in genealogies and origins. Poor man: if he had enrolled in al-Azhar, if he had received an education, he would have been somebody important today. May God mete out punishment to undeserving people. But God has recompensed him well by blessing him with good offspring. He has always told me that if he had to beg for alms near al-Husayn's mausoleum so that his two sons could finish school and get an education, he would do it. But he would always follow that by praying to God to spare him from being dependent on anyone. My hands are getting tired. My health is not what it used to be, but the shop is better for me than retirement. I hope that God will call me home from here, from this place. I fear a lying down that might be a long one. Here I sit and wait for my friends who keep me company. They come and sit. We don't talk much but I feel I am not alone, by myself. For fifty years I haven't changed my perch: clients change, strangers come and do business, and thousands of passersby pass before my eyes, but the shop remains the same. As for the days in the distant past, we have nothing but nostalgia for them. Days without company, however, are hard. Cheer is only possible in numbers. Once they depart loneliness and desolation set in. It's the beginning of absence.

O Ahmad! What a good man!

I looked at him. It was as if he understood. I bent toward him to see him. It was as if he were very distant. I brought my glasses closer but I didn't see his features. I called out to him, "O Ghitani!"

I felt his voice but I didn't hear him. Wonder of wonders, I reverted to who I was and once again was Gamal. I came back, panting as if I had climbed a steep slope when I had a bad heart. When I recovered my ability to see, my father was gone, as was the shop. It was hard for me to be separated from him without seeing his features, but that secret mysterious voice told me it was no use, that it was hopeless.

I learned that human features changed every moment, that a single face contained countless faces, and that no features remained fixed, ever. I found out that they changed with the change of place, light, cold and heat, sadness and joy, being in a bad mood or a good mood, being focused or unfocused, that we spent long stretches of time looking at the face of the beloved who was nearby, getting our fill of it, remembering it, being stirred by it, not knowing that what we were seeing now would not be the same as the one we would see in a few moments or tomorrow, that human inattention would hide the content of those features and what they truly held. I also learned that those features at which we were looking at the moment and which we imagined would never be erased from our minds and our burdened memories, those very features would grow faint one day with separation and distance. It would never occur to us that we would struggle one day to recall the features of those closest to us. But that would be in vain. The memory of things that we never imagined one day would grow faint, would actually fade. As the Qur'an says, *Everyone on earth will perish, but the countenance of your Lord, in all majesty and nobility will remain.*

There was no hope of recovering the features of my father at that specific moment or in any other moments. When I remembered him or imagined him I was recalling something different, a faded sign saying: "My father was here." That sign would be quite distant, but the reality would be long gone, finished. The secret mysterious voice told me that I had seen the most I could of my father through the eyes of Hajj al-Sawi, the owner of the store that was gone, whose appearance was totally obliterated during my time on earth. It was now a boutique selling imported toothpaste, dairy products, sweets, shaving supplies, and costume jewelry. All that my father had seen has changed, all that which had been imprinted on the pupils of his eyes has now changed just as his features have changed for me. And because the fading of the memory and its weakness weakened the heart, my nostalgia grew so strong I was unable to get any rest in any position, standing or sitting. As for escaping through sleep, that was impossible in the Diwan. Nostalgia assailed me like the fragrance of a closed, deserted place where musk has been entombed for seven thousand of my earthly years. I learned that nostalgia brought about affection and mercy. But unfortunately when those two feelings came at the wrong time and in the wrong place and under the wrong circumstances, they fed nostalgia, which was transitory, blowing like passing thoughts, which were also transitory and impermanent. They stayed with one only as long as they blew in, but left behind invisible pain, the worst kind. Has anyone heard of a passing thought that took up permanent residence in a heart? Thoughts would stay in the heart only during the time they passed through, an interval not calculable by our human arithmetic. My Sheikh al-Akbar, Muhyiddin ibn Arabi has said that God had ambassadors to the heart named passing thoughts and that they did not stay in the heart of God's servant except the time they took to pass by it, and they delivered what they were sent to deliver without taking up abode because God has created them in the form of that which they were sent to deliver. Thus every thought was its own proper form.

I learned that nostalgia would be proportionate to how much I saw, and more important, how much remained alive deep down inside me from the distant days. I longed for the company of my master al-Husayn, for his appearance, for his extending me a helping hand, for his compassion, and for his companionship. The resting place of his head has always been my destination. When traveling I would make sure to visit it before my departure. Then it would become the focus of my nostalgia and homesickness and immediately upon my return, I would rush to it as if coming to renew my residence in my own home. When I sought him out in the Diwan, I abandoned everything. I didn't entrust my affairs to anyone, nor did I consult anyone. I didn't think of kin or progeny. I came to the Diwan stripped of everything: I left my immediate surroundings and went there just like a dead person, leaving behind family and possessions. Therefore, I felt I was entitled to desire to see him. I hoped he would grace me with a quick peek, but he didn't appear, didn't even look from afar. I felt thwarted and abandoned.

Then my nostalgia abated somewhat, enabling me to see a crowded road. I looked more closely and I saw my father accompanying my brother and me on a visit to a retired police officer whose name was Abu Hashish. He was taking us to an apartment building somewhere near al-Gaysh Square, but whose exact location I didn't know now and wouldn't be able to recognize even though I remembered it was painted yellow and had a high staircase. I also remembered the brown wooden door and the long corridor leading to it. I saw my father and my brother and I saw myself. I was walking behind them; not once did I precede them or even catch up with them. In the formal living room I stood in a far corner. A man—it was Abu Hashish—entered. I didn't see his features, but I could feel my father's joy as he pointed at us, "Gamal, my older son, and this is Ismail, the younger."

I didn't know at the time that Abu Hashish was the officer who saved my father's life. I found that out after my father's departure. My maternal uncle was talking about my father's childhood, when he mentioned the name of the officer who gave my father protection in the police station. There my father was, looking at him as if saying: had you not saved me from my very own family, had you not exacted from my paternal uncle the promise and the pledge not to harm me, I would not have begotten them and I wouldn't have been alive today.

I saw my father accompanying us to Khalaf Bey's house in al-Zahir, a large home with many rooms including a large formal living room with a valuable tapestry hung on the wall. There was a large bookcase made of expensive wood and filled with volumes of law books in Arabic and foreign languages. I wanted to look more closely but, afraid of making an unintentional mistake, I didn't. I saw Khalaf Bey's older son playing with a small automobile that would run when he pushed it. We watched but didn't take part.

I saw my father taking us to the stores on Muski Street. He bought for me a fire truck and for Ismail a tram with passengers and a conductor with his leather bag. That was one of Father's customs that continued until we grew up, to get each of us a toy in each of the two eids, and new clothes. I saw my father stretching out in our only room, saying that he would get us a bird that could fly in the room. From time to time I asked him about that marvelous bird, but we never saw it. I saw him accompanying us to Cinema Olympia on Abdel Aziz Street and a scene from a film whose title I didn't remember: a boat in a sea, and Shukuku singing. I saw the back door of the cinema's front row seating area: the walls painted yellow and the red fire extinguishing equipment hanging on the wall, an old odor, perhaps from the humidity in the long corridor which never saw the sun. I saw the large vegetable market and Hajj Umar al-Makhut's fish store. There was a small trench in front of the store where washing water coming from inside was poured. From where we sat we could see the heavy wooden cover of the icebox. Workers were piling up pieces of ice on top of the fish. There were several small round brass tables with metal legs on which were arranged glasses of sharbat and tea and

160

a small glass in which were stuck several stalks of green mint. Hajj Umar was sitting in the shadiest part of the store, wearing a baladi gallabiya and a red fez. Nearby stood his private carriage, to which two black horses were hitched. They had shiny saddles and in front of each was a sack full of hay or barley, I didn't know which. On a high table near the entrance of the store was a phonograph with a big horn. Hajj Umar al-Makhut had come back from Hijaz where he had gone on pilgrimage for the fourth time. My father was listening with great interest as the Hajj talked about Zamzam, the crowd of pilgrims at Mena, and the standing at Mount Arafat. My father listened and I didn't know that he wished and wished he could do the same.

I saw the old Parliament Hotel overlooking Ataba Square, with its gray paint, the arches delimiting the entryway alley, its entrance and rectangular windows, its big rooms and their high ceilings. There I saw Hajj Mahmud Ahmad from our village, resting after a surgical operation. My father was visiting him twice a day. This time we accompanied him. The Hajj looked at us and said, "Praise God, Ahmad. Your sons have grown!" Next to the bed was a basket in which there was a fetira and next to it a large watermelon. The Hajj asked my father to cut the fetira and the watermelon. My father hesitated, while I was salivating for some of it. The Hajj encouraged me, saying, "Go ahead, Gamal, have some. Your father is a generous man and wouldn't say no."

I saw my father in the office of the secretary of the Abdel Rahman Katkhuda Primary School, Ibrahim Effendi. I saw his face with a round green prayer bruise in the middle of his forehead. He said the tuition fees were fifty piasters. My father said that he would pay on the first of the month, the following Saturday. Ibrahim Effendi said, "You can avoid paying altogether if you submit a certificate of poverty." My father said, "That would be a bad omen. These would be the first tuition fees I pay for the boy."

I saw Ataba Square. My father was taking me to the ministry. In the middle of the square was the bus stop where the green and white Thorncroft buses were standing. I looked through the rear window and saw Qasr al-Nil Bridge then I didn't see much after we got off.

Near the expansive square there was a presser's shop. To get to it we had to go down three stairs below street level. My father was carrying three white collars that belonged to Khalaf Bey.

I saw my father taking me to the Cairo Railway Station. He was waiting for my maternal uncle coming from Said. I didn't, at the time, catch the nostalgia in his voice when he said the word, but many years later I understood. It was also much later that I figured out why, while lying down to rest, he would visualize the train traffic by saying, "Now the eight o'clock train is starting to move. It stops at the small towns, unlike the twelve o'clock train, which stops only at provincial capitals because it's an express train. Now the newspaper train is about to enter Tahta. Now the four-thirty is starting at Asyut."

I saw the train platform again. My father was holding my hand and shouting, "O Muhammad Ali, Muhammad Ali." I could see my maternal uncle peering from the train window and then handing my father the basket containing the 'visit.' In the foyer of our little apartment, my mother ripped the cloth covering of the basket. On top of the sun-baked bread and dried dates were slaughtered squabs and a goose. My uncle told my mother to boil them so they wouldn't go bad. My father began to fidget. He kept coming and going, whispering to my mother, begging her not to complain to her brother, to let his days in Cairo pass in peace, that he would do what she wanted and would not yell at all.

The first evening my father took my uncle to Ahmad Afifi's coffee-house so he could smoke the narghile. The following day he took him to the mausoleums that provided the last resting place for members of the Prophet's family: Sayyidina al-Husayn, al-Sayyida Zeinab, al-Sayyida Nafisa, al-Sayyida Ruqayya, and Sidi Zayn al-Abidin. My uncle looked bored, his face pale and his features tense. My father understood. He went to al-Club al-Asri Hotel, approaching it timidly, hating and fearing what he was about to do, but he wanted his brother-in-law to be happy. He whispered in the ear of Umar the servant, entreating him to procure a small piece of opium for his brother-in-law who had come from the village. He added repeatedly that it was not for himself and he swore to that. At home he whispered to my mother, "I brought him what he wanted, just for your sake." He asked her if she was satisfied; my mother nodded that she was.

I saw my father accompanying me on a late afternoon to the tomb of a man whose name I didn't know. The tomb was built of stone and had an iron gate. There was a marble basin filled with plants, mainly basil. That was why I have always associated the smell of basil with death.

I saw the roof of our old house. We left the room. My father lifted me up in his arms to be able to see. We looked at the horizon burning with yellow flames. My father said that that one was in the environs of Ghamra and that one was close to Qasr al-Nil. My heart raced. That was a date I could pinpoint: the twenty-sixth of January in the year nineteen hundred and fifty-two, and my memory had nothing to do with fixing the date as it was a well-known date recorded in history books that keep track of momentous events.

There I was, sitting on the roof. My father was talking about a young man from our village whom they caught "milking his organ." My father said that whoever did that would go crazy or die. Still on the roof, my father told us about a man who bothered him, an official in the ministry whose name was al-Ayat. He sounded pained and seemed to be complaining. I stood between the two edges of the sheet hanging to dry on the roof's clothesline and I recited a prayer against that man. My heart had sympathized with my father's pain and suffering, but he told me not to wish any harm on anyone. He did not want me to pray against the man because heaven responded to children's prayers promptly. I realize how tired he was and that he was just letting off steam.

I saw my father grab a broom, with which he killed a snake that he saw creeping next to the bathroom. He told my mother to get him some kerosene to burn it and get rid of its smell completely, otherwise the snake's mate would come looking for its missing partner. My mother feared snakes and geckos and if one appeared it was always my father's job to get rid of it. It was also my father who would open the door if someone knocked unexpectedly. When we walked together he would let us walk on the sidewalk while he walked on the street itself. When we ate, he would be the last to get his share. My mother would sit in front of the door, wearing a white gallabiya and a colored kerchief around her head. We would listen for his footsteps, which were uniquely his, on the stairs and then his knocks on the door.

I saw us sitting, waiting for him in the small living room of the house in al-Darb al-Asfar where we had moved and would live for some time. I saw myself after coming home from work, waiting in my room, now that I had my own room. The bell would ring and I would hear my father's voice in the living room. I would either get up to get the door or I'd stay put until he opened the door. I saw myself visiting the house after I had my own house and family. I heard his voice in the living room saying, "I've come early to see Gamal."

I saw my house. The bell would ring several times, the way it never rang after his final departure. My father would come into the salon and sit in the same chair. There would be long intervals of silence. He would pray that God provide for me and protect me, which would signal to me that he was about to leave. He would get up, saying that he had to go. I would ask him to stay but he would say that he had to go visit someone who lived nearby. I would say that he had a long way to go back to his house, that he would be late, and he would say that he would return early. Before he opened the door he would say that he would pray for me, my wife, and my son at al-Husayn's mausoleum. Then he would raise his hands and ask God Almighty to grant us health and vigor and to protect us from evildoers and to shower us with His blessings. I would stand at the top of the stairs, expressing affection and repeating words of leave-taking several times and asking him to take care of himself. I would hear him returning the blessings and saying, "Go inside, son, it's cold." I would go inside, tired. When I went to bed and lay my head on the pillow, I would miss him and blame myself, "I should have made him stay. He should have spent the night here with me. I shouldn't let him go so early." I kept telling myself, "Next time I won't let him go like that, next time . . . ." But that next time never came and he never experienced it.

Once again I listened for his old footsteps, his coming and going, drawing near and going far. I heard them then they were gone. I looked around in confusion. Maybe I should seek those sounds in the Diwan, in the House of Lingering Sounds, searching for those steps, their echoes. But how and when? At that point my feeling that I had been abandoned and become empty increased, as did the abject poverty of my soul. The sounds were not responding to my packed memory. They were not granting my wishes and the flare of nostalgia was causing me great distress that might bring about irrevocable forgetfulness, which in turn would lead to estrangement, which would mean death. And I would also be forgotten. I myself forgot and today I would be forgotten. My life was divided into two distinct lives: one in which I heard my father's footsteps, harbingers of stability and security, and another that was devoid of those steps.

I realized I was about to slip into the Station of Disappointment and Remorse, that my stay there would last a long time and my agony would extend over stages. I begged and implored. I beseeched my master and guide to delay my getting to that station because my heart was heavy, my conscience bloodied, the fragrant source of my affection had been cut off and my nostalgia had reached its zenith. "O my master: if you don't help me, to whom can I resort? To whom can I confide my faithfulness and my betrayal? To whom will I offer my reasons and my excuses? With your help I have seen and learned, so have you heard my nostalgia and my hopes? Will you have mercy on my shortcomings and inability to withstand my overpowering nostalgia?" I recalled what one of my venerable sheikhs had written. The memory came back to me as I was in the thrall of longing: "I greet the breeze that extended from the beloved to a heart on which all doctors had given up. Yes, and a greeting to a soul that used to lead to acceptance and pleasure, but was now sad and regretful of the past. A greeting to a night in which the two parties were wrapped in affection and cheer that all human and jinn envied. A greeting to a look that has revived many a stumbler and with its light guided the lost. A greeting to an intimate space breached by neither informer nor censor, and unpenetrated by the prying eyes of untrustworthy relatives or strangers. A greeting to messages that replied with a gentle rebuke that caused the heart to melt and tenderness to keep the soul alive. A greeting to signs whose mere apparition awakened old desires and broke the chains. A greeting to a handshake that shook the soul and an embrace that revived hopes. A greeting to a reunion filled with sweet talk with the beloved that no one had a chance to intrude upon. A greeting to wakeful moments totally devoted to yearning for the beloved. A greeting to a sleep in which the dream revealed the beloved much more clearly than the heart longed for."

In this meager existence we hope for life,
Though we've known only toil and strife.
What good is life when beset by fear,
For bounty missed, or the death of one dear?

Thus I was shaken to my foundations, and making a safe landing was the farthest thing from my mind. I was assailed by nostalgia for nostalgia, a nostalgia for that which I had lived and learned and a nostalgia for my nostalgia. I was torn, scattered. And because I, because I . . . I was deserving of punishment. At that moment God allayed my troubles and blessed me with an epiphany.

A Passing Epiphany
This is a passing epiphany, a point between two stages, a moment to catch my breath, between two torments.

I began to ascend to the highest heights without fearing that I would be sent back to the lowest depths. I settled on a high point. I stared with keen sight. I saw our whole terrestrial world, round and beautiful and breathtaking. I saw within its circular shape all forms with respect to length, breadth, straightness, crookedness, squareness, and triangularity. I saw all the continents, overall and in detail. I saw the seas and what they contained and the mountains and what they concealed. I saw the meteors and their destinations and the clouds. I saw the cities and their traffic. I saw the villages, their well-trodden trails and all the streets and curves. Then my eyesight became totally pliable, so I could see whatever I wanted or wished for, without losing sight of the whole, as if I were seeing the whole world, and at the same moment seeing a small traffic light on an unknown street corner. I would see the whole city and colorful flowers peering from a white metal basket hanging from a second-story window in one of its buildings, or wooden miniatures atop the door of an old house. I was even able to read the titles of books in the bookstore windows. My glances hovered and then landed like a tired pigeon on the places that I had known as a child, a boy, a young man, and then a man. At that moment I was exclusively blessed with an ability surpassing that of those who had epiphanies before me: namely, my ability to see the same place at two different times or at several times, simultaneously in the same glance.

The first person I saw was my father, walking in the early morning while dewdrops were still forming and at midday in a crowded place, then on a deserted road between two villages. Then I saw him accompanying me. There he was on his way to work, to the chapel located on the lower floor of the ministry building, to the nearby garden where he would stretch when he got tired. There he was on Qasr al-Shawq Street. It was winter and he was wearing just a gallabiya. Then he stopped, displaying that anxious look that characterized humanity from the earliest times. The stores were closed except for one belonging to the bearded man who sold bread and flour. My father took a long look, clasping his hands behind his back. A man was holding the hot loaves of bread that had just arrived from the bakery. My father waited for him to leave then stepped forward and greeted the bearded man in a soft voice that was unusual for my father, a voice I hadn't known in my long voyage except after his marriage and begetting me, begetting us. He asked for six loaves then told the man, "This way we owe you thirty piasters. The first of the month is coming soon." The bearded man said, "Don't worry, Ahmad. May God extend His helping hand." At that point, my father was emboldened and asked for an additional five piasters, "Now it will be thirty-five piasters." I looked closely and saw the little hairs on his hand and around the knuckles of his fingers, as well as the pictures and ornaments on the little banknote. I saw my father at the same time extending his hand with an empty bowl to Sayyid the ful vendor. There he was going back home, having brought us the day's breakfast.

I saw my father entering a coffeehouse, stopping at the entrance and saying, "Peace be upon you," whereupon all the men sitting responded with, "And on you peace and God's mercy and His blessings." I was seeing all of that at the same time, not missing observing the clouds depart, the snows form, the earth revolving on its axis, the cold of the earthquakes, and the blowing hurricanes and which would take too long to explain now.

I saw him approaching a hearse standing in a side street in the town of Tahta. I was happy for him. He was in the same form and shape in which I had seen him leaving the village in the Ephipanies of Travel. My father got close to the hearse and asked the driver, "Who's the dead person?"

"A man from Banha."

"Will he be buried in Tanta?"

"No, in Banha. I am taking him there tonight."

"Would you take us with you?" my father asked.

The old driver, tired of loneliness, looked at him.

"Where are you going?"

"To Cairo. We will try to make a living."

The man, beginning to like my father or take pity on him, said, "Come, son. It's a long drive. We'll keep each other company."

Umar al-Makhut stepped forward and asked, "How much will you charge us?"

The old driver smiled. "Your good company is enough."

Makhut went back to my father, expressing dissatisfaction. Were they really going to Cairo in a hearse? That would be a bad omen. My father said that matters of life and death were in the hands of God, that those things had been determined, that if God willed that they go to Cairo, riding that vehicle, who were they to disobey His will? I followed them with my eyes, in surprise, totally astonished. That was the first time I learned how my father came to Cairo. In a hearse! At that point I heard a reproachful voice, "Did you care enough to inquire at all?"

Oh! It was my master al-Husayn revealing his luminous face to me after a long absence, looking at me with the two eyes I had seen in Karbala the moment he received his eleventh wound. My joy was tempered with pity for my beloved and master and I was devastated with the shock of it all!

The Station of Encounter and Reception

Peace be upon you and God's mercy and His blessings. I came to, my dear beloveds, from my total devastation and shock and found myself in Bab al-Hadid Square. Year, unknown. Month also unknown and a day of unknown name. I didn't care to ask. It seemed that was an early signal of despair and despair was a step toward forgetfulness. I realized that I was being placed in the Station of Encounter and Reception, which was another phase of the torment inflicted upon me and which I accepted humbly and without question.

There are several branches of learning associated with this station. They include the knowledge of addition and multiplicity; the knowledge of division, length, and width; the knowledge of originals and shadows; the knowledge of time, conjecture, fear, and ignorance of what will come. Of the moments of the day, it has the moment of the break of day; of winds, violent storms. Of the phases of the fragrance, the moment the scent is born. Of the human condition, it has staring. Of hand movements, greeting and shaking hands. Of states, it has astonishment and caution together. Its equivalent house in the Diwan is the House of That Which Was and That Which Will Be.

I learned from knowledge that I acquired that I was at a time in which I had not yet been born, that I was still scattered among the elements, that I didn't have tangible existence yet; rather that I was here with my old consciousness, that I was awaiting my father, and that meant I was the receiver and the received all at once. Before I had any opportunity to inquire, I looked at the entrance of the square from the south. The hearse stopped, its right side door opened, and my father got out. Upon seeing him I became him; I became my father. I became the lamp, the niche, the wick, the glass, and the flame all at once. I felt tired from the journey and the dust, and fear of the land on which I had not set foot before, and eagerness to visit the mausoleum of the beloved al-Husayn and members of the Prophet's house. I wondered what would happen to me and where I would be at this hour when tomorrow came. I also wondered who was passing at this very moment on the bridge leading to the bend in the village road that has become remote. I was worried, too, and wary of evil people who were lying in wait for strangers. But first and foremost, I was filled with deep affection for the old driver who had shared his food with us, which he kept in a large red kerchief, and who throughout the way made room for us, me and Makhut, next to him so that the three of us would fit on the narrow front seat. Whenever we passed by a town or large city he would point it out to us and tell us about it and about some of what happened to him in it. He stopped at the small coffeehouses outside towns and invited us to get out and swore that we would not pay a single millieme for the hot tea and lentil soup that he treated us to, saying, "You are about to start your lives away from home and that will need every millieme that you brought from the village!" He stopped only at the shops of the undertakers whom he knew, one by one, exchanging greetings and expressions of friendship and affection with them, inquiring after their health and families. He introduced us to them as if we were his dearest friends. He told us that these were the only people he could visit with, that they provided him with companionship on his long trips as he accompanied the dead, since others were not anxious to keep him company, unlike us. He pointed at us and said, "These are my road brothers." He was a good, kind man whom providence sent our way. He allayed my anxiety and made the beginning of my exile easier to take, having come as I did from being a stranger in my own village, which did not open its arms to me and closed all doors in my face and, bitterest of all, hardened the hearts of those closest to me.

The old driver opened the right-hand door of the car, saying, "May God bless you on your journey and send good and virtuous people to help you."

I said, "It's hard to say goodbye to you, good man, but that's the way of the world."

Then I noticed that al-Makhut was silent so, fearing that the good man might interpret it as unfriendly, I said, "If I and my friend, Umar, were to come to Banha, how can we find you?"

He laughed and said, "There's only one undertaker in Banha; ask for him and you'll find me."

I said, "I swear that if God opens the doors for me and enables me to earn an honest livelihood, I will come and visit you."

He shook hands with us. The car shook when he turned the engine on. From the narrow opening I could see the edge of the coffin attached to the floor of the car. He waved goodbye to us with his arm. I turned to look at the huge square and the crowd of people of all races and walks of life. "Cairo is big," I thought to myself: "Its roads seem endless. May God make it possible for me to make an honest living and spare me the need to ask anyone for alms. Your opportunities are myriad and you have al-Azhar and learning. Please God, help me memorize your book and understand it and be among its reciters. Protect me, God. There is a huge building surrounded by an iron fence. The buildings are tall and the streets are hard. There are many people. I'll ask one of them."

At that point I became both my father and the man whom my father asked. I was a public scribe on my way to the religious court to sit in the place I haven't moved from in twenty years; my briefcase where I kept official revenue stamps and the white writing paper was under my arm. I carried a small box in my pocket where I kept the stamp and small pieces of blotting paper to dry the ink. A young peasant from Said approached me and asked where the Cairo Station building was. I pointed at it quickly and he said, "May God increase his blessing to you." After I passed him I turned and saw him speaking with a friend of his. I said to myself, "Maybe this is their first visit to Cairo."

I looked with my father's eyes. I noticed that al-Makhut looked anxious and fidgety, seemingly lost in thought. I decided to ask him, fearing that something I did might have bothered him. I also wanted to comfort him, so I asked, "Are you afraid of the city? Or are you worried about the days to come which are still hidden from us?" I wondered whether he was thinking about the family he left behind in the village. I begged him not to worry, that if there wasn't enough to eat, I'd give him my own food and deny myself, that if there was a shortage in clothing, I'd take mine off and give it to him so he would cover himself. I told him that He who created us would not forget us and that there was no need to fret.

He suddenly interrupted me, "Listen, little brother . . . ."

I spoke in al-Makhut's tongue, thus I got to find out the real, secret plan and the deferred wish. I said in his voice, postponing disclosure of what I really had in mind, "Come on, Ahmad. Let's have breakfast and drink Cairo tea."

I said, in my father's voice, "We only have a few pennies, Makhut!"

My heart, my father's heart, was telling me that al-Makhut was hiding something from me.

We went into a ful and felafel place. My very first meal in Cairo. "In the name of God, the merciful, the beneficent. May it be blessed."

From where we sat we could see those going and coming and the Cairo Station building. It was here that trains traveled back and forth. I didn't know the day that I would sit inside this building and wait for the train to Tahta, to Juhayna. I said, "There was no need . . . ."

I looked with Makhut's eyes and his mind became my mind: "After we finish the meal I'll pay the check. I will not ask him for a single millieme. When I find an appropriate moment, I'll say 'Goodbye! We should go our separate ways.' I haven't and I won't tell him of Mi'allim Haridi's address in the fish market. I don't know where that market is, but I'll ask and if you ask, you don't go astray. The mi'allim is my relative and will help me, and can give me shelter the first few days. I'll be his guest, if not at home, then I'll sleep in his store. Being one person is less of a load on someone than two. If I were to go to him with Ahmad, perhaps he'd say: 'He doesn't think he is burden enough and is bringing another person with him; this is what's wrong with people from the village and their onerous burdens.'"

After we left the restaurant, Ahmad seemed content, but before he forgot the treat and before its effect wore off, I said, "Listen, cousin . . . ."

I listened with my father's ears and with his hearing and heart that had begun to put two and two together. That tone foretold a decision that had already been made. I listened to al-Makhut. He said he had to leave me here, that he was going on an errand that might mean a livelihood for both of us. I felt miserable. I'd be deprived of his company and I'd meet Cairo all by myself. Al-Makhut was lying to me, to one who was bitten and hurt by the days of his life. I understood what it was about. He had it all arranged while still in Juhayna, he had fully intended to do it, but he didn't confide in me. I didn't wish to burden him or to stand between him and his making a living.

"May God make it easy for you! It's hard to say goodbye after all we've been through, but go ahead, look after yourself."

I hear al-Makhut with my father's ears, "It's a matter of a day or two and I'll come to you."

He was lying to me. Where would he come to me? I had no roof over my head, no address, not even a destination. It was hard for me to see him go. There was a lump in my throat but I shook his hand and wished him safety and told him to take care of himself, when I was the one who needed someone to wish me that. I prayed to God to save him from evil people and their company. He nodded and turned his back to me, hurrying away as if he wanted to be rid of me, quick. He even forgot to shake my hand. Who would I go to now? Where? I would get a grip on myself and ask for the way to the mausoleum of al-Husayn, to visit him and ask him to protect me and look after me in my exile and to keep evil people away from me, for I was an orphan: no father, no mother, and no one who cared to ask about me or inquire after my affairs. If I got hit by this tram or that car, I'd be a goner and my story would end there, as I am the last of my line. I didn't know what fate was hiding for me in Cairo.

At that point I became a messenger working in a fabric and clothing store. I was on my way to the post office to buy a few stamps when I was approached by a peasant, a Saidi, fresh out of the village.

"Which way to al-Husayn, Amm?"

He looked confused and lost and had I not been in a hurry, I would have laughed at him and got myself some free entertainment. I said to him, "It seems you're a brand new Saidi!"

He looked at me as if he didn't understand. Quickly I pointed in the direction of Ataba Square leading to al-Husayn mosque.

For a fleeting moment I was surprised and sad that I had addressed my father in such an improper way and because I had upset him, even though he didn't seem upset. I was mad at myself despite the fact that it had been someone else's tongue. But what could I do? That was what happened and what had been decreed for me in this strange situation.

I became my father again. I followed the man with my eyes. I must ask someone else, but only after this one had disappeared from my sight. Maybe he was misleading me. Didn't he laugh at me?

Oh, those Cairenes! I felt like a corn plant in a cumin field. Nobody was paying attention to me and the streets were so crowded and yet I felt the people were so distant from me. When a stranger appeared in Juhayna at the bridge, people would gather around him and they'd show him the way and would invite him into their homes at nightfall and feed him if it was time for a meal. Here, all those I see around me are strangers to each other. Look at this square: it's huge. I'll ask any effendi. But before asking, let me fill my eyes, for this was the first I was seeing of Cairo. What destiny was Cairo holding for me? I didn't know.

At this point something unusual happened to me, and it was one of the secrets of this station. I was my father. Yes, I was used to that and knew all that he had suffered. But I also became everything that he was seeing for the first time. So, I was and I was not. I spoke in my silence and was silent even as I spoke. I walked as I stood in my place and stood as I walked. I became a barefoot boy in tattered clothes, holding a tin can, and I was my father's heart that took pity on him. I became a very old porter, carrying a heavy sack on his back, trying to keep it balanced. I became a horse-drawn carriage driver, sitting and waiting, and when I looked at that confused Saidi I didn't bother to dwell much on him for he didn't look like someone who would take a ride in my carriage—he looked like one of those who appeared every day in the square and, after a period, long or short, would be making the rounds of the coffeehouses carrying a basket with soft pretzels and cheese and eggs. Perhaps he would be carrying a bag full of shirts and underwear and cotton socks and combs. He might hit it big and end up a big powerful mi'allim with gold teeth, riding in the evening a horse-drawn carriage other than the one drawn by the spoiled horses he had ridden in the morning. It's all a matter of luck.

I became the question that occurred to my father: I wonder how much he would charge me to take me to al-Husayn Mosque? I was also the answer, "No need, Ahmad. Save your pennies for the coming days. No one knows what's awaiting you."

I became a pickpocket getting ready to get on the tram, then I was a plainclothesman wearing a gallabiya and a coat. I became a Nubian soldier in the border police, the camel troops. I was also a thought in my father's head: did they also have camel troops in Cairo? The image that had come to his head was that of dozens of black soldiers riding camels, attacking the village, shouting and calling out to men as if they were women, to get back inside their homes. I became a woman wearing a pair of anklets. Then I became a lupine seed vendor stacking little paper bags in tall rows on a wooden handcart and I was also one of the customers. I became a fruit grocer, then the doorman of an ancient, two-story hotel. I was the questions: how much would it take for me to spend the night there if I had to? I became a grocer, the lone patron in a restaurant, a traffic policeman, a truck driver, the driver of a small car, a man riding a bicycle, a tram driver wearing a fez and a khaki suit and placing a handkerchief around his neck. I became a train engineer crossing the road in a hurry to make it to the Cairo Station, a little girl rolling a hoop in front of her, an old sheikh hurrying to lead the prayers, a seller of old manuscripts, a pupil kicking a little stone, a vendor of cotton candy, a leader of a zar ritual, and a musician car-rying a lute covered with a green cloth heading for a coffeehouse to wait for someone to hire him for a wedding or a party. I became a man smoking a narghile sitting in front of a store selling empty velvet cases for jewelry. I also became a cloth dyer, a fireman, and a judge walking slowly in a dignified fashion, and a young woman who had run away from her village in Northern Egypt, trying to walk steadily and show no fear to fend off male predators and to blend in. I became a worker for the city, who lit gas lamps at sun-set and put them out in the early morning. I became a fat pasha wearing a fez and ceremonial suit riding in an open car. I was a cool breeze relieving my father's exhaustion. I was his wide-open eyes taking in what he was seeing in pristine surprise. I was the feeling of surprise itself and the puzzling question, the cryptic answer, the vague feelings, and the onset of fear. I was his hurrying steps as he crossed the roads, his slow and deliberate steps before everything new that he saw, and his striving steps. I was the ground under his feet, the ramp for his bridge, the sidewalks he took, the entrances of houses he passed by, the walls of houses he looked at, and the grass of Azbakiya Garden on which he rested. I was a stone, a plant, and a forgotten store sign. I was a bow, a turn of the head, a timid nod, and a first impression. I was a passing thought, a puzzlement, and a wondering question: what should he do? And what should he say? I was the sudden hastening of the heartbeat following a fright, the realization that a part of one's life was gone and would not come back. I was the feeling of grief following that realization. I was the fear of tomorrow, the weakness of the legs, thirst, the silent supplications to the resting place of Imam al-Husayn at which he would arrive shortly for the first time. I was everything that my father suffered those first moments and that was my torment in that station.

The Station of What Was and What Will Be
I saw sunrise and sunset together and I leaned on the place where the sun sets.

This is a station in which causes for things are varied and numerous. Sometimes they seem clear and at other times they become so fine that they are hidden. Some find comfort in being with their beloveds and others get that comfort from vanquishing their enemies and then there are those whose comfort lies in abandonment and flight. I am all of these. Before being in this station I have been made to understand that I would meet two beloveds and that the two beloveds would remain one and that I would enjoy being close just as much as I would suffer because of that closeness, for everything that I've seen and would see is ephemeral; just as the Holy Qur'an tells us, *Everyone on earth will perish, but the countenance of your Lord, in all majesty and nobility will remain.* Praise be to the One who placed me in this wondrous station in which I have assumed a form and an appearance different from mine, then pushed me into a time other than my own time, but indeed a wondrous time in which

177

different times coexist: for there are things that I see now from a bygone era and something else that I see from an era that hasn't come yet and the two times exist side by side and I am in between the two, not knowing exactly in which time I am actually living. But to avoid confusion on your part, my sagacious reader, the imam of those striving on the path of God has authorized me to give a brief explanation and to that end I say: I have come during my father's maturity. I came as a man over forty-five years of age, which is an age I had not reached when I began to write down these epiphanies, whether in the first writing, which I tore up, or the second writing, which I haven't finished yet. Besides, I do not know whether I'll make it to that age or whether the thread of my life will be cut before I get to that age. That's because my life has been difficult and the time during which I lived has been desolate. Bad luck has been heaped on me and my era and we were thwarted. My country was polluted and humiliated and my own endeavors bore very little fruit. I suppressed my screams and avoided being violated even as the scum of the earth threatened my honor. My own people took the easier and the lighter way out, straying from integrity and honesty. They thought by staying away from the vicissitudes of time and the reversal of fortune they would achieve peace of mind and security. They succumbed to shameful and humiliating arrangements, and were content with whatever was available. They eschewed wisdom and the wise and as a result friendliness fled and affection vanished. As for good qualities, they sought home somewhere else. Virtues were crippled and hopes stumbled. The future turned into a dead end. Please forgive me, sagacious reader, if I tend to be long-winded and verbose, for these are symptoms of our condition in our twisted times, but that's a long story that would take me too far afield. Please allow me to go back to what I was about to narrate.

That Which Was and That Which Will Be
And thus I found myself at the age of forty-five even though I hadn't been born yet. I was a supervisor at a large bakery belonging to Hajj

al-Rimali when a man from the environs of my village came accompanied by a shy young man, new to Cairo. He said he hoped I'd help that Ahmad get a job, any job where he could make a living, spare him the need to beg and keep him away from the clutches of swindlers. One of his relatives tricked him out of the pounds that he had saved and brought with him close to his chest, actually sewing them into his clothes. That thieving relative promised to help him enroll in al-Azhar then kept evading and stalling him. Ahmad was on the point of begging in the streets just to stay alive but he didn't because he was a proud man. So he took all kinds of cruel, backbreaking jobs. He carried stones from ships to the harbor at Rod al-Farag; he worked in a sugarcane juice shop where he broke off the thistle tops and peeled the canes; he worked in a thread-dyeing house. All these were temporary jobs that lasted only a short while. Besides, he was still hopeful to find the time while working to go to school and start his education.

I gazed and my eyes both saw and heard: I saw my father in the sugarcane juice place when the man mentioned that; I became tired and saw his legs tremble on the ramp extending from the bank of the Nile to the boat, weighted down by the heavy stones. The smell of the dyes in the dye house filled my nose when he talked about my father's work there. I looked at my father, suppressing my longing, just as a homesick person would hide his yearnings for home. I asked my father, who had not yet become my father, what kind of education he had in mind and he said that, if God willed it, he would learn reading and writing and then return to the village as a teacher of religion, that his stay in Cairo was temporary. He said that Cairo was a big city, that a stranger would be lost in it and he was not made for it, that his goal was to go back to Juhayna. At that moment I had a lightning revelation: I was shown a secret aspect that I never knew while he was alive. I found out how he had lived since the day he arrived in Cairo and up to the day of his final departure: he considered his stay in Cairo as temporary. His secret thoughts came to me as he told himself in various decades: "I'll finish school and go back."

"After I get a job in the ministry I'll request a transfer to the village."
"After the boys finish school in Cairo, I'll go back to the village."
"After Gamal's graduation."
"After Ismail's graduation. After I make sure Nawal is okay, and little Ali."
"After the end of my service, I have no business staying in Cairo. The kids have grown up and have no time for me. I'll go back to die there, to the place I left, so I wouldn't burden my children with my burial and funeral. I would go lightly to meet my maker."

None of that came to pass.

I found out from this revelation that my father lived in Cairo for forty or fifty years and that that lifetime was temporary for him. That was why he didn't mix with Cairenes, did not marry a Cairene woman, kept his rural dialect, and always sought out people from his village in Cairo.

At that point the lightning revelation came to an end and I went back to my father full of compassion, grief, and pity, but I didn't show any of that. I told him he would ride every day a horse-drawn carriage, green and covered, with two back doors closed by an iron bolt. Inside that carriage were shelves on which racks of bread would be arranged: fresh round loaves that had to be delivered hot to the houses, which requires speed, nimbleness, and honesty. That was the carriage delivering subscribers' bread to houses of notables who had power and clout. The deliveries would be made three times a day, at breakfast, lunch, and supper. It was a long route and by day's end he would return to the bakery exhausted and would go into a far corner that I gave him permission to sleep in when I learned from him the he hadn't found lodging yet. I gave him the permission when he promised to look for a room. I was comfortable with the decision, then I began to trust him even more when I found out that he was diligently looking for shelter. Then my outlook changed: I looked at him as my father who would be, so I was filled with kindness, yet I was not able to tell him who I was because I was not permitted to do so. When my wish grew stronger, so strong that I decided to speak despite the lack of permission, but when I started to tell him who I really was and what was going to come, my tongue grew heavy and I would lose my words. Dumbfounded and my thoughts scattered, I would be unable to see and veils would arise between me and the future.

Then my role changed and I was in a different position: I became the driver, holding the reins, lashing the horses, stopping in front of the homes until Ahmad—my father—opened the back door of the carriage and picked up the loaves to be delivered. I watched his diligence and how he averted his gaze when he stopped at open doors, even though they were outside doors that led to big gardens or courtyards. But what drew my attention was his inquiring after the owners of the houses: pashas, sheikhs, men of learning, and big merchants, his questions about their families, their in-laws, and about important events they may have taken part in. It seemed to me that he was thinking of something that he was about to express right away, but he didn't. His face would light up and look serene whenever we drew near al-Husayn Square. Every time he would say, "God's will, O Husayn!"

He beseeched him to protect him, to save him from hardships, and to keep evildoers away from him. I would listen to his many stories, about men from Juhayna, masters of great houses who filled the world with awe, who took pride in themselves and who were very generous and for whom the world opened up, but then they departed. Some of them did not leave behind much to be remembered by and some gave the world a bad progeny. After our daily delivery routine we would go back together. He would accompany me to the stable where he would unhitch the horses and we would together push the carriage to its corner, then we would walk together. He would go back to the bakery by himself, tired to exhaustion. There he would eat his simple supper, which changed only on rare occasions: when he went to visit an old man who just came from Juhayna or when he was invited to a wedding or to a dinner. It was then that he would eat meat and sauces and fetir.

But his daily supper was one of the bakery's loaves and a piece of cheese, with a bell pepper or a slice of pickled cucumber. He would then enter the bakery, filled with the smell of fuel and smoke, rising dough and sawdust. Then he would climb over the dough racks, turning over the last one on top so that remnants of dough and flour would not stick to his body or clothes.

Slowly and in measured steps, I acquired an ability that was of great importance to me, a penetrating ability by which some of his night thoughts and the sounds he heard were made available to me. These sounds included the crawling of rats and crickets, a mysterious whistling that sounded at a specific hour, steps coming closer then moving away, a door being opened then closed somewhere or another, an unknown call, the footsteps of the night-beat policeman making sure locks on stores were secure, a muffled moan, the whistle of a train in the distant wilderness, the sound of yearning, the call to the dawn prayer from the old mosque, the sound of the night slinking away, other vague sounds of which some were probably coming from the depths of the universe and the sounds of the morning's breathing.

My father would then get up, feeling his way in the dark of the bakery, avoiding stumbling over the containers, racks, and other obstructions, to the sink. He was forbidden to light a match or any light for fear of fire. He could not leave the bakery for two reasons: fear of thieves and because the door was locked on the outside. It was more like a prison.

As for the nighttime passing thoughts, they began as soon as he stretched his exhausted body and closed his eyes, reciting the Fatiha to keep away the devils. His thoughts at night passed before me in this revelation and I saw them exactly as they presented themselves to his mind's eye, eliciting in me what they elicited in him the moment they came to him and the moment they departed. If the effect on him was sad, I was saddened, and if it was one of longing—and that was the case most of the time—I longed for the same things. If the thought was one of joy and merriment I rejoiced with him. If he vented his exasperation by suddenly exclaiming, "O Most generous, most kind! Give me strength, O Husayn!" or if he would suddenly sing or hit his knee with the palm of his hand, I would do the same thing. Of his constant thoughts I was aware of his homesickness for the bridge, the days of the flood, and the honey-like aroma of the figs and the taste of ripe dates that had fallen under the palm trees, his visualizing of his palm trees and the times of harvesting them. One of his thoughts was how he took the clusters of dates to the good man who saved his life and by whose hands he had been granted a new life, the Master Sergeant Ahmad Husayn. He wondered where they were right now, he and his good and kind wife, may God grant her a child! All they ever wished for was to have a boy or a girl. He decided to pray for them at al-Husayn's mausoleum after the noon prayers on Friday. When circumstances permitted and he could afford to travel to Juhayna, he would stop on his way at the village of Hajj Qandil on the eastern bank and buy soap, rice, and fabric for a gallabiya for the good woman who was kind to him as if she were his own mother, and who offered him milk and makhruta in the morning. He would get off the train at Deir Mawas then cross the Nile at Hajj Qandil. The man would be happy to see him and when the people of the village came to greet him he would say in front of them all that a whole new life was granted him at the hands of his uncle, Amm Ahmad Husayn, and he would sit politely in his presence and would never walk in front of him or cross his legs in front of him if he sat on a bench, and before leaving him he would kiss his hand just as a son kissed his father's hand. When he got on the boat he would say to him out loud, "Please pray for me." Then the boat would sail and the bank would be enveloped in fog and the features of the good people would disappear.

Among the features that would appear and persist would be those of the face of the good driver who gave him a ride from Tahta to Cairo. If he passed by Banha he would look him up, as Banha was close to Cairo. The man might not remember him but he would tell him, "I am the one who rode with you. My friend was with me."

He wondered how Makhut was doing. He hadn't seen him for quite some time, but he heard news of him related by men from Juhayna who met after Friday prayers at the Ajam coffeehouse in front of al-Husayn mosque. After he worked only a few days with Haridi, the fish merchant, he heard someone saying that he was going to the British army camps in Abbasiya and he asked him, "Will you take me with you?" The man nodded. There they found an auction to sell old things: chasses of cars, boxes, and uniforms. Makhut didn't have a lot of money. At the end of the auction a glass box with wires and short tubes was left. Others said it was an unknown body of steel and glass. Makhut bought it for one pound and thirty piasters. Maybe he liked its appearance, or maybe it was Makhut's strange sense. At the door of the camp a fat man got out of a private passenger car. He went inside and returned quickly, catching up with Makhut at the intersection. He asked him, "How much did you buy it for?" Makhut, lying, said, "Ten pounds." The fat man said, "Here's twenty." Makhut paid no attention and turned his back to the man who said, eagerly, "Here's forty." Makhut moved away even further. This went on until the fat man took out a wad and swore that he did not have one millieme more than the three hundred pounds. At that point, Makhut turned and wet the tip of his finger and counted the banknotes, one by one, then handed the man that strange contraption. People were saying that Makhut was now almost bigger than Mi'allim Haridi himself. They said that he had contracted with a big hotel to supply them with fish. Well! What a world! What luck! Anyway, may God be generous to him!

The Said train came into view. The black locomotive was spewing steam and smoke and emitting successive thunderous noises as it began to move, as well as a dull whistle presaging exile or return. He was at the platform; he often went and stood there watching the trains as they departed, bidding them farewell with his eyes until the last car disappeared at the bend. Then there was that empty silence that followed the departure of trains and those saying their farewells, of the porters and the railroad employees. All of that left him sad and with a lump in his throat.

Then he would go back to al-Azhar, to the courtyard lined on all sides by the different aisles, and the shadow of the columns in the late afternoon, and the swallows flying to the tops of the minarets, the cool feel of the marble floors. It was the late afternoon lesson by Sheikh Salih al-Ja'fari, a venerable-looking man who leaned his back against one of the columns in the covered courtyard, surrounded by disciples, a virtuous and blessed man with a few miracles. He came from Sudan and never left al-Azhar except to pray in the beloved al-Husayn's mosque. One of these days he would be able to attend regularly, to keep up with the lessons and understand everything being said, but before that he had to learn how to read well. He cursed his luck: if only he had more time! In any case that was a temporary job and of the four piasters he was going to save one piaster every day so that he might spend a little on himself. He would live on as little money as possible, and, God be praised, he didn't have any responsibilities except for himself.

The streets leading to al-Azhar, al-Husayn, and to distant Juhayna got mixed up in his mind, as did the coffeehouses, the clothing stores, the rug warehouses, the copper shops, and those dealing in burnished silver; also the visions of peasant women sitting on sidewalks with chicken cages and baskets of cottage cheese in front of them, and skins of butter, piles of green onions, sweets, and body wraps, the well defined contours of women's buttocks, women's veils with or without gold ornaments, a round face, and eyes highlighted with kohl. Ah, the women of Cairo! One of these days he would have a house and a woman awaiting his return and children who would be overjoyed when he came home. They would ride on his back and he would happily play with them. He would take them to the parks, to al-Husayn, to al-Ajam coffeehouse, to the museum, to friends and relatives. They would be children who would not know the hardship he had known nor the humiliation he lived through. He would get them whatever they wanted or wished for.

At that point the revelation ended. My father fell asleep and it was not part of this epiphany to enter into his dreams or know their contents. As the revelation ended I felt a great pain: the last images he saw before he slept, before he slid into the world of dreams, were visions built around a house with a wife and children and a door that provided protection for him and them against the outside world, the smell of food awaiting him when he returned home from a job hitherto unknown to him. I found myself in a strange emotional state, tormenting to me, cruel by being gentle with me. After the end of that revelation I was overcome with a strange fear, especially since I didn't know what the following step in that station might be. My fear grew and an ice-cold chill seeped deep inside me. I felt my strength being sapped and my core all mixed up, as if I were standing at the end of the world on the point of total loss without any hope of recovering my losses. At that point of near-collapse, I was called by the voice of a woman I was in love with a long time ago to allay my fears of loneliness. I became nostalgic for that voice and wondered why I heard it in that station. I didn't know what was being asked of me but I calmed down, even though my torment was not alleviated and my loneliness was not allayed.

After a while, how long I didn't know, Gamal Abdel Nasser appeared to me. I found out that he was going through many ordeals, that he was being pursued mercilessly, and that they were almost catching up with him, that he was trying to find a hiding place but no one was helping, that he had been deserted by his friends, by the era in which he was the be all and end all, in which he stood very tall, in which he constructed and built. I stared at him and found that he was walking in the street leading to the bakery where my father worked. I learned that Gamal Abdel Nasser had two appearances in this station: a natural one, since he was a secondary school student in Alexandria, wearing a fez, thin and tall with a big nose. So, I could pinpoint the time marker—the first half of the thirties—but I was turned back without success when I remembered that each existent in this station had its own time, that times coexisted in close proximity with each other, that actually they intersected. Thus there were no time borders, no tomorrow or yesterday and no separation: no before or after, no demarcation, and no natural phenomena. There were no specific events that could be used as a marker. Therefore I didn't know how much time he had spent in Cairo even though I did see the moment of his arrival and suffered all he had suffered, on the whole and not in detail. Undoubtedly that was so for a reason hidden to me and because of something I could not fathom.

As for the second existence of Abdel Nasser, it was his presence in these epiphanies and that was a gathering filled with secrets. I saw him stop in front of the bakery around sunset as the sky appearing above the houses was red and night was standing nearby on alert. My father went out to meet him. He knew him, which was evident from the way he received him kindly with a smile, shook his hand, and asked him, "Hungry?"

There he was, nodding to my father's question. My father walked next to him. At that moment I discerned a trench extending below the walls in which pure, clean water was running. My father asked him to wait for him under a post holding a gas lamp that had not yet been lit. My father headed for a place selling ful and falafel. He knew the vendor and called him by name even though I didn't hear him. My father asked him to be generous because he had a dear friend visiting from the village. My father did not want to divulge the name of his guest or how close their kinship or friend-ship was. So, my father knew what I knew, that Abdel Nasser was being pursued, that they were closing in on him, that being with him constituted danger. And even though my role at this point was to observe and nothing more, it was possible for me to recall some of what I knew. My father was affected and grieved whenever he heard of someone who was in an elevated or mighty condition once but who had fallen to the vicissitudes of time or whose situation had changed and whose people forgot him, those who had once gathered around and supported him now deserting him.

I recalled my father's sorrow when a former minister—I forgot the name that he told me—was standing at the information desk, tired and old, leaning on his cane and the employees of that desk were asking him to show his ID. My father happened to enter and he recognized him. My father, now getting on in years, was called Amm Ahmad and they didn't assign to him specific jobs, so he spent all his time in the prayer areas, either performing prayers or stretched out on the floor, traveling with his eyes across the ceiling to a distant unknown. Some old employees asked him to read the Fatiha at the mausoleum of al-Husayn. He got to be known during these years, which turned out to be his last, as one of the lovers of al-Husayn. My father said to the employee at the information desk, "Don't you know his excellency, the minister? Please, please, Pasha, come in." The man looked at him quizzically, "Do you know me, son?"

He addressed my father as "son," even though my father was older, but that was how people who had been in a position of authority for a long time behaved. My father said loudly, "Your picture is hanging upstairs in the minister's office. Who doesn't know your excellency?" My father would say at the end of that story in sorrow, "Imagine! No one recognized him! What a world!" He looked sorry every time he came back from the observance of the anniversary of the death of a former political leader in Said and would say to me, "Imagine, the anniversary was attended by only three people! Even his children don't attend and once his wife dies, that anniversary will not be observed at all."

Here was my father turning around, carrying hot loaves of bread, some cheese, and halva. He headed for Abdel Nasser and they both walked in the shade. My father said to himself, and I was able to hear his silent talk, that he has always lived in fear of being fired, that any boss could fire him for the most trivial of reasons, depriving him of his livelihood and that of his children, but after Abdel Nasser came all of that ended. He told himself as he had told me repeatedly in the same tone, using the same words, that Gamal Abdel Nasser protected the weak from the strong, and the poor from the rich, that if he had done nothing else, that would have been enough. He was now walking, greatly moved. Here was Gamal Abdel Nasser, whom he had seen only in crowded processions, now defeated and pursued. The time I was seeing now was during the thirties; that was certain, for my father was still single, not having married yet. He was working in a bakery and his daily wage was four piasters, no more but it could be less if he made a mistake. As for Abdel Nasser, he belonged to an era that would come later. My father recalled what happened in the future as if it were in the past, thus everything had happened already. That was strange for me and beyond my limited ability to understand outside my human ken. I couldn't understand how each of them belonged to a different time and yet they were walking together, talking and eating together, each looking at the other.

As their steps continued to move forward I had to postpone the questions, the surprise, and the awe. My father was now accompanying Abdel Nasser to a small room in the old house with a large courtyard in which stood an old neglected car covered by a wide fishing net with seashells on the edges. The entrance was lit by a small lamp whose wick danced with the slightest breeze. They entered the house. I went back to the entrance of the alley: al-Inshaa Alley, I was able to read the sign. But when did my father live in that room and when did he rent it? These were questions for which I had no answers. If my masters in the Diwan had wished to let me in on this information, they would have.

Here I recalled something that had puzzled me. After my father's final departure, several official forms had to be requested in order for the family to start receiving the government pension. My brother Ismail had to do all this paperwork since I was absent on that ill-fated trip. One of my father's old ID cards had an address of which we had not been aware and it had never come to our attention that my father had lived there: Inshaa Alley, Sayyida Zeinab. We were at a loss. When did my father live in this place that he had never mentioned? When did he sleep here? When did he set eyes on it, eyes that were now just two dark holes? He didn't tell us about that nor did he share with us the days that he spent at Inshaa Alley. It was negligence on our part that we hadn't asked him. I tried to explain the whole matter to myself by saying that perhaps it was the address of one of his relatives or acquaintances that my father wrote in his old ID card when he had no address, no lodging of his own, no key to lock the door behind him and go to sleep in safety.

But there he was before me at that same address and the same room. I was apart from the two of them. I could see and hear them but they didn't see me or smell me or hear my breathing. I realized that I was sitting in the middle between them but in a strange posture. I wasn't touching the floor with my chair, rather I was sitting in the air, in an empty space, leaning on nothing. The room looked desolate because there was no furniture at all. My father had driven three nails into the wall on which he hung a gallabiya, a vest, and long underpants. On the floor there was a rug woven from remnants of old cloth. My father left his shoes at its right edge and used them as a pillow.

My father appeared to be ashamed of how desolate, small, and dark the room was, but Abdel Nasser looked content. He communicated with my father by his eyes: no sound was coming out of their mouths and their lips were not moving to form the letters and the sounds, but I understood what they were saying. Abdel Nasser was saying that exile had exhausted him but that he never imagined one day that he would suffer the pangs of exile in a land on the two banks of the Nile. My father answered him with a glance, reassuring him without uttering a word. Abdel Nasser said that the hardship he was going through now was beyond anything he had known. He never imagined that his eyes would see that flag in the land of Egypt nor read in an Egyptian daily newspaper an advertisement inviting Egyptians to spend their summer vacation in the state of Israel. Near the square that was still called Tahrir Square he stopped before a travel agency whose name was pronounced in English but which was written in Arabic characters; he read a sign hung on the glass façade giving the fares for individual and group travel, times of departure for air-conditioned buses and planes from Tel Aviv to Cairo and from Cairo to Tel Aviv. My father pointed to the food so that his guest would continue to eat, while he, my father, chewed slowly, eating as little as possible for fear the food would not be enough. Besides, my father would not finish first before the guest had had his fill. Abdel Nasser continued to express his innermost thoughts through his eyes. He said that when he came back to that time he found that people were astonished but that after he was put in jail, escaped, and moved around among them he observed that the astonishment was wearing off, that many people were getting used to news of the Israelis' travel and their presence, to reading about some officials here in Egypt, and to seeing those officials praising the cordial relations between the two countries.

From where I sat I said, speaking the words, "Some of these people you know well. They were close to you." I noticed that my voice did not reach them, so I fell silent, even though I noticed my father bowing his head. It seemed to me that he wanted to say that which I said but that he chose not to add to the man's pain in his ordeal. When I understood that, I blamed myself for my rashness. Abdel Nasser said, "Only a few followed me." My father said, "The few are the beginning of the many." Abdel Nasser said, "People's faces are sullen. Features have changed." My father said, "These are difficult times." Abdel Nasser said, "In my old tours I used to look at the feet of passersby and I'd see that they were wearing shoes. Few were going about barefoot. That used to reassure me and I went to bed feeling at ease, knowing that I was on the right track despite the great difficulties." My father said, "Yes indeed, you protected the poor from the rich." Abdel Nasser said, "Today on my way to you, I saw a woman in a black gallabiya carrying a baby and holding the hand of a little child, maybe five or six years old. The child was barefoot even though the sun was blazing and the ground burning. Things are very bad and I feel like a stranger here." My father extended his hand, touching the place of his heart, "And I am a stranger like you, but as they say: to a stranger a stranger is a relative. When strangers get together they are no longer strangers." Abdel Nasser sighed, wondering, "How has all of that come about?" At that I couldn't help speaking so I said, "You've left us a bad successor. It was you who handpicked him." He didn't hear me. I decided to keep the question to myself until the obstacles between us had been removed, then I'd face him and demand an answer.

I followed my father as he got up to shake the dust off the rug. He spread it and with a glance bade him to stretch out. Abdel Nasser asked him, "And you? Where will you sleep?" My father said that he was used to hardship all his life, that nothing was more comfortable than the floor. Abdel Nasser said, "Sleep beside me." My father begged him to sleep, for tomorrow they were going on a big, big trip. That was how my father described that journey. I didn't know about it or the route or destination, but I was afraid of a sudden attack. My father said, "If you get up at night, or if you need anything, please don't hesitate to wake me up." Abdel Nasser did not answer but lay down in silence, touched by my father's feeling toward him. The world was still a good place. Here was a poor man who couldn't even extend his hand to touch mine; we had been worlds apart and look at him now, exposing himself to grave danger without worrying, providing me with food and shelter. As for those who knew me, who tried to get closest to me and to follow me, they were now in hot pursuit of me, trying to nip my return in the bud and to banish me from an era that were enjoying.

Abdel Nasser stretched out, his stature seeming taller as he slept than when he stood up. He slept and my father slept but I didn't sleep, not even for a second. And here I must point out a benefit. For ever since the Diwan became pleased with me and gave me permission, I've lost physical characteristics that are part of human nature. My constant vigilant wakefulness was a result of that, the absence of the need to sleep. No sleep and no slumber, rather a full alertness during which my consciousness glowed the whole time, like a nightlight. That was something that no human had ever known or experienced. Perhaps that light would fade a little or grow weaker but it never stopped burning. As for transitions, they were sudden. And here I must divulge a little bit, noble reader and close supporter: all obstacles before me have been lifted since I entered the Diwan. No more time. No more place and no more physical, emotional, earthly, or cosmic barriers. Among the newly acquired abilities was also the ability to move easily from one condition to another, from one time to another time, from one space to another with the change of my breathing: with inhaling I would move to a coming era, with exhaling to a past era; or I could become a child, then an old man—praise be to the One, who in the Qur'an told us, *Everyday exercises universal power,* saying also, *We shall dispose of you two dependants* [man and jinn].

It must be pointed out, though, that my desire or ability did not provide the moving force behind my mobility or vision. Rather I was at the mercy of those that God had given the ability to determine my fate and who sometimes tormented me and at other times gave me bliss. I was granted whatever was granted to human thoughts and feelings. Among these would be wondering, regret, astonishment, fear, sadness, nostalgia, awe, panic, physical and moral pain, as well as curiosity, irritation, resentment, and all the conditions native to human nature. Thus, that night I didn't sleep a wink because sleep was a stranger to me in my constant travel. I sat, suspended in space, overlooking their sleeping bodies, counting their breaths and listening to the night. I became like a watchman, guarding their sleep against any sudden intrusion or terrifying nightmare or unwelcome dream or pain or anything causing them discomfort. What I feared most was a sudden attack, so I wanted to be able to alert them before it was too late. However, my watching over them and my anxiety for their wellbeing ended, like everything else. *Everyone on earth will perish, but the countenance of your Lord, in all majesty and nobility will remain.* Dawn peeked and broke and the morning threw off the remaining covers. My father got up, cautious not to wake up his guest. He went out, then came back carrying a tin can filled with hot milk. He poured its contents in two glasses and gently shook Abdel Nasser's shoulder. They left together before the streets became crowded with passersby and traffic and before it became dangerous. I followed them and was astonished when they took some steps and I took some steps behind them. They went out and I went out after them. Then al-Inshaa Alley disappeared and so did the houses. It was a totally different terrain, a totally different era. It was a barren stretch of land leading to Karbala, to Kufa. When I came up next to them to look more closely at their features, I saw that they had the imprint of that distant period, for each era had its own human look. I knew that this station was about to end and I bade it adieu.

The Station of Regret
Let no one go through the travails of this struggle
Except the successful, happy one
Who walks this earth alive as a martyr.

When my father, in the company of Gamal Abdel Nasser, arrived at Kufa's old time, he had been fired from his job, thus losing his only source of income. The reason for that was a letter sent to him by one of his relatives in the village, who addressed the envelope thus: "To the Respected Rimali Bey, Owner of al-Rimali Bakeries and from him to the Respected Ahmad al-Ghitani." The bey asked in astonishment, "Who is that?" He was told he was a worker in the baladi bread bakery. He got very angry, incensed at the impudence: how dare a simple worker make of him an intermediary through whom to receive a letter! Then he told the foreman to settle the account of that Ghitani and to let him go.

My father told Abdel Nasser as the houses of Kufa loomed in the horizon in the midst of the towering palm trees, "I swear, sir, that I hadn't given my address to anyone. It was a scheme from my uncle so that I would lose my job and my livelihood." He told Abdel Nasser, "The best years of my life were those I spent at the bakery." Abdel Nasser said, "Every past seems beautiful to whoever lived it no matter how many difficulties filled it."

My father looked sad. Abdel Nasser told him in an attempt to soften the blow, "Had it not been for the job, you wouldn't have gotten married and begotten your progeny from which four have lived." With distress in his voice my father said, "Four, what have my four children done for me?" Abdel Nasser said, "You have raised them well and given them an education. Don't regret what's past and forgive them and pardon them." My father, in an attempt to modify his position, said, "I am not being unfair to them. I am just reproaching them lovingly. Before my final departure from the world I said to them, 'Forgive me,' and they forgave me. Regrettably my breaths didn't come to my aid and my heart got weaker and I did not say my forgiveness for them out loud. They never heard it from me, but God knows to this day that I still love them and from time to time I ask permission to go visit them one by one. I see them but they cannot see me and I hear them but they cannot hear me. My eldest son, Gamal, was not there the moment I made my departure from the world. I was apprehensive about my departure to a destination I didn't know. So, as my soul left my body I let out a scream that awakened him in that distant foreign country. Yet I rocked his soul just as I rocked him as a child and I calmed him so he went back to sleep."

My father sighed, "Oh, the kids! How I miss them!" At that point I ran until I caught up with him. I turned my face to him and shouted, "Look, I am next to you!" But he didn't hear me and didn't see me. My eyes welled with tears and I once again followed the two of them. I realized that one of the secrets of this station was the barrier between us: I could see them and hear them, but they would not be aware of me, that the condition of my being was that of a follower, that I could never go ahead of them and that everything I saw would be lit by that degree of weak light, pale and slightly red, like that in the middle of high clouds immediately after the setting of the sun, and that the smell accompanying me in this station would be the smell of old rain that had fallen some time ago and whose drops had gathered in soft holes or the folds of a plant. That smell evoked painful sorrow and nostalgia and everything I heard was from the Saba melancholic melodious mode. As for the sciences of this station, they were all extinct and encrypted and had no equivalents among the names of sciences known to us. Abdel Nasser said, "I am as sad as you are because the one I trusted betrayed the trust and the one I had confidence in broke his promises to me."

Here my father said in a wondrously firm tone, "You gave us a bad successor."

Abdel Nasser fell silent then said, "We've gone too far."

The second of two going deep into the night of Kufa, my father, said, "Do not be sad. God is with us."

From that moment, immediately after he said that, they separated and each went a different way. I also lost sight of them and was cut off from any news about them. Once again I became a total stranger. I said to myself that I should reflect on what I had been through and examine what I had written and try to recall what I remembered. I also decided to use the things I had seen to guide my inner eye and use my secrets to enrich my innermost core, for I could sense the ordeals creeping closer and the times of tribulations approaching. If I managed to find my way then I would have attained knowledge and if I pretended to be blind and ignored what I had seen, then at least I had been given the choice. I heaved passionate sighs of longing for the two of them just as I had a big lump in my throat when I saw them the first time for fear of separation from them. I grew more and more pale and was overcome by an endless distress and I wondered, "Would my son or one of my grandchildren seek me out and go to the Diwan in search of my memory after I had been buried and forgotten, after my whole era had gone as if it never was?"

My position changed: I was now sitting in an old mosque in Kufa. Its floor was covered with mats and its roof with palm tree trunks. I was sitting among others, facing my father who was directly in front of me and whom I could see with my eyes. At this stage in the station I was permitted to see him with all my senses. He seemed to be at an age with which I was not familiar: he was neither young nor old and he was talking to a gathering in the mosque, reminding them that they had let al-Husayn down, causing them to blame each other, and fanning the flames of remorse.

Then my position changed and I became an observer at a session in an expansive house that belonged to one of the notables of Kufa, Sulayman ibn Sard al-Khuza'i, one of the companions of the Prophet, pbuh, who knew him, sat with him, and heard directly from him. As for the other men they were al-Musayyib ibn Najbat al-Fazari, a close companion of Ali, Abdallah ibn Saad ibn Nufayl al-Azdi, Abdullah ibn Wayl al-Tumaymi, and Rifaa ibn Shaddad al-Bajli. My father was speaking to them in Classical Arabic that I had never heard him use. My father, who lived about a half century in Cairo, never gave up his Saidi dialect, and never spoke the Cairene dialect, so much so that I was too ashamed to use it in his presence or in the presence of my mother, but spoke like him ever since I became aware of such things, even up to that time when we said goodbye at noon on that Friday before my ill-fated trip when he looked at me for a long time.

My father addressed the notables gathered in that house in Kufa, "God has tested you by giving you a long life in which you'd be exposed to distractions of long duration. So pray to God that you don't end up like those of whom He said in the Glorious Qur'an, *Have we not granted you a long life for those who reflect? Then the warner came unto you.* The Commander of the Faithful Ali has said that the respite that God has given humans is sixty years, and you are all past that. You have received al-Husayn's messages and his messengers and he has asked you to support him in the beginning and the end, in public and private, but you denied him until he was killed right here. You neither supported him using your hands, nor argued in his favor using your tongues, nor did you offer him strength by giving him the support of your sons or the help of your money. So, what is your excuse before God and when you meet your Prophet, when his beloved grandchild, his own progeny and posterity, were killed in your midst? No, by God, you have no excuse not to kill his killer and his allies or die attempting to do so."

Then my location changed and I found myself listening with other people to my father. The place was the Kufa market inside a camel-hair tent. He was saying, "By God, I fear that we might be witnessing the time when life becomes a burden and catastrophes multiply, a day in which injustice extends to those of merit among us. You were so looking forward to the arrival of the family of our Prophet, promising them victory and urging them to come. When they did come, you wavered, you sat back, and you waited; you waited to see what would happen until the grandson of our Prophet, his progeny, his descendant, his flesh and blood was killed right in front of you. He kept crying for help but his cries were not heeded, asking for justice but he was denied. The evildoers used him for target practice with spears and arrows until they killed him."

As soon as my father finished, one of those present, whose name was Khalid ibn Saad ibn Nufayl stood up and said, "For me, I swear by God that if I knew that killing myself would erase my sin and would be accepted by God, I would do it. But that was something that people before us did and was forbidden to us. So, let God and all Muslims present be my witnesses, I hereby give everything that I own, except the weapon with which I fight my enemy, as alms to Muslims, to strengthen them in their fight against the unjust."

A man by the name of al-Mu'tamar Hanash ibn Rabia al-Kinani got up and said, "And I do the same and you be my witnesses."

Then another man whose name was not revealed to me rose and said, "And I too."

Another, a black man, said the same, as did several others. Silence descended and the twilight deepened. When I looked again, my father was gone. I felt a gash in my chest and so did the people gathered there. They stared shedding copious tears, tears of regret and of pained hearts, "If only we had stood by al-Husayn! If only we had died with him!" My eyes went around looking for my father but I was thinking: "Why the regret now that it was too late? He was there among you and when he was gone, when he died, your consciences awoke and all these feelings came to torment you. Man was created to regret."

I kept looking for my father but couldn't find him. I couldn't see where I was going and I got deeper and deeper into exile. I became confused; sitting gave me no rest nor could I sleep. Standing did not take my mind away from my worries, nor did walking. Seeking him out did not lead me to him. Regret and remorse ganged up on me from all sides and I succumbed to the murkiness obscuring my days and my outlook. My whole being focused on a past moment that had left me behind. It was the Wednesday preceding my departure. That Wednesday I did not know that all my father had left were thirteen days. I hadn't known the day I started on my trip that he had ten days remaining. The days preceding a specific day would seem ordinary; they would pass, whatever they were loaded with, without any warnings or omens, though it might be different for the person about to make his final departure. There would be something mysterious stirring inside him and warning of the approach of death without specifying anything, just suggesting it and intimating its secret steps, hinting that he was getting close to an unspecified area, that it was getting closer and that soon it would have him in its grip. Later on I found out that there were many signs that indicated that my father had felt his day drawing near earlier than I had conjectured. I will get to that and mention it if God, the Generous, gives me enough time to live so I can write it down. *No soul knows in what land it will die.* I asked myself again about that land where I would rest my head and I closed my eyes in preparation for departure. Where was it? What part of the world? Everything that happens to us in the few days preceding death does not give us pause, but when death does happen, we recall things, we remember the conversations and the minutest details, gestures, movements of the hands. Everything said or every glance exchanged becomes a significant portent of what was coming. It was very much like the first time one saw the face of the beloved and the last time after which there would be no meeting, no contact, no more times of joy, good news, surprises, differences, or ecstasy. One always remembered the beginning and the end.

On that Wednesday I was visiting a friend, conducting some kind of business. My friend's office was about a quarter-hour walk to my father's workplace. It was after one o'clock in the afternoon when I left and walked a few yards. Then it occurred to me to stop at the ministry, for my father usually went to the department where he worked to sign out. The idea delighted me, for he was always happy to see me. He would be confused at the beginning because of his sheer delight then he would ask me to stay a little and have some tea or coffee. He might ask me to accompany him to greet some of the old employees. He would introduce me as his eldest son to those who had known him for dozens of years, withstanding hardships and suffering just to raise his children. I told myself that he used to take us everywhere in our childhood and on the way he would grant our wishes. Now that we had grown up and had our own independent worlds and expanded our horizons with numerous relationships, we deserted him and no longer accompanied him. We did not know who his friends were or with whom he overcame his loneliness. I was happy with the idea of visiting my father and started on my way to the ministry. I stopped at the intersection before crossing the road. I looked around for fear of speeding cars. I saw an unoccupied taxi coming. I bent a little and the moment the driver was parallel to me I shouted "Bab al-Luq?" I didn't expect him to stop, especially since the roads leading to Bab al-Luq were always crowded and taxi drivers refused to go there. However, the driver stopped and motioned to me to get in. I repeated my question, "Bab al-Luq?" and he nodded. It seemed he was just starting work that day, as some drivers avoided refusing a fare at the beginning of their day, thinking it would affect their ability to get customers for the rest of the day and fearing surprises of the road. I quickly passed before the building of the ministry where my father was at that time. Now, however, he was gone forever from it and there was no possibility of my ever seeing him by chance when crossing the square leading to the entrance.

I looked at the building. My plan was no more than a passing thought, an unrealized idea and a desire that never materialized. I said to myself I'd visit him some other time. Thus I begrudged him a surprise that would have pleased him, killed a little joy that would have come unexpectedly to him on the thirteenth day remaining for him. If only I had known! If only I had done it!

I was in the city of Kufa at a time hundreds of years before my time when I was overcome by crushing regret so I cried, but my crying did not alleviate my anguish. How did I waste what I wasted when it was within reach, in my hand almost? Has the world so taken me away from him or have I gotten too preoccupied with the world? I made a fist. I gritted my teeth and my pain increased. At that point, with me close to perdition and facing extinction, I felt a kindly hand touching my head. I looked and saw al-Sheikh al-Akbar Muhyiddin ibn Arabi. I looked at him. He gave me permission and I got up from my fall and followed him as he walked. His image inspired me with great awe. The hair of his head was jet black. His silence continued for a long time and I was puzzled by the significance of his appearing to me at this stage in the station. Strangely enough, despite my focus on him and repeating to myself, "God has blessed me with the best companion and the best company after my suffering! May God enable me to follow in his footsteps and to emulate him so that I might attain his standing, amen!"—despite this, my regret was not alleviated or erased. Rather it grew stronger and more bitter, for now I was no longer in the shade, protected, but was rather out in the open, burning heat. Suddenly our master spoke and said, "Do you have anything for me?"

I immediately stated my secret desire, "Please intercede for me, O grand sheikh, at the Diwan, with its pure president and two luminous members, with my beloved, my companion of my migrations and the guide of my travels who has been away from me, even though the likes of me should not be asking for . . . ."

My Sheikh kept looking at me, "Do you have something?"

I cried out, "I would like this moment to be changed for good, that when I remember it I would remember that I dropped in on my father and visited him, when I recall it I would see him welcoming me and rejoicing at the sight of me and bidding me to sit next to him."

The grand sheikh said, "That's difficult to arrange."

"But nothing is too far from God's reach," I protested.

The grand sheikh said, "Yesterday you forgot, today you'll be forgotten!"

Then he added, "Use your sagacity, for we have indicated to you what was expected of you. We have stated it explicitly, bearing the consequences of doing so."

I said, "But today I am all alone."

He disappeared and I shouted, "Please give me an audience with my master, the martyr."

I was immediately filled with regret so strong that it knocked me out. After a while—I didn't know how long—I came to. My regret just kept rising, from the moment I realized my mistake and crime and shortcoming, increasing until I lost consciousness, and then I came to only to go through the whole process again with regret reborn stronger and stronger every time. I was unable to rid myself of it or to alleviate its impact, because it was inside me, so how could I get it out? Whenever it wore off, it came back stronger and I could find no relief from its fires burning me. I shouted, "Can't you alleviate my pain?"

No one answered me and no voice was heard in reply. At one point, our sheikh appeared again. He approached me in the midst of my torment, then he stood near me as I lay prostrate with regret, my head near his feet. I waited and when I heard him asking, "Are you sticking to your request?" I said, "Is that so impossible?"

Thereupon he took out of the folds of his cloak a sharp white blade. He held me by the hair of my head, and brandishing the blade, he brought it down, severing my head from my body. Then he detached it and held it in his hand. I was now looking at my headless body as the blood dripped from my neck and poured from my severed veins. I felt his hand relaxing its grip on my hair and for a moment I thought he was holding my head. Then I realized that I was floating, suspended. I was now in a different form.

The Station of the Star
I swear not by the positions of the stars. That, if only you knew, is a great oath.

I became a head without a body and a body without a head. I bewailed my condition and had great pity for myself when I saw with the eyes in my head my headless body the first time, then saw with the eyes of my sense my floating head, separated from its root. I realized that the beauty of the human body and its perfection were functions of its integrity, that it was together, that if one organ was separated from the rest of the body, it would appear meaningless, strange in itself, weak in appearance, fragile in essence, pitiable and sad. I now had two shadows after I had had only one that I followed and that followed me, folding it, extending it, and sometimes with it enveloping me. But now my arm appeared estranged from me, especially my hand that I had often clenched and opened and in which I held paper and pen. In the isolation of my organs was embodied the weakness of human nature given to unity, togetherness, oneness. I lamented my foot, my chest, and my penis that I had fondled in my childhood and beyond, which I had thrust into various vaginas. Now it was beyond my reach, disobedient and unresponsive. My hand couldn't play with it, encircle it, or rock it. It no longer went ahead of me, crossing feminine worlds. It now felt limp as if it were made of an old rag. I pitied myself. Each of my organs had its own orientation. Thus my head rose after I cast a lamenting glance at myself.

I was now floating in the sky above the city of Kufa. From on high I saw the city compressed, tightly held together by palm trees and other trees. Then I flew higher and saw Kufa and Karbala together. I recalled in sorrow my states in the Station of Thirst, seeing my beloved and master al-Husayn under siege, prevented from access to the waters of the Euphrates. I gazed with my new sight and saw the spot where my master's pure head was severed, a spot that no other mortal besides me knew now, and which no human could pinpoint except me—but I can't divulge it in this present written recording. I was given it exclusively during my ordeal and that which was given to me exclusively cannot be disseminated without permission, and that has not been given. Therefore I will hold my tongue.

I could not land at that spot and stay there and express my grief for what took place there. I also was not able to land in Karbala to stop at the resting place of my master and the master of my masters. How could I land when I had no feet to walk with? How could I knock on one of its doors when no hand obeyed my command? I couldn't shake hands and I couldn't point. My flight continued through gloomy sunset moments and I didn't know what I was going to do when the night came. Would I just land at random or take refuge in the peak of a mountain that would protect me from harm from unknown quarters? Or resort to a place that wouldn't harm or adversely affect what was left of me? I didn't know how I would lie down and how I would sleep and wake up, stretch out or kneel. I was governed by my terrestrial background and had no ability to visualize what would become of me. I said with my tongue, "Let me patiently endure what has befallen me." My flight continued for a long time and I was floating in the midst of the clouds, which I went through and which went through me. When the twilight began to deepen, I began to experience a strange, suspicious kind of hunger that was totally new to me: a pale but heavy kind of hunger that I had never experienced before, brought on, not by emptiness of the stomach nor fasting for a long time nor just an appetite. And because I was still capable of coining similes and metaphors, I tried to find something to compare it to. I had great difficulty but the closest thing to it was like when the bladder was full and one was unable to empty it. It probably was like the prelude to a fainting spell, yet it remained a hunger unlike anything I had ever known. At some point that I could not fix in time or place, I was called, "Gamal!"

I looked toward a distant point in the sky and, since I had no neck, I moved my eyelid and my eye impotently, like someone lying down, looking around but unable to change his position or his body. I saw a green dot, not emerald, not light green as in plants, not springtime or autumnal green, not close to yellow or blue (green, as we know, is a blend of the two primary colors, yellow and blue, and the predominance of one or the other determines the degree of greenness). It should be pointed out that among the sciences of this station was that pertaining to colors and their secrets. The green of that dot, however, was something that I had not seen the like of: radiant, shiny, but also subdued, as clear as the blue of the sea in deep parts and the silver of the moon on clear nights and the morning light. I gazed as the green dot kept coming closer to me. I stayed still and I saw that it was a bird, but I couldn't quite make out its features, coming from the direction of the qibla, going right then east then flying south and moving away to the north. It did all that as it constantly drew near me until it was now directly in front of me and, lo and behold, it was pure radiance, absolute light and from that were formed human features to which I clung in disbelief. When the human face of the bird was complete I shouted, "It's you! It's you!"

I didn't know him except in the published and broadcast pictures from the trial, clad in white behind the bars of the iron cage and also from shots of the attack as he rushed in broad daylight with his bare-chested companions into the core of the danger zone, storming the reviewing stand to save an era and a whole nation. I knew him from the televised short that showed him getting off the transport truck, lobbing the grenade, then going back in a few seconds to grab the machine gun. I knew him in my imagination and there he was in front of me, free of any shackles, unveiled on all sides, a green bird of light. There he was, fixing his wings to stay suspended in the air. I said with great sympathy, "Khalid! I spoke and you acted! I wished and others wished, but you performed!"

He nodded with his head whose features had become so fine and small, the size and form of a bird's head. He didn't answer me but brought his mouth close to my mouth. I was unable to embrace him because I had no arms and couldn't get closer to him because I was deprived of my free will, constrained by the one who controlled me, who willed for me to move forward, higher, or farther away. There was nothing I could do on my own. My position was fixed, facing him. I could embrace him only with my eyes and my gaze. I had great sadness in my heart that I wished I could express, but my mouth looked at his mouth just like a baby eying his mother's breast before nursing. Thereupon he dropped into my mouth three drops of a sweet delicious syrup which tasted like pure honey, even though it was not honey. I tasted it and liked it very much. I knew he had fed me something like manna from heaven. I opened my eyes, quite full, with hunger only a distant memory. I forgot the taste of any other food I had ever had. Khalid flew higher and stopped at a certain spot above me, looking at my head as if reassuring himself about me. At that point I saw a red gap in his chest, a spot of deep red light shedding real blood as if the light had veins, exactly in the heart. I cried, "Was it painful?"

His voice came to me from the east, "God gave me the strength to do what I had to do, but He also gave me the strength to bear the pain."

I saw the blood drops blending with the cosmic space, orbiting with the planets, getting born with the new ones and not dying off with those doomed for extinction. I saw the blood extending the redness accompanying the break of dawn on the two banks of the Nile, dyeing the tips of palm trees and the tops of the towering trees.

In the dark of the night, one drop settles in the form of a star in the sky, a small star among those crowding the sky but it has unique characteristics and special, fine features, some apparent and some hidden. Among these characteristics is that that star appears only in the sky above the Nile Valley and can only be viewed and monitored from the hills of that valley: the Muqattam hills, Attaqa Mountain, Galala Mountain, Mount Moses, and from the dunes of the Western Desert, never disappearing in autumn or spring but moving a little, just a little farther during the summer and winter. It shines as the crops reach full ripeness and trees full bloom, when the veins of mines sparkle in the light of the stars. Unlike all other stars, you can pinpoint its position and its dark red light in the sky crowded with stars. Here I will try to convey to you some of the characteristics exclusive to this star, wondrous among its kind. In food, for instance, the Pleiades are assigned sweetness; Ursa Major bitterness; Alcor sourness, and Sirius unctuousnesss, but to the star Khalid is assigned good-tasting food. In colors, jet black is assigned to Alcor; Ursa Major yellowish white; Sirius blondness, the Pleiades what results from the mixture of two colors; and to the star Khalid, dark red, blue of the sea, and foggy green. In places, Ursa Major is assigned barren mountains, deserts, and prisons; Sirius rough terrain, sites of fires, and fortresses; the Pleiades plains, plateaus, uninhabited depressions, houses of kings and sultans; Alcor sands, dunes, permanent and seasonal markets, houses situated by roadsides and street corners leading to orchards; and the star Khalid even grounds, well-trodden footpaths, dewy places, shores and banks, and ancient buildings. In birds, Ursa Major is assigned cranes, swans, and ostriches; Sirius roosters and turtle doves; the Pleiades evening birds and night birds; Alcor migrating sparrows and flocks; and the star of Khalid eagles, nightingales, and vultures. Of the phases of life, Ursa Major is assigned old age; the Pleiades youth; Sirius early youth, Alcor childhood, and the star Khalid the beautiful age that is gone. In body parts, Ursa Major is assigned the head; the Pleiades the chest, the waist, and the buttocks; Sirius the liver; Alcor the arms, fingertips, and the legs; and the star Khalid the heart and the veins. In kinship Ursa Major is assigned grandparents; Alcor, siblings; the Pleiades, mothers; Sirius, fathers; and the star Khalid the children and the children of the children. In moral character, Ursa Major is assigned confused thinking; the Pleiades thinking and reflection, Sirius anger and foolishness; Alcor pride, individualism, intelligence, and discretion; and the star Khalid dreaming and revolution. In trees Ursa Major is assigned camphor; Sirius Persian roses; Alcor pines, cedars, and white sandals; the Pleiades ebony; and the star Khalid palm trees and willows. In sounds Ursa Major is assigned mumbling; Sirius speaking in a low voice; Alcor whispering; the Pleiades shouting, and the star Khalid the baby's first cry.

Dear reader, this is part of a larger whole and that itself is but a portion of the entire picture. The secret is great; raise your eyes, gaze at the east, and you will see. Don't give up; its faint light will draw your attention and the longer you look the more clearly its nature will reveal itself to you and show you little bits of its secret. Remember, this star is a drop of the blood of Khalid who saved you and saved me. This is what I have learned as I floated in the air across space. Among the things I wish to say is that there will come a time when it will guide everyone traveling by land and sea or on the Nile. Discovering it as a fixed landmark, however, will require time, expertise, experience, long familiarity and precise observation, exactly as it took mankind a long time and many untold years to discover the positions of Ursa Major, Alcor, the Pleiades, Sirius, Cassiopeia, Saturn, Jupiter, and the borders of the galaxy. Here I am pointing and alerting, not begrudging what I've learned nor holding back that which I've come to know and that which has been exclusively revealed to me at the peak of my ordeal after my head had been severed from my body. Here I am screaming in the hope that my people will see what I've seen and know what I've known and be guided to the position of this star as I've been. So, please take heed.

The Station of Distress
And from the evil of darkness as it grows intense.

O God, All Hearing and All Knowing, please alleviate the pain of my wounds. I wished my conversation with Khalid had lasted longer, but he soared higher, leaving me behind. However, contentment and satisfaction after that wondrous fullness I felt after he fed me let me know that I had received some mercy and that I might not be condemned to the eternal anguish of regret. May God make me, the readers, and the listeners worthy of the utmost mercy, amen. I learned that the temporary blessing I was granted could be attributed to my time on earth, even though I was not given its details but was promised knowledge of them later on, for mysterious, hidden reasons. I consigned my ignorance to a corner of my head and gave in to my floating condition. Things kept changing; I bent with the harsh wind and swayed with gentle breezes until I saw, from a very high vantage point, scenes from ancient history. I swirled in space and, given my sharp vision, saw my father and Gamal Abdel Nasser walking in the desert, close to the Euphrates. With them was a group of men whose number I couldn't count, but I estimated it to be no more than a few dozen. I was able to make out some features. I could see my friend who was martyred at midday on Friday. I also saw Mazin Abu Ghazala and a number of his companions who were martyred after him, some of whose photographs were printed and posted on the walls, then ripped out when the enemy became a friend and their delegations came to us in droves without fighting. I saw Khalid's four companions. I came to understand that they had exerted great efforts, that they planted the seeds of regret in people's minds and awakened the consciences of those who did not lift a finger to aid al-Husayn. Regret now grew stronger and stronger and some people here and there rose, demanding revenge for al-Husayn's blood. I didn't know where they were heading or whether they were seeking out one person in particular or some of those responsible for the murder of al-Husayn,

209

especially since Gamal Abdel Nasser had identified them and indicated where they were to be found. He sent secret scouts after them to monitor their every movement so that it might be possible to pounce on everyone who had shot an arrow or slingshot at the beloved or wounded him or any of his family and supporters.

As for my father, he sought out those who had forsaken the beloved. He lit a fire in their chests that was difficult to put out. That was the beginning of the people's regret and sorrow for failing al-Husayn and causing his death even up to this day and until the end time comes. I noticed the onset of night and hovered in the darkness around them. My sense of smell led me to my father and I recalled anew those distant moments when we embraced and were close to each other in harmony. I saw my right hand leveling the rough floor for him to lie down and my left hand shooing the night insects away from him and his friends. That felt strange and novel to me, to see a part of my body not subject to my orders or my control, moving on secret signals from me even though it was unconnected to me or to parts of me. I hovered above them, watching the dangers of the night; perhaps I could warn them or alert them. How would my voice reach them? That I didn't know, but I said to myself that perhaps intentions would find ways. As the morning drew near and broke, Gamal Abdel Nasser got up and thanked and praised God. After the morning prayer he spoke to the gathering. His voice was sad and his tones full of grief, reminiscent of his appearance on the eighth of June, a Thursday evening, when he announced the defeat then his resignation. That was how he started now: "God has willed that we separate today, so please be patient and bear the hardship. . . ."

Then he arrayed them for battle. They numbered about seventy, some mounted, some not. It seemed to me that they were fewer. He placed Mazin on the right and Husayn, Khalid's friend, on the left and gave the banner to my father. Then he ordered firewood and reeds to be placed in a low-lying patch of ground that looked like a trench in case they were attacked from the rear. This proved useful.

From where I hovered in space I looked on in surprise and dis-
gust: I saw the one whose name I couldn't bear to pronounce,
the one who succeeded Abdel Nasser in ruling Egypt, may he be
damned by God, approach and stay in the back, much the same
coward he was when he lived. I saw him scheming and pushing
others to carry out his machinations while at the same time saving
his own skin. He had with him several thousand troops, servants
of foreign monopolies, troops wearing uniforms of the army of
Yazid ibn Mu'awiya, the murderer of al-Husayn, soldiers wearing
the Mossad's secret service uniform, troops from the American
Rapid Deployment Force, mercenaries of unknown identities,
bankers, owners of soda-pop companies, contractors, brokers, and
antiquities dealers. They were raising their banners, which bore
advertisements for heating and cooling air conditioning, side-by-
side refrigerators, cars, silk cloaks, fighter jets used in forty armies,
a new nail polish for women, electric shavers, and an advertised
bank interest. Mazin wanted to shoot an arrow at them but Abdel
Nasser prevented him, saying that he didn't want the first shot to
come from his side.

He looked at their huge numbers, their weapons, and heard
their calls for surrender. One Israeli announcer was shouting in a
megaphone: "Stop and think. Surrender and you will be saved. We
guarantee you a drink of water, food, and medicine." Thereupon
Gamal Abdel Nasser raised his hands in supplication and said, "O
God, you've given me confidence in every calamity and hope in
every hardship. I have been through so many ordeals weakening
the heart and burdening the mind, misfortunes in which friends
were defeated and enemies gloated. In these catastrophes, I have
resorted to you for help and support. I didn't know that all of these
enemies were uniting with one purpose: to get rid of me, to wipe
me out, and to distort my reputation. I was not aware of the one
leading them. It was I who pushed him to stand next to me and
appointed him as my deputy during my absence and presence. I
confess, now that it's too late, that there was a veil covering my

eyes for some time and that the price I paid, that my country and people paid, was exorbitant."

Silence prevailed for a few moments, then someone among them shouted. It turned out it was an Israeli officer wearing the paratroopers' crimson beret. He shouted, "Is Ibrahim al-Rifai among you?"

My father shouted in reply, "Yes, there he is," pointing to my friend who had been martyred midday, Friday the nineteenth of October.

The Israeli officer shouted, "Is Ibrahim Zaydan among you?"

My father answered, "Yes, there he is," pointing at my friend who was martyred on hillock number seven, east of the Suez Canal, on the morning of the tenth of October.

"Is Ibrahim Abdel Tawwab among you?"

"Yes, there his is," pointing to my friend who was martyred on the twenty-fourth of January, one hundred and thirty-four days after the siege in Kabrit, east of the canal.

The Israeli officer started laughing uncontrollably. "Why did you fight? Why did you train and struggle? Why were you killed? Our flags are flying high in your country. My soldiers have passed in front of your houses. They have taken photographs of your tombs. They have flirted with your daughters. As for you, you have been forgotten and no one will ever remember your names. In days that you have not even witnessed, your countrymen are afraid of praising you or even mentioning you."

My father shouted, "I'll burn you!"

The Israeli announcer kept repeating, "Stop and think. Surrender and you'll be saved."

My father said, "May God take him to the fires of hell!"

The Israeli paratrooper riding a horse dashed ahead. Between him and where my father was there was a low-lying stretch, so the horse stumbled on a stone and his foot got stuck in the stirrup. The horse kept hitting every stone and tree until the officer was killed. Ibrahim al-Rifai was standing on a hill, looking distressed, his hands on his hips exactly as I had seen him during the long days of the war. There was, however, an annoyance that made his features unfamiliar to me. He approached my father and asked him, "Is what that Israeli officer said true?"

My father fell silent and was at a loss for what to say. Al-Rifai looked at the body of the Israeli officer quizzically. Richard Allen, an American intelligence officer who had followed the situation said, "I was in the front among the mounted troops that stepped forward to fight Abdel Nasser and his friends. I had been appointed as a special guard so I advanced, hoping to hit him in the head and get a bonus and a promotion, but when I saw what happened to the Israeli paratrooper I thought it was a bad omen. I remembered the daring they displayed at the reviewing stand after all the reports had asserted that his people had lost their will to fight, that they had gotten preoccupied with their daily bread to the exclusion of all else after we made it hard-to-get for them. So my enthusiasm waned and I backed out. Now I'm not going to get myself into the trouble I got myself into then."

I saw an awe-inspiring venerable old man, born in Cairo, where he lived and died. It was my mentor of great esteem and honor and it was he who advised me to stick to the epiphanies because a sleeping person would see that which a wide-awake person did not. Ibn Iyas came close to Abdel Nasser and asked for permission to speak. He was given permission, so he stepped forward and spoke to the gathering, "Listen, people. You are being led by the lowest of the low, the likes of whom I have never known. If he had one-tenth the courage of the most cowardly among you, let him step forward now. He can hear me. You brutal, perverse lout: didn't you rush to Abdel Nasser on your knees? Weren't you too cowardly to meet him alone or to contact him except through an intermediary? Have you even addressed him with just his name and without titles as you claimed? Didn't you hail everything he did or caused to happen? Then he appointed you successor and you turned your back on all he stood for. You became hostile to the poor and the destitute and those who worked hard on their behalf. You incited people against him and against his principles after he was gone and couldn't answer or defend himself. And you've given up a lot, worse than Khayr Bek, your predecessor who handed Egypt over to the Ottomans. You didn't respect the blood these men have given and you did not cherish their memories and now you come, hiding behind their numbers and weapons as they try to avenge the killing of the son of the daughter of the Messenger of God, preventing them from reaching the water of the Euphrates just as the murderers of our beloved and master did. You deny water to this gathering that has the purest of purposes."

Al-Rifai shook his head in sorrow and regret, "So what the Israeli officer said was true! We died for nothing!"

The Zionist announcer kept repeating, "Stop and think. Surrender and you'll be safe."

Shabath ibn Rab'i, one of the killers of al-Husayn shouted at Ibn Iyas, "Shut up, you senile old sheikh! You've talked a lot, so quit. Aren't you content with what you've written in your obscure books that nobody reads? Let everybody get thirsty like those before them."

Ibn Iyas's voice rises, "May God keep you thirsty on the day of judgment. You are the worst of the worst!"

The brutal lout ordered that he be shot. An arrow hit him in the shoulder and Ibn Iyas was wounded.

I saw my father shouting, "O followers of the murderers of al-Husayn. You, slaves, dregs of all nations, servile informers, brokers, murderers of the children of the prophets. Treachery is an inherent quality in you, the worst fruit."

William Casey, director of the CIA, asked, "Who's that?"

He was told that he was a poor man, that the newspapers did not publish his name, that he had not been seen in receptions, that none of the higher-ups had followed his funeral cortege, nor was it led by a representative from the presidency, and there were no wreaths; throughout his life he had never held a dollar, had no knowledge of travel agencies, had seen the sea only twice when he went to Alexandria on official business, had never spent an entire hour in an air-conditioned room, and that all his life he wore clothes made of local fabrics.

Moshe Dayan, laughing, said, "Are we fighting people like that? We'll surely be victorious."

The announcer kept repeating, "Surrender and you'll be safe. There's a comfortable life ahead of you. Don't be a loser. Those who called you have abandoned you. Those who promised you support have betrayed you. You are surrounded on all sides. There's no hope for you. Fighter, stop and think. Put down your spear; destroy your sword, hand over your arrows."

My father stepped forward, carrying the banner in one hand and brandishing a sword in the other. He was the first to step forward in the fighting. He fought hard, killing more than forty men. Then they ganged up on him. I saw a blade cutting his leg. It was then that I learned where that deep scar in his right leg had come from. I had often looked closely at it as a child, and when I sat in front of him playing with him I touched it. As an adult I saw it when his gallabiya rose a little, but I averted my eyes and didn't inquire. That scar must have disappeared now that his body had decomposed in the grave and been lost forever like the rest of his features.

I flew high and I flew low and when the dust settled I saw the banner in the hand of my friend Ibrahim Abdel Tawwab. There was no trace of my father. I busied myself with looking for him but I didn't see him and I wondered, even though my wondering now was less than before because of how much I had seen and how strange it had been. Let me tell you, intelligent reader, that I'd been made to understand that I'd meet my father other times, that that would not be my last experience with him, that what I was witnessing and what I had witnessed would not be the last stop, for the journey was still on-going and only God, may He be praised, He whom I worship as the One with no partners, knew where it would take me. Realizing that reassured me and I considered it evidence of mercy and kindness toward me, even though my head had been severed from the nape, I had no body, and my blood was dripping and mingling with the clouds, the rainbow, and the twilight preceding sunrise. I didn't know how I was going to meet my father.

Would it be as I have met him before or would I hover around him, separated by a long distance while I was lost in exile, observing what was happening? I saw Mazin Abu Ghazala stepping forward, fighting like a lion until he was killed. Abdel Nasser prayed for him, "May God have mercy on him. May he go to Paradise."

Ibrahim Zaydan stepped forward. I looked more closely trying to follow them but I couldn't. The dust was stirred up, blood flowed, arrows came down like rain. I heard Abdel Nasser tell his companions, "Rise, may God have mercy on you, to inevitable death. These arrows are messengers to you."

Lieutenant Colonel Muhammad Ebeid and a baker, name unknown, who had been killed on Marasina Street in the neighborhood of Sayyida Zeinab during the 1919 Revolution, stepped forward and said to Abdel Nasser, "Peace upon you, Abu Khalid. We've come to be killed before you and to defend you."

"God have mercy on your souls," Abdel Nasser said and motioned to them to come closer. They did, their eyes full of tears. He said, "Why are you crying, my dear soldiers? I hope you will soon be happy!"

They said, "May God enable us to ransom our nation with our lives. We are not crying for ourselves, but over you. We see you surrounded by those who once claimed to be loyal to you and to your principles, standing between you and the water."

"May God recompense you well," he said.

They said, "Peace upon you and God's mercy, friend of the oppressed and the weak."

He said, "Peace upon you and God's mercy and His blessings."

They engaged the enemy close to where Abdel Nasser stood and were killed.

At that point I heard Ariel Sharon say to the brutal lout, "Do you know who we are fighting? We are fighting the valiant knights of this age, men of discernment who are willing to die for their cause. Despite their small number and the difficulty of their circumstances, they kill all our men seeking combat with them. I thought our sudden and surprise appearance would eradicate them, I thought they'd surrender."

Then General Moshe Dayan attacked Abdel Nasser's right flank but they stood their ground and got down on their knees, pointing the spears. The horses did not move forward and when they turned, Gamal Abdel Nasser's companions shot them with arrows. They felled John Foster Dulles, Mordechai Gur, and dear Henry. Then a formation of the Rapid Deployment Force attacked Abdel Nasser's left flank. By the time the thick dust stirred up by the attack had settled, Mustafa Abu Hashim, the petroleum worker who grew up and died in Suez, Oweis the radish seller, and Murgan the Nubian, had all been killed.

Abdel Nasser walked over to them and said, "God have mercy on you."

General Abdel Moneim Riyad approached them and said, "Losing you gives me great pain. May you all be blessed with paradise."

Mustafa Abu Hashim said, "May God recompense you with good news."

The general said, "Had I not known that I'd be soon following you, I'd have asked you to entrust me with all that you deem important to you."

Mustafa said, "I entrust you with this," and he pointed to Gamal Abdel Nasser's banner, then recited, "They supported you during their life / And at their death they passed on the torch of support to those who followed."

Then Jimmy Carter and a group of his companions attacked Abdel Nasser's companions. Ahmad Urabi with ten of his companions rose to fight them and they defeated them and killed Alexander Haig while eight of Abdel Nasser's supporters, including Ahmad Urabi, were killed. Each man would approach Abdel Nasser and say to him, "Peace upon you and God's mercy, friend of the poor and defender of the fatherland." Abdel Nasser would answer by saying, "And peace be upon you." Then he would recite from the Qur'an: "*. . . and among them are those who paid with their lives and others awaiting [but] they have not changed at all.*"

Before long they were all dead except for seven who stood to protect Abdel Nasser from the final attacks. Only seven, among them a shoeshine man who had been killed during the indiscriminate shelling of the city of Port Said and who had been buried under the rubble and about whom nobody asked even after a long absence, because he was a stranger. His body was not recovered at the time of his death. Also among those killed was a boy wearing an old costume and a small green turban. I didn't know to which era he belonged, but I saw him after receiving a broad and deep wound in his collarbone. I also saw General Shafiq Sidrak, one of those I had known from before and who had been martyred on the sixteenth of October. Among those killed were also Gawad Husni, Isam al-Dali, and a man whose name I didn't know. There was also a Moroccan man who had come to Egypt for a temporary stay but who had lived there some time ago. He had heard of the threat posed by the Franks so he went out to engage in a struggle on the path of God and fought and was killed. Each of these stepped forward one after the other until only the boy was left. He embraced Gamal Abdel Nasser tightly, then stepped forward on foot. General Rafael Eitan went up and hit him, whereupon the boy was felled and as he was dying called out, "Dear father, peace be upon you from me!"

Arrows and blazing shots rained down, making Abdel Nasser's shield look like a hedgehog. He lay on the ground for a long time and if they wanted to kill him, they could have. The brutal lout shouted from a distance, "What's wrong with you? What are you waiting for? Kill him!"

They ganged up on him from all sides. General Ariel Sharon hit him on his right shoulder. John Foster Dulles hit him on his left shoulder. Ronald Reagan hit him on the shoulder, then Menachem Begin took out the spear and stabbed him in the side of his chest. Gerald Ford shot him with an arrow that hit him in the throat. Then they signaled to the brutal lout, giving him permission. He advanced, protected by them, his chest covered with a bulletproof vest. On his wrist he wore a watch that warned him of impending danger and he held a baton that shot a paralyzing substance at anyone who got near him to try to do him harm. Later on the *Washington Post* said that protecting him had cost American taxpayers three billion dollars, thus making him the most expensive slave ever in history. When he got close to Abdel Nasser, they gave him a sword. He closed his eyes and in one fell swoop severed the neck. Thereupon they all took part in despoiling him. General Alexander Haig took his shirt. The contractor Uthman Ahmad Uthman took his pants. Menachem Begin took his shield. A velvet scarf was taken by the wife of the brutal lout, may God damn them both. Eliyahu Ben-Elissar took his ring. The announcer who kept shouting one warning after another took one of Abdel Nasser's sandals.

I was hovering, feeling slaughtered by pain in addition to being truly slaughtered. There I was, hearing and seeing but not doing. I couldn't. Here was a beloved whose cycle had ended. My anguish reached its apex and I was unable to cope. I felt a total loss enveloping what was left of me. His absence was going to be a very long one: I was not going to listen to his promises nor would his voice be able to dispel my sorrow, nor would I be able to see him. When his name would be mentioned we would say, "He was here, alive, and here he gave a speech and here he appeared and promised. He was."

I suddenly came to and became aware of my immediate surroundings. I found that I was rising high in the air. I saw all around me, from east to west, enveloped in utter blackness. I looked more closely to make sure and then I saw a great wonder: all the women of Egypt, from successive and different eras: from tents, bamboo huts, and mud-brick homes. They had different modes of dress and head coverings. The one thing they all had in common was that they were all dressed in black and were wailing, crying, supplicating, lamenting the passing of the departed lion, saddened by the ship that was now stranded in the mud.

I saw my grandmother as I had known her in my childhood, tall and thin, wearing her long Saidi robe. I saw my grandmother, my father's mother, blind. I saw a great-grandmother who had lived a long time ago. I saw my mother, my sister, our old neighbor, my wife, my female colleagues, and all the women I had chanced to see on the streets of my city and the villages I had been to. I saw poor old women sitting on the ground near mausoleums, shrines, and fountains for the dead. I saw Potiphar's wife and Shagar al-Durr and women in poor neighborhoods who went out in demonstrations. I saw women with uncovered hair and veiled women, women who read and spoke various foreign languages and others who could not tell one letter from another. I saw women who came out of the alleys on that dark night on which Gamal Abdel Nasser declared he was stepping down. They were barefoot and didn't know where they were going in the dark in the frightened city.

I soared even higher and couldn't hear their voices. I realized that I had seen a gathering the likes of which hadn't been seen in our terrestrial world and that if they had stood in one line they would have encircled our planet earth seven times at the equator. I wished I could've wandered among them, listened to their languages and dialects, some of which were already extinct and which I couldn't understand, and some of which had letters as yet unborn. However, I moved away, alas, and slowed down, sadness having lodged in my heart. I told myself: Patience in the face of these catastrophes!

I thought of my father: where was he? Where? As I almost closed my eyes in despair and turned my face away from my very existence, I caught a glimpse of my master, so I lowered my eyelids as I couldn't lower my face. I said to myself: Rejoice, my heart, and sing. I still have room between the sky and the earth. My condition immediately changed and I experienced summits of human joy. I wished I could postpone the moment of meeting so that its sweetness would not be over and become a past I couldn't recall. I moved toward him slowly, postponing the moment of bliss and ecstasy. Seeing his face made me forget all my travails and troubles. I hovered around him and when he gave me permission, I landed on his right shoulder, wetting his clothes with my blood because my neck never stopped bleeding. I calmed down; my consolation was that I was like him, with a severed head. I was not concerned with asking about my fate or what would happen and whether my head would be reunited with my body. I was so happy to see him that I became a conduit between the rough and the smooth, the hot and the cold, sadness and joy, and the dark and the light. I was all movement inside, so much so that my severed head became big enough for the whole world. I couldn't stay within myself. I understood the good news. I took shelter on my master's shoulder just as a child would seek shelter in the embrace of his father who had returned after a long absence.

I looked and saw Gamal Abdel Nasser's body, naked and without a head. I was made to understand that my father was walking now, that he was struggling in a hard place. Once again I started enjoying being close to the beloved and breathing longingly in his embrace. I said, "A stranger is one shunned by his beloved."

My master and master of my masters replied, "Rather a stranger is one who is reunited with his beloved."

I said, "That being so, please allow me to cry over conditions that led to the separation." I began to weep, repeating, "*God is sufficient for me and the best support.*"

The Station of Togetherness

Perhaps the flowing of tears would cure passion,
Or give comfort from troubling, secret thought.

Creator of the original and the shadow and everything between them! If He wills it, He withholds and if He wills it, He bestows! Splitter of the fruit and the pit! If He wills it, He brings together and if He wills it, He divides! Re-weaver of the hole, if He wills it, He brings closer and if He wills it, He will rend asunder! He answers the prayers of those who call on Him, giving to whomever He wills and denying whomever He wills. He placed me in the Station of Togetherness even though I was incomplete and he who is incomplete should not ask about what made him incomplete.

221

I was just a head, my body being far away. I couldn't settle down. I had no side to lie on. The most difficult kind of travel is when a man travels inside himself. The world, in that case, passes him by without him attaining it. This is one of the torments of life in this world. He placed me in this station when I had no legs or arms. Thus I moved from the Station of Distress to the Station of Togetherness, which was a difficult station.

Of the days of the week this station has Friday. Of the moments of the daylight it has that between one second and another; of the night, the moment it reaches the middle: does it belong to the day just passed or to the one to come? Of the months it has February, the shortest: all other months precede or follow it, surrounding it as older brothers surround the youngest. Of the colors it has the rainbow with all its hues. Of nature, the maturing of the leaves in the summer before their separation from the branches in autumn.

It has many branches of knowledge, among them the knowledge of meeting, the knowledge of adding one letter to another to have meaning, the knowledge of planets aligned in a straight line, the conjunction of the sun with the moon, the appearance of stars, and the knowledge of tracing things back to their origins, the knowledge of cessation and the reason for it, the knowledge that *everyone on earth will perish*, the knowledge that *no soul knows in which land it will die*, and *no soul knows what it will earn tomorrow*. The Station of Togetherness also has the knowledge of ancient moments, knowledge of length and width and what happens when they get close to each other, the knowledge of lovers' talk, the knowledge of those fond of reunion, the knowledge of the certainty of separation, the knowledge of the last moment after which we will not see beloveds that we know or places to which we were attached or in which we've spent some time. The knowledge of our silent repetition, "Are we going to see what we've seen again?" "Will there be a return?" To this station also belongs the knowledge of recalling old times, over and over again; knowledge of unknown longings and the knowledge of veneration when passing old ruins, uprooted trees, water that has dried up in old canals, ancient waterwheels that have stopped moving, and coffeehouses that have closed their doors, dispersing patrons, strangers, and itinerants. To it belongs also the knowledge of the passing of time, the knowledge of lips touching the first time and the last time, for who remembers those two moments of being together with his beloved?

As for the branches of knowledge that have to do with me in this station, they are numerous. They include the knowledge of my weakness and lack of resources. For I'll have you know, perceptive recipient, that I am weak, weaker than you imagine, and gentler than you think. My heart cannot recall old times or my love that will not come back. I also cannot reconnect a tree leaf with the branch from which it has been separated. Among my branches of knowledge is knowing the difference between a day at the end of which I expect my father to come home, or his coming to my house when I became head of my own household and a father in my own right, or passing by the ministry building, knowing that he is there—and a day that will pass while knowing that I'll never see him, my certainty that I will never hear his footsteps on the staircase, his knocks on the door. I have also been given the knowledge of forgetting voices, their flavors, their reverberation, those voices with which we've lived a long time, listening to and conversing with them; when they depart we think they are with us, that they'll never be absent, until that moment comes in which we discover suddenly that we'll recall them, that we've forgotten them, that they are gone forever, that their sounding from time to time in the human memory does not indicate their presence at all.

I remembered how I was blessed when I went through the House of Lingering Sounds, but, like all blessings it was temporary. These are abundant branches of knowledge; if I were to elaborate on them and explain them in detail it would take me a long time. This would satisfy, please, and calm me, but I am afraid, dear recipient, that that might cause you to be bored and impatient. Therefore I will move on and tell you about my departure, in this station, to a time when I had not been born yet, a time whose air I hadn't breathed and whose spatial formation and features had not been seen by my eyes.

My head floated in the thirties of our twentieth century in which I was born and in which I might die; *no soul knows in which land it will die.* I saw a vision that pleased me since it never happened to anybody else: I hovered in the sky above al-Husayn Square in Cairo, seeing but unseen by anyone. I went around the thin, graceful towering minaret and I trained my eyes on the shops and the old coffeehouse. I saw him, my origin, the trunk from which my branch grew. I saw my father, the nearby beloved who went far away. With his departure and death, part of my life that might be longer, richer, and deeper than the remaining part, was gone. Part of my history died. *Man has only that for which he has striven.* Yesterday I forgot and tomorrow I'll be forgotten. I was now without a roof and the wind could sweep me away. I was ready for things to come full circle and the vicissitudes to take full hold of me. I was no longer at a safe distance from them.

I saw my father, to whose voice I would not listen in my remaining terrestrial life. I won't have conversations with him, as the time for pleasurable exchanges and joy at seeing him, especially in my childhood, was gone. I used to take delight in my early years and be happy and have sweet dreams, reassured that tomorrow would come, when I slept next to him and opened my eyes in the morning and found him by my side. My joy would increase when I learned that the day was a holiday and that he would stay home with us. But when I grew a little older and became a big boy, the times of closeness were gone and I no longer slept next to him. If only the old days would come back, if only I could be near him, talk to him. I wish I were granted a meeting! I was saying that as I saw him from where I was hovering and following his steps as he crossed the square. I saw him at a time when it was impossible for anyone else to see him. He was coming from the Station of Distress where he was carrying the banner and brandishing his Yemeni sword. I saw that the scar on his leg had not healed yet. I stared and saw dust in his hair. Those were grains of sand from the desert where he had been under siege with his companions. I knew where those grains of sand had come from but I didn't know where they would go after they left his hair. At that point I was given an accounting suitable for the situation, so I saw those grains of sand scattered over seventy spots on earth after leaving his head and after his final departure. If I were to list all of those spots, if I were to recount their different courses from then until now, it would fill a volume that would be too heavy to carry. I traced the journey of every grain and knew how they made it to where they ended up. With the accounting completed, I landed on the balcony surrounding the minaret. And, given my ability to be aware of several things at the same time, such as listening to many conversations and following each separately or seeing what was happening in two or more places far apart, I saw my father standing in front of al-Ajam coffeehouse. It was an old coffeehouse that disappeared in the fifties of our twentieth century. In its place now, during your time, gentle recipient, several shops are standing. Their features changed and different buildings were erected, but the ground on which he stepped remained the same. Many were the places he frequented, the doors he knocked on, the cushions he leaned on, and the chairs and benches he sat on that vanished or were disassembled and their parts scattered. I wished I could follow the traces of everything that my father had touched or his eyes had seen, as perhaps they would preserve a faint trace of him, but my wish was not granted. I, however, received a beautiful promise that it might happen at the right time and place.

There he was, my father, hesitating, not entering the coffeehouse. If he sat by himself, he would have to order a cup of tea or coffee that would cost him five milliemes at a time when he needed every single millieme. He had been without a job for some time, since his hands let go of Gamal Abdel Nasser's banner, since he left that battle somehow, and since he was selected to remain behind to tell several generations at different times what happened so that it would not be lost like so many other things. But currently he had no source of income. He was alone and his previous savings were running out as the big hopes began to fade and he wasn't getting any younger.

There my father was, catching a glimpse of his relatives: Ibrahim, a man I had known when I was young and later on in life. This relative of my father was the last one my father visited on the night of Tuesday, the twenty-eighth of October. My father was encouraged, so he entered the coffeehouse and shook hands with Ibrahim, who asked him how things were. My father told him that in the whole world there was nothing to look forward to, that things were very tight. Ibrahim said that hope for an easing in the situation was at hand, that Khalaf Bey was coming soon. There, Khalaf Bey was listening to my father. My father was now bowing his head in silence. This bowing of the head was one of several events that had led to changing many things that he had thought would not change, to an easing in a situation he thought would never improve. There were different occasions on which he had bowed his head thus in silence, each taking place at a different time. Some of those times he was aware of it and at other times he was not. He didn't make a connection between them and the order in which they happened and their consequences, each leading to something he hadn't expected or to a change in intentions that he didn't imagine. Those were moments that we experienced without noticing, but sooner or later the change took place. There he was, hiding his fear and anxiety, while deep down he was hopeful. Those were feelings of which we were ignorant, about which we had no inkling. Such was that particular moment, which had recurred to my father several times. The last time that he recalled it was Sunday the twenty-sixth of October. One of the amazing things was that he had recalled the moment in my presence several times, but I didn't notice or didn't pay attention. And how could I make the connection between an almost imperceptible change in his features and what was going on in his mind? That, by the way, was a self-contained, mysterious branch of knowledge with countless secrets. Amazingly, my father, as he recalled that moment, always feared that it might not end the way it had in that distant past time. I myself, dearly beloved, experienced such a feeling in a different situation. That happened while spending the evening in the house of an intimate friend who invited us to dinner one night then brought out a projector and we watched six short films, one after the other. We saw the car pulling the 130-millimeter cannon stopping in front of the reviewing stand and Khalid getting out of it, then his lightning-fast return to grab his machine gun and his daring assault to put an end to that despicable time and to finish off the brutal lout, to avenge what happened and what was happening and what he had done in the Station of Distress when he denied access to water to those calling for avenging the killing of our master al-Husayn. Every time we saw a new film and the car stopped I was afraid that the moments would not end the way they had actually ended. I was afraid that Khalid would be obstructed, that he would not finish that which he had begun. As if, every time, I was living the event without knowing the outcome.

Khalaf Bey was listening with an earnest face like someone in authority who could get things done. After listening, and without looking at my father, he asked him to write an application and bring it; perhaps it might work. My father raised his voice in a prayer and afterward he left. I saw him nearby holding a white blank sheet of paper. He was at a loss. He had to catch up with Khalaf Bey before he left. That was an opportunity that might not be available another time. But, who would write the application? If . . . if only he had received some education, if only he had enrolled in al-Azhar! It was not proper for him to ask Khalaf Bey to write the application for him.

At that point something amazing happened and even though so many amazing things had happened to me that I was no longer amazed by anything, what happened really left me dumbfounded as I was in my condition, a head without a body. Yet I saw my body proceeding before me, before my father, getting attached to a head that was not my head, bearing a face other than mine. When I looked more closely I imagined I saw the features of Gamal Abdel Nasser, but I was not sure it was him. I was certain, however, that it was my body, as I felt it in my perch on the edge of the round balcony of the minaret of the mosque of my beloved, pure, and most faithful intercessor. That was my hand, and that my chest, and those my fingers. I was overcome with a rare longing, the longing of a soul for itself. I felt a terrible loneliness enveloping me. My head yearned for my torso and for my root. That was a feeling I was given exclusively: no human had ever experienced it, not even my revered sheikhs since none of them had stood in that very station.

My feet were going toward where my father stood. He was now moving toward me. He was asking for a few moments of my precious time to help him write that short application; thereupon my hand reached for the pocket of the clothes that covered my body and picked out a pen and removed its cap. On a small brass table in front of a shop selling colored beads and ancient ceramics, my hand began writing the application as my father gave me its contents orally. My hand, independently of me, wrote the following:

To his Eminence the Undersecretary of the Ministry of Agriculture:
Greetings.
I have the honor of approaching your eminence begging your help in obtaining a job as day laborer, category 'porter,' since I am a poor man who supports a large family.
Peace be upon you and God's mercy and His blessings.

Submitted by:
I extended my hand with the pen. My father took it and slowly signed: Ahmad al-Ghitani

I was touched by the simple formula and the few words. I was also surprised by something I had never known before, and many were the things I didn't know about my father. Woe is me, dear perceptive recipient, I was not ungrateful, I swear by God Almighty. It was the bad time in which we lived and careless human nature. I found out that my father applied for work as a porter, that he spent some time carrying sacks of cotton seeds in the seed department. I had always known that he was a messenger who carried letters and delivered them. That was true, but it didn't begin and wasn't realized until four years after working for the seed department. This fact belonged in the category of modesty of hopes, a branch of knowledge that applied to all of us, but my father's share of it was great. His hopes grew modest when he started working. After he got married, moving from his job as a porter carrying sacks to that of a messenger delivering mail was a struggle worth undertaking, more important than enrolling in al-Azhar, his first wish.

In that branch of knowledge I've come to understand there are several subcategories of meanings: not everyone who holds out his hand will get what he wants, not everyone who sleeps will dream of what he wants to dream of; not everyone who brings a suit will win; not everyone who prays for something will be granted that for which he prays; not everyone who offers his affection will be offered affection in return; not everyone who cries will be satisfied; not everyone who is denied something will feel frustrated; not everyone who swims will drown; not everyone who is scared will be frightened; and not everyone who is given security will feel safe.

In this station of mine, I recalled something that took place before it took place and was finished before it started. It occurred to me when I went to the ministry and went upstairs with my younger brother to the legal affairs department. I passed by the corridor where my father used to sit and went into a room to finish the paperwork for my mother and unmarried sister to get their share in my father's pension. I sat at an employee's desk. And, to tell the truth, they showed me kindness and averted their eyes when I shed tears of grief after I saw a list of workers containing the names of those who deserved bonuses. My father's name was there but a long line in red ink crossed out his name and all the columns opposite it, ending with a statement saying that he passed away on 28/10/1980. I leafed through his service file: requests for leaves of absence, lists, my father's signatures on cold winter days, summer days, rainy days, clear days, in the morning, the afternoon, in the evening, while sad, while happy, when thinking of us, and when he was not thinking of anything in particular.

I turned the pages until I saw the first sheet in the file that gave me pause: it was my handwriting, the application I wrote with my hand when my head was severed from my body. I was touched by the simple formula. I saw one of the moments of my father's existence, one of those preliminary moments that led to my terrestrial existence. I read the signatures and remarks on it and stopped at a remark written by a fancy hand in red pen: "Appointed for a daily wage of five piasters." Five whole piasters! I went back to my station. I recalled that which hadn't happened yet. I saw the application after my father's death, the color of old ink and the white sheet whose edges had turned yellow, filed away now in a place unknown to me: an ancient government safe or a warehouse in the basement somewhere.

I saw my father at the ministry during his first days of work. There he was summoning his will and his strength. I saw his legs shaking under the weight of the sacks, their veins tensing up, and the bottom of his feet clinging tighter and tighter to the ground. I was able to pinpoint the spots at which he paused for a few passing moments to adjust the heavy load on his back. He would place the front hem of his gallabiya between his teeth and raise his hands to the back while the sack filled with seeds rested on his bent back. At some point my father's legs were replaced by my own legs, as was his spine, beginning with the seven neck vertebrae down to the coccyx. His burden became my burden, his groans my groans, his suppressed pain my pain, and his shaking my shaking. I found that to be great especially that no sigh escaped his lips, so that they wouldn't think him to be weak and unable to endure. I suffered under the weight of the first load, under which my father almost fell, had he not gotten hold of himself and God's mercy intervened. The difference between my back and my father's back and my legs and my father's legs was that he had suffered for a long time, carrying water skins and his relatives' sheep and crossing irrigation canals with them on his shoulders and back. As for me, my back and legs were not used to weightlifting because, through his hard work and toil, he had spared me that. When the officer and plain-clothesman arrested me and took dozens of my books, it was my father who carried them on his back to the gray car that stood waiting at the entrance of the alley. I was afraid to let my father down: if my back could not stand the heavy weight of the sacks or if my feet got twisted then he would lose his livelihood, and that was one of the worries that added to my torment. Then I got stronger so I carried at one time a weight equal to what my father carried all day long, then all week long, then a whole month, and then all that he carried throughout the time he worked as a porter.

Despite my great hardship and the toll it took on my body, my bliss was in my tribulation, my medicine in my sickness, my rest in my fatigue. That was because I saw that part of my body was one with my father's body. So much so that I dreamt of a bliss after which there was no deprivation, a union after which there was no separation, and a sense of security unaffected by fear. I now possessed the proof that even though my head and body were separated they were still connected, for my head suffered all that my other organs did and it was receiving their signals. Thus I knew there was a possible reunion, that an invisible thread remained unbroken, that there was still a wholeness, a togetherness. I accepted what happened to me for that was fair punishment for my estrangement and my not inquiring about the deep wrinkles in my father's face, or about a sad look that I came to understand only after my father's disappearance, his final departure, the impossibility of give and take between us, and total despair of ever meeting again.

I hovered over him upon his return from the ministry in Dokki to his lodging close to al-Husayn. I saw him but he did not see me.

He walked by himself from Dokki, crossing the bridges on the Nile, walking slowly, looking around sometimes. Occasionally he would sing some Saidi tunes full of nostalgia for the place he was born and where he grew up, to amuse himself and fend off the feeling of loneliness. By walking he would save the tram or bus fare. I saw him getting up energetically in his room that contained nothing but an old mat, the same room in which Gamal Abdel Nasser took shelter one night before they both appeared in Karbala. Soon after getting up my father would perform his ablutions and prayers and he would pray to God to provide for him, to keep evildoers away from him, and to bless his belongings. There he was making his way from Utuf to Dokki on an early morning still moist with dew. He would arrive before they arrived and wait, then he would begin carrying his loads and I would suffer what he suffered.

I saw him on Friday waking up energetic, happy because it was the day he spent mostly next to the mausoleum of the beloved, al-Husayn. After prayers he would go to the coffeehouse of al-Ajam. He would see Khalaf Bey and would walk over to him, greeting him politely and standing at some distance but without humility or any sense of inferiority. He had great affection for him, as he was his benefactor. This kind of visit and wait was the beginning of a relationship between the two of them with its ups and downs and which continued until the day of whose significance I was not aware before it came, the twenty-eighth of October. Khalaf Bey was now asking my father how he was doing. My father praised God and prayed that God give Khalaf Bey a long life. My father would sometimes say, "Please, God, don't make his day before my day." And I actually was afraid lest Khalaf Bey should die suddenly, because I knew that my father's grief would be enormous and because I had a vague sense that somehow their destinies were connected. God gave Khalaf Bey life for a year and a half after my father's departure. My father's precious effects, which comprised his clothes and various pieces of paper, still contained a silk scarf with a drawing of the Kaaba that Khalaf Bey had given my father upon his return from

Hijaz. My father cherished that scarf dearly: he would spread it and fold it carefully and keep it well protected, airing it from time to time and wrapping it around his neck only on very rare occasions. He also kept a page of *al-Musawwar* magazine in which there was a feature dating back to the early fifties about the Khalifa district and its judge. If I were to leaf through the old bound volumes of the magazine, I would find it, but I haven't done that yet. As a child, when my father was in a good mood, I used to sit and read out to him the feature, to which he listened in obvious pleasure. When I grew up and our paths diverged, I never read to him.

Now I was asking myself to no avail: why? I was close to him in my heart, so why didn't I speak? Why didn't I express what I felt toward him? What he got out of me in that regard was so slim, so scanty. That was a guilt that was too much to bear, but there was nothing to do about it except to cry for forgiveness.

On Fridays like that, my father would meet men from the old village, those just coming in or those who had been living in Cairo. He would welcome them and spend what he had to treat the newcomers to drinks. He would also sometimes insist on accompanying them to his modest lodging if they needed some place to stay. He did that with many of them who had come from the village destitute and who stretched out on the mat their first few nights in Cairo, then left. As days went by some of them became quite rich and powerful. I was about to mention many of the names of such men but I abstained, dear perceptive reader, since I knew that would not please my father in his eternal absence from me. Perhaps he would consider such an act an attempt on my part to slander people for whom he had done small favors. The truth be told, I didn't hear those stories from him, but rather from my mother and my uncles and others after his passing, may God have mercy on us.

There my father was, embarking on a visit to one of his sick relatives or acquaintances or taking part in a wedding or performing one duty here and another there. He would laugh whenever he found himself in jovial company, telling stories of old incidents, listing genealogies and degrees of kinship, the posts that famous men occupied before becoming ministers or pashas or political leaders. He would sometimes say that the one closest to his heart was Gamal Abdel Nasser, because he protected the poor from the rich and because his father was a simple man like himself.

I awoke while hovering as somebody would after a period of inattention. I detected the passing of a moment that my father had experienced like the blinking of an eye, a moment in which weakness crept into his old, deferred wish to study at al-Azhar, not the cessation of the wish or its burial—I was hoping to find the right words to express what I saw from where I was floating. It was a fleeting moment undetected by consciousness and unnoticed at the time, then it got repeated after intervals, short or long, causing determination to weaken, ideas to falter, and decisions to waver. Putting forth old intentions didn't bring them to fruition all at once, just as merely wishing things did not make them come true. Such matters took time, they sneaked up on you slowly, then suddenly flickered into being like the lighting of a candle. At the beginning it would appear to be steady, casting its light around for some time, then it would glow for a second, then flicker away and fade out.

I was able, however, to witness the first moment when my father's determination to pursue his original intent was shaken. That moment passed like any other fleeting moment as he passed between two trees that are still standing today along the Nile in the Agouza district. However, he never shook off the old feeling that all he was going through, all the hardships and difficult circumstances he was living under, were temporary, that a better situation awaited him, that one day he would enjoy a comfortable arrangement with life. I hope I've been able to explain what I'd seen.

My head continued to float and hover over Egypt. Shortly before sunset I traveled to the south, to Juhayna. This was my father's first visit there since he was forced to leave after a number of years unknown to me because my master and the pillars of the Diwan did not let me in on the date of his departure or return, as a form of punishment for not getting that information directly from him. I saw my father's eyes, his longing and his eagerness to see all the places that had significance in his growing up. I listened to him as he was talking in a clearing in the middle of the houses. He was sitting with Sheikh Abdel Latif Muhammad Ali and Sheikh Hashim the Elder. Sheikh Abdel Latif was saying it was time for my father to complete half the obligation of his faith, time to get married, that he wasn't getting any younger, or was he waiting for one of those crafty Cairene women to hoodwink him? Why would he think of that when the village in front of him was quite full, even crowded? Sheikh Hashim said that that was true and that if God had made it possible for him to make an honest living, what was he waiting for? My father fell silent, his thoughts going hither and yon, then said that his work was hard and that it paid little, five piasters. Would that be enough to support a household? He said that marriage was a responsibility.

I got close to them. I was there and not there at the same time. I could see them but they couldn't see me. There was my father's face and that was the perplexed look I was quite familiar with. I don't know why all of a sudden I was gripped with grief, so I rose to soar above the village, shedding tears that fell on the path separating the two rows of houses. Nobody took notice because my tears were scant and because it wasn't yet the rainy season. I looked at the village from above and saw that it was compact, surrounded by palm trees. The houses were small. In one of them my father was born and he was now sitting in another house. I was not aware of where my body was as I was still separated from it, feeling like a stranger, totally alienated. But regardless of the present situation, that feeling of alienation had been a constant with me in my time on earth: my conditions, states, and moods never remained the same for long stretches of time: I wasn't blessed with peace and tranquillity at all times. Even in music I was never enthralled by the melodies of a composer or a singer. I was always subject to some mysterious, unenunciated rebuke, and a feeling that I was constantly being tested that never stopped nagging me. That sense of ordeal assailing me started in recent times with my father's departure, a heavy burden that could never be lifted. Then there was the vexation and heartsickness because of the presence of my enemy in my homeland, breathing the same air as me. I had this longing to see Gamal Abdel Nasser that right now seemed like an unattainable dream. I blamed myself for being upset with him while he lived, and that seemed like man's fate: not to know the essence of something until it was gone. My remorse over the loss of my beloveds was as hard on me as the remorse of those who had let al-Husayn down, who did not support him while still living and breathing, while his heart was beating.

My consciousness was torn, my thoughts scattered. My strange time united and disunited. When my soul blossomed with hope, my mind was beset with doubts, and when my hopes were refreshed by expectation, my goals got engulfed in a fog of difficulty. When my will was stirred up, it threatened to wither. Memory was always overtaken by forgetfulness. Just as I forgot, tomorrow I would be forgotten. There was no love that was not shriveled by fading interest. There were feelings that filled me one day, made me proud even to the point of arrogance, thinking they would never fade or diminish, then those same feelings just evaporated, leaving me empty, the fire now gone cold.

As I continued my hovering, these ideas kept turning in my mind: there is not a single passion that does not suffer from faltering; no heart that is not beset by doubt; no attentive ear that does not get tired and does not quit listening; no eloquent tongue that does not stop speaking; no eye that cries forever; no fleeting thought that slows down and stays in the mind; nothing near that does not become far; and no beloved who does not become a stranger. I also reflected on the Qur'anic verse part of which says *Has there ever occurred a time when man was not something. . . ?* All of us and all beings are nothing but fleeting thoughts in the memory of time. But which time? What is time?

In my night flight, going hither and yon, without destination and without shelter, I cried, "O Beloved! O master who heard my father's cries!"

Al-Husayn did not disappoint me. He appeared to me in perfect human shape displaying none of the defects of humans.

I said, expressing my perplexity, "Where should I go? In what space should I move? What force is propelling me? Why the transience? Why the forgetfulness? Why don't I choose the time of my setting sun before my twilight appears? Is it time? Is it time? What is it?"

He looked at me in silence. I was shaken. I understood him. That was my second act of disobedience. It was my heart that tempted me and my mind that betrayed me so I spoke and asked about things I should not ask about. If I were to ask a third time about things of which I had no knowledge, my whole being would be threatened and I'd go back to where I had been before. All the epiphanies would be erased as if they never were. I shut my eyelids penitently, begging forgiveness, imploring pardon. I felt his moving away in steady steps, the departure of the beloved. I was overcome with that hunger that no stomach brought about and the deprivation that no appetite fed. A shadow fell on me. Khalid in his eternal flight came to me. I expressed innocent astonishment, "Do you know this time also?"

Without his saying a word, without an answer from him, I received information and facts. Ever since he stood blindfolded early that Thursday morning before the firing squad, the morning of that Thursday belonging to my time, he and his companions were freed of all constraints. He was put in charge of all the time of education; his first companion was entrusted with the time to come; his second companion with the time that has departed; his third companion with the time of signs and symbols; as for his fourth companion, he was among the few in charge of the present time. They have turned into birds of light, into flowers, dew, fog, and shade.

Khalid was fashioned of light. When you saw Abdel Hamid you would be about to shout, "Look at this bird and its strange feathers," but once you got near him you'd find petals of the world's flowers. As for Husayn, he was fashioned of that fog seen at dawn. Ata was of the dew drops which would get close to the sun but never evaporate or vanish, he would hover around lovers at the peak of heat and would moisten and cool them. As for Abdel Salam, he was of shade and lovers' secret whispers.

Their permanent abode became time and their sojourn across eternity. Khalid was entrusted with many important tasks, of which I will mention only by way of example: watering all kinds of plants in the land of Egypt. It was he who watered those shady willows and palm trees through eternity and that single sweet basil branch that grew near my father's tomb. He was also entrusted with carrying pollen from flower to flower and with warning of danger when it loomed, be it an earthquake or cosmic bolts. His voice was used for that secret, mysterious voice that called people in the middle of the night, the one that called me at the beginning of my epiphanies and invited me to start my journey, which I did. He was also the one charged by the president of the Diwan to feed me.

I gazed at him, expressing my gratitude with my eyes and my admiration of his daring and courage and his exacting our revenge on the brutal lout. I was about to ask him when was the time allotted to talk, for me to ask and for him to answer, when to engage in a real dialogue, but he dropped in my mouth sweet manna and quail. Then he pointed with his right wing in that direction and I gathered he was pointing to my father. So, once again I started looking at my origin. I saw Juhayna's hot midday. I smelled the aroma of freshly baked bread, the fired ovens, the sacks of flour, the waterwheel scoops made of leather and perfumed with water coming from the depths.

My father was sitting with Sheikh Abdel Latif as the sun was going down. There was a breeze crossing the palm trees to the north. An old man was yawning in the nearby mosque. My grandmother Aisha was telling my mother who was still a virgin, "Take these loaves to your grandmother Najma." My mother wrapped the hot bread in the tip of her black shawl and stepped outside the house. Before turning right she hurried up, it seemed that she had seen the two men sitting in the shade. At the seventh step after she went out of the house, my father saw her. A mysterious feeling, confusion, ecstasy, specters of the world of women that was still unknown to him, came over him. Before she disappeared at the bend he asked, "Whose daughter is she?"

Sheikh Abdel Latif answered, "The daughter of Ali Basha."

"Sheikh Ali Basha the singer?"

"Yes, God have mercy on his soul. God has not granted us another voice like his," replied Sheikh Abdel Latif.

After a short silence he asked my father, "Listen, Ahmad. Shall I ask for her hand for you?"

My father looked baffled and shy and didn't answer.

Glossary

Ah ya bouy lit. "Oh, my father!"; an exclamation of pained grief typically associated with southern Egyptians

Ahmad Urabi (1841–1911) Egyptian army officer who led an unsuccessful revolt in 1879 against Tawfiq Pasha, the Khedive of Egypt. The revolt was crushed in 1882 when Britain invaded Egypt in collusion with the Khedive.

al-Ahram Leading, state-owned newspaper in Egypt

al-Azhar mosque and university built in CE 970. Currently the world's leading Sunni (mainstream; orthodox) Islamic university.

baladi an adjective meaning 'of the country,' 'indigenous.' Positive or negative connotation depends on context.

Diwan as used in this work, refers to the mythical-mystical council that oversees all affairs and all existing things and creatures of this world

eids lit. 'feasts'; refers specially to the Islamic Eid al-fitr and Eid al-Adha

Eliyahu Ben Elissar Israeli politician and diplomat; the first Israeli ambassador to Egypt

faqih a Muslim man learned in religion

Fatima al-Zahraa the Prophet Muhammad's daughter, and wife of Ali ibn Abi Talib, cousin of the Prophet, and mother of al-Hasan and al-Husayn

fetira an Egyptian pie (pl. fetir)

ful medammis slow-stewed fava beans, a staple food in the Egyptian diet

gallabiya a loose-fitting gown worn by men and women in Egypt

General Muhammad Naguib (1901–84) one of the main leaders of the July 23, 1952 revolution in Egypt. He became the country's first president, serving from June 18, 1953 to November 14, 1954.

General Rafael Eitan former chief of staff of the Israel Defense Forces and government minister

Hajj refers to the Muslim pilgrimage to Mecca; also used as a term of address to a male who has performed the pilgrimage

al-Hasan son of Fatima, the daughter of the Prophet Muhammad and Ali ibn Abi Talib, the fourth caliph (successor of the Prophet)

al-Hurr ibn Yazid military commander in Yazid ibn Mu'awiya's army, fighting al-Husayn in Karbala who changed sides and joined the latter's small band of followers and family members

al-Husayn grandson of the Prophet Muhammad and son of Ali (the fourth caliph) and Fatima, daughter of Muhammad

ifrit a jinn (genie)

keddah variant of qadah; dry measure equal to 2.062 liters

Khalid a reference to Khalid al-Islambouli, the Egyptian army officer who participated in the assassination of Egypt's president Anwar Sadat and who was sentenced to death and executed

Khayr Bek the ruler of Aleppo during the reign of Sultan al-Ghuri (the penultimate Mamluk ruler), whom he betrayed by collaborating with the Ottoman invaders

the legendary beloveds Salma and Layla women immortalized in Arabic lore by poets who idolized them

makhruta a type of homemade noodle, usually eaten with milk and sugar for breakfast

mastaba built-in bench or couch traditionally part of the outside wall in the front of a peasant's house

mi'raj according to Islamic tradition, the Prophet Muhammad's journey when he ascended to Heaven

Mordechai Gur Israeli politician and chief of staff of the Israel Defense Forces

al-Mustafa lit. 'the Chosen One'; another name for the Prophet Muhammad

Saba one of the maqams, or systems of melodic modes, in traditional Arabic music

Saidi adjective deriving from 'Said,' or southern Egypt

Sayyida Zeinab granddaughter of the Prophet Muhammad and daughter of Ali ibn Abi Talib

Shaaban eighth month of the Islamic calendar

Shagar (Shajar) al-Durr widow of the Ayyubid sultan al-Salih Ayyub. She became the sultana of Egypt in CE 1250

sharbat flavored sugar water served on happy occasions

Shukuku, Mahmud popular Egyptian comedian, actor and singer

Sidi Zayn al-Abidin son of al-Husayn

Uthman Ahmad Uthman (1917–99) famous and influential Egyptian engineer and contractor. He founded the Arab Contractors, the largest Arab construction firm between 1960 and the 1980s.

Yazid ibn Mu'awiya CE 645–683, second caliph in the Umayyad dynasty

zar a dance ritual alleged to exorcise demons believed to 'possess' certain women

Qur'anic Verses

The following Qur'anic verses or parts of verses appear in the novel in italics. All translations are the translator's own.

Page 3
He [Moses] said, "So what have you got to say for yourself, Samaritan?" And he [the latter] said, "I perceive what they do not perceive." (20:95–96)

Page 8
And wishes have deceived you. (57:14)

Page 9
And if you repeat the crime, we will repeat the punishment. (17:8)

Page 11
And they sold him for a measly price, a few dirhams, for they held him in low esteem. (12:20)

. . . And God has full power and control but most people do not know that. (12:21)

Page 15
This is the parting between me and you. (18:78)

Page 16
And we have set a bar before them and a bar behind them. We have covered them so that they do not see. And whether you warn them or do not warn them, they will not believe. (36:9–10)

Page 18
Dawn and the ten nights. (89:1–2)

Page 23
There is not a thing that does not sing God's praises, but you do not understand what they sing. (17:44)

245

Page 42
Man was made in haste. (21:37)

Page 57
Number of years and the reckoning.
(17:12)

Page 58
Man is given to haste. (17:11)

Page 85
*It is God who created you in a state of
weakness, then gave you strength after
weakness. Then, after strength, gave
you weakness and gray hair.* (30:54)

Page 117
Slumber nor sleep. (2:255)

Page 124
Man can have only what he strives for.
(20:15)

Page 134
*They are in doubt and confusion
concerning a new creation.* (50:15)

Page 148
Lord, increase me in knowledge.
(20:114)

Page 153
Be not among those who despair. (15:55)

*The sight did not deviate nor did it
overshoot its mark.* (53:17)

*Have we not given you a life long
enough for those who want to reflect to
do so?* (35:37)

Page 157
*Everyone on earth will perish, but
the countenance of your Lord, in all
majesty and nobility will remain.*
(55:26–27)

Page 177
*Everyone on earth will perish, but
the countenance of your Lord, in all
majesty and nobility will remain.*
(55:26–27)

Page 193
Everyday exercises universal power.
(55:29)

We shall dispose of you two dependants.
(55:31)

Page 203
*I swear not by the positions of the stars.
That, if only you knew, is a great oath.*
(56:75–76)

Page 209
*And from the evil of darkness as it
grows intense.* (113:3)

Page 217
*And among them are those who paid
with their lives and others awaiting
[but] they have not changed at all.*
(33:23)

Page 221
*God is sufficient for me and the best
support.* (39:38)

Page 222
Everyone on earth will perish. (55:26)

*No soul knows in which land it will
die.* (31:34)

*No soul knows what it will earn
tomorrow.* (31:34)

Page 224
*No soul knows in which land it will
die.* (31:34)

*Man has only that for which he has
striven.* (53:39)

Page 236
*Has there ever occurred a time when
man was not something. . . ?* (76:1)

Translator's Acknowledgments

I would like to thank my wife E. Kay Heikkinen and the following friends and colleagues for help with various aspects of the translation: Ahmed Hashim and Kelly Zaug, and from the American University in Cairo Press, Neil Hewison and Nadia Naqib.

Modern Arabic Literature
from the American University in Cairo Press

Bahaa Abdelmegid *Saint Theresa* and *Sleeping with Strangers*
Ibrahim Abdel Meguid *Birds of Amber* • *Distant Train*
No One Sleeps in Alexandria • *The Other Place*
Yahya Taher Abdullah *The Collar and the Bracelet* • *The Mountain of Green Tea*
Leila Abouzeid *The Last Chapter*
Hamdi Abu Golayyel *A Dog with No Tail* • *Thieves in Retirement*
Yusuf Abu Rayya *Wedding Night*
Ahmed Alaidy *Being Abbas el Abd*
Idris Ali *Dongola* • *Poor*
Rasha al Ameer *Judgment Day*
Radwa Ashour *Granada* • *Specters*
Ibrahim Aslan *The Heron* • *Nile Sparrows*
Alaa Al Aswany *Chicago* • *Friendly Fire* • *The Yacoubian Building*
Fahd al-Atiq *Life on Hold*
Fadhil al-Azzawi *Cell Block Five* • *The Last of the Angels*
The Traveler and the Innkeeper
Ali Bader *Papa Sartre*
Liana Badr *The Eye of the Mirror*
Hala El Badry *A Certain Woman* • *Muntaha*
Salwa Bakr *The Golden Chariot* • *The Man from Bashmour* • *The Wiles of Men*
Halim Barakat *The Crane*
Hoda Barakat *Disciples of Passion* • *The Tiller of Waters*
Mourid Barghouti *I Saw Ramallah* • *I Was Born There, I Was Born Here*
Mohamed Berrada *Like a Summer Never to Be Repeated*
Mohamed El-Bisatie *Clamor of the Lake* • *Drumbeat* • *Hunger* • *Over the Bridge*
Mahmoud Darwish *The Butterfly's Burden*
Tarek Eltayeb *Cities without Palms* • *The Palm House*
Mansoura Ez Eldin *Maryam's Maze*
Ibrahim Farghali *The Smiles of the Saints*
Hamdy el-Gazzar *Black Magic*
Randa Ghazy *Dreaming of Palestine*
Gamal al-Ghitani *Pyramid Texts* • *The Zafarani Files* • *Zayni Barakat*
The Book of Epiphanies
Tawfiq al-Hakim *The Essential Tawfiq al-Hakim* • *Return of the Spirit*
Yahya Hakki *The Lamp of Umm Hashim*
Abdelilah Hamdouchi *The Final Bet*
Bensalem Himmich *The Polymath* • *The Theocrat*
Taha Hussein *The Days*
Sonallah Ibrahim *Cairo: From Edge to Edge* • *The Committee* • *Zaat*
Yusuf Idris *City of Love and Ashes* • *The Essential Yusuf Idris* • *Tales of Encounter*
Denys Johnson-Davies *The AUC Press Book of Modern Arabic Literature* • *Homecoming*
In a Fertile Desert • *Under the Naked Sky*
Said al-Kafrawi *The Hill of Gypsies*
Mai Khaled *The Magic of Turquoise*
Sahar Khalifeh *The End of Spring*
The Image, the Icon and the Covenant • *The Inheritance* • *Of Noble Origins*
Edwar al-Kharrat *Rama and the Dragon* • *Stones of Bobello*

Betool Khedairi *Absent*
Mohammed Khudayyir *Basrayatha*
Ibrahim al-Koni *Anubis • Gold Dust • The Puppet • The Seven Veils of Seth*
Naguib Mahfouz *Adrift on the Nile • Akhenaten: Dweller in Truth*
Arabian Nights and Days • Autumn Quail • Before the Throne • The Beggar
The Beginning and the End • Cairo Modern • The Cairo Trilogy: Palace Walk
Palace of Desire • Sugar Street • Children of the Alley • The Coffeehouse
The Day the Leader Was Killed • The Dreams • Dreams of Departure
Echoes of an Autobiography • The Essential Naguib Mahfouz • The Final Hour
The Harafish • Heart of the Night • In the Time of Love
The Journey of Ibn Fattouma • Karnak Cafe • Khan al-Khalili • Khufu's Wisdom
Life's Wisdom • Love in the Rain • Midaq Alley • The Mirage • Miramar • Mirrors
Morning and Evening Talk • Naguib Mahfouz at Sidi Gaber • Respected Sir
Rhadopis of Nubia • The Search • The Seventh Heaven • Thebes at War
The Thief and the Dogs • The Time and the Place • Voices from the Other World
Wedding Song • The Wisdom of Naguib Mahfouz
Mohamed Makhzangi *Memories of a Meltdown*
Alia Mamdouh *The Loved Ones • Naphtalene*
Selim Matar *The Woman of the Flask*
Ibrahim al-Mazini *Ten Again*
Yousef Al-Mohaimeed *Munira's Bottle • Wolves of the Crescent Moon*
Hassouna Mosbahi *A Tunisian Tale*
Ahlam Mosteghanemi *Chaos of the Senses • Memory in the Flesh*
Shakir Mustafa *Contemporary Iraqi Fiction: An Anthology*
Mohamed Mustagab *Tales from Dayrut*
Buthaina Al Nasiri *Final Night*
Ibrahim Nasrallah *Inside the Night • Time of White Horses*
Haggag Hassan Oddoul *Nights of Musk*
Mona Prince *So You May See*
Mohamed Mansi Qandil *Moon over Samarqand*
Abd al-Hakim Qasim *Rites of Assent*
Somaya Ramadan *Leaves of Narcissus*
Kamal Ruhayyim *Days in the Diaspora*
Mahmoud Saeed *The World through the Eyes of Angels*
Mekkawi Said *Cairo Swan Song*
Ghada Samman *The Night of the First Billion*
Mahdi Issa al-Saqr *East Winds, West Winds*
Rafik Schami *The Calligrapher's Secret • Damascus Nights • The Dark Side of Love*
Habib Selmi *The Scents of Marie-Claire*
Khairy Shalaby *The Hashish Waiter • The Lodging House*
Khalil Sweileh *Writing Love*
The Time-Travels of the Man Who Sold Pickles and Sweets
Miral al-Tahawy *Blue Aubergine • Brooklyn Heights • Gazelle Tracks • The Tent*
Bahaa Taher *As Doha Said • Love in Exile*
Fuad al-Takarli *The Long Way Back*
Zakaria Tamer *The Hedgehog*
M. M. Tawfik *candygirl • Murder in the Tower of Happiness*
Mahmoud Al-Wardani *Heads Ripe for Plucking*
Amina Zaydan *Red Wine*
Latifa al-Zayyat *The Open Door*